Sylvia went up to take another shower and looked at the crumpled bed sheets. It seemed like weeks, months, since she had left the house. David had left her a note in fine, clear handwriting, 'Sylvia, I've taken down your number and will call tomorrow, David.' She smiled to herself, tomorrow was too long, she needed him tonight. . .

D1740638

JO HARRIS

Never Say Always

GRAFTON BOOKS

A Division of the Collins Publishing Group

LONDON GLASGOW
TORONTO SYDNEY AUCKLAND

Grafton Books
A Division of the Collins Publishing Group
8 Grafton Street, London W1X 3LA

A Grafton Paperback Original 1988

ISBN 0-586-07357-4

Printed and bound in Great Britain by
Collins, Glasgow

Set in Times

To Tina

Chapter 1

Sylvia rushed from the office and was rained upon whilst grabbing a cab, dressed in her smart black cocktail outfit which was now crumpled up under an over-sized trench-coat. She sat back and, looking out at the rain, touched her damp hair attempting to see her reflection in the cab window, trying to decide if she liked it scraped back from her face and swirled up into a bun. They stopped at lights next to a dark van and she caught her reflection, a stark white face which only seemed to show black eyebrows and very black hair with a severe centre parting. Sylvia recoiled from the image and fumbled around in her black bag for a mirror, her eye make-up was too much and she was deciding what to do about it when the cab swung right and stopped with a lurch at the Savoy.

The young man was ferociously attractive and Sylvia could not help but watch as he came across to her. She had only come to this party, this gathering of the famous and would-be famous, to see how Yolanda would cele-brate her success. A new film, talk of an Oscar, talk about rising from the dead! Sylvia was intrigued by it all but not quite taken in, even when Yolanda smiled most warmly and thanked her so very much for coming along. Sylvia watched her up close then, watching the wheels turn, the flawlessly oiled control, everyone was Yolanda's best friend that day. Everyone in love with Yolanda and Yolanda in love with every one of them. You could almost taste the love for her, it clung in the smoky atmosphere and showed in the glittery smiles and the shining eyes of the people.

'Hello,' the good-looking youth was talking to her now, 'are you alone or what?'

Or what? Sylvia thought, looking into his very blue eyes. 'Hello,' she said, and could not stop smiling back at him. 'I came by myself if that's what you mean.' She felt a little uncomfortable, a little off guard, a little ridiculous.

'I had a bit-part in the film,' he continued, holding his hands about six inches apart. 'This much,' and then he laughed. 'Bunch of stiffs this lot, aren't they?'

She laughed as well. 'I haven't actually seen the film yet, will I miss you if I blink?'

'Right,' he agreed, and then held out his hand to her. 'My name is David Christensen.'

Sylvia offered her own and felt it being pulped. 'I'm pleased to meet you.' She caught a glimpse of Yolanda laughing recklessly and suddenly looking her real age. 'I'm Sylvia McLeod.'

'The agent?' he asked, smiling even more.

'No.'

'Do you know Yolanda?' he asked after a pause.

Sylvia nodded. 'Through a mutual friend.' That sounded odd to her and a little dishonest, a bit out of place.

'I thought you were in the business,' he said after another moment.

'No,' Sylvia turned to him, 'afraid not.'

He shrugged and continued to smile at her.

An hour passed and they were still together on a very comfortable sofa, he was telling her all about his life as a struggling actor whilst Sylvia, after accepting several glasses of champagne from passing waiters, felt drunk and was trying to decide whether or not she was enjoying herself. A great many people had left by now but Yolanda was still at the centre of those who remained.

'She *is* wonderful,' Sylvia said without a trace of sarcasm. 'I don't know how she does it. All those people and she can't really know any of them.' Champagne slopped from her glass and dribbled on to her wrist, the sleeves of her awful dress acting as blotting paper.

'Just another great performance,' he said knowledgeably.

Sylvia nodded. 'She is terribly good at it though, isn't she?'

Yolanda left soon after, waving all the way through the ornate glass doors, bright camera flashes surrounding her like diamonds.

'I could murder a cup of tea,' she called to him above the sloshing sounds as he swabbed around her bath like Norman Bates in *Psycho*. 'What are you still doing here?'

Vanny came to the bathroom door wearing bright orange rubber gloves which almost exactly matched his hair. 'I had to take Frank to a hairdressing contest this morning, had to help him set everything out.' He leant against the door frame looking at her.

Sylvia kicked off her black patent shoes with their silver wedged heels. 'I see he's had another go at your hair.' She looked at it for a moment. 'I'm not sure if I like it as much, you were divine as a blond!'

Vanny grimaced. 'Who did yours, then?'

Sylvia's hand immediately went up to her head. 'Why, don't you like it?'

'Makes you look like a teacher,' he said, pulling off a rubber glove. 'And how did your star-studded do go, then? Did you get a close-up of Yolanda? I bet the mortician's wax was in evidence . . .'

'Oh, you know, all right, very crowded . . .' She began to unzip her dress. 'Haven't you nearly finished, Vanny? I want to take a shower.'

He went back in and came out again carrying a mop-pail and a plastic box full of cleaning things. 'I'll make some tea,' he said, 'and you can tell me who you met.'

Sylvia nodded and moved unsteadily towards the bathroom door.

Vanny was impressed that Sylvia knew Yolanda and was always asking her to invite the famous 'friend' to the house. 'Who else was there?' he demanded.

'Oh, no one very much . . . I did meet a young actor who starred in the film with Yolanda.'

Vanny looked interested. 'Who was that, then?'

'David Christensen,' she said casually, sipping the black tea Vanny had poured into the pint mug for her. She loathed tea from mugs.

'Never heard of him,' he said dismissively. 'What does he look like?'

'Well, now, let's see, he's very young, very blond, well-built, terribly handsome . . .' She began to laugh.

'For God's sake, Mrs McLeod,' Vanny was laughing too, 'I bet he's not famous at all, fancy you picking someone up like that . . .'

'I haven't done any such thing,' Sylvia protested her shock at such a suggestion. 'Anyway, why shouldn't I? I'm not nearly as decrepit as you would make me out to be. Some people are still attracted to me,' she said, half as a joke.

Vanny didn't look very convinced. 'How old?' he asked. 'How old is your actor?'

'Twenty-three,' she answered defensively, 'and he's not *my* actor but, if you want to continue as *my* cleaning person, you'd better get a move on because Molly's coming here tonight.' She put the pint mug down on to the old pine table-top. 'Have you done in the lounge?'

Vanny nodded. 'I'll come in extra early tomorrow, it's Frank's half-day.'

'Not too early, Vanny,' she said firmly, 'I don't want to be woken at the crack of dawn like last time.'

He nodded and started to leave, pausing at the kitchen door to grin back at her. 'Twenty-three, eh?'

Sylvia threw a handy teaspoon across at him.

Molly looked at her sternly. Sylvia hated it when she did that. 'Tell me again,' she commanded.

'He's an actor who appeared in Yolanda's film,' Sylvia said as casually as she could.

'What kind of an actor,' Molly asked bluntly.

'An actor-actor, what do you think?'

'Twenty-three? You must be mad,' Molly concluded.

'I'm only meeting him for a drink, you know, social intercourse . . .'

'Stop being so obtuse, Sylvia . . . What does he look like?' Molly was watching her friend closely.

'Well, he fills his trousers out really well if that's what you mean.'

Molly raised her eyes to the ceiling. 'For God's sake, Sylvia.'

'You're surely not thinking about propriety, no one mourns for a year anymore, I'm not in purdah . . . In any case, Douglas wasn't my husband, we were hardly even together at the end.' Sylvia regretted her anger. 'I'm sorry.'

'Don't be, it's none of my Goddamn business, I'm just slightly concerned, that's all.'

'I know you are and I love you for it but don't worry,'

11

she sat next to Molly, 'he's just another young actor . . . Perhaps I can help him, write a piece about him.'

'Oh God, not more strays, you said that about the wretch who cleans your house. I never understood how Douglas put up with him.'

'Douglas never emerged from his pit until after noon, besides, I think he really was quite fond of Vanny and Vanny was very good to him.'

'Vanny may be a very nice boy, Sylvia, but he doesn't exactly clean very thoroughly . . .'

'Who cares about a bit of dust. Vanny understands the way I work and he's away a good deal which is fine, and he does know how to clean, *I* showed him how! You're so rude, Molly.'

Molly laughed and reached for her coffee cup. 'I know I'm rude. If you were married to Jack and had all of my brood you would be, too!'

'I pity your students . . . at least you have that, your career.'

'Ah, yes, that, teaching English to a bunch of snotty undergraduates, the same thing as last year and the year before that. Your job is creative and interesting, changing, challenging.'

'Writing bits for *Arts Monthly* is hardly the pinnacle of creativity, Molly.'

They were silent for a moment. 'Tell me some more about the boy,' Molly said, sounding a little dangerous. 'I bet anything you'll be in bed with him by the end of the month.'

'Don't be absurd,' Sylvia replied. 'What do you bet?'

'Ten pounds, no, let's make it twenty.'

'You must have money to burn then, you may as well write me the cheque now.'

'End of the month.' Molly poured them both a large brandy and they toasted one another's victory.

Molly left just after midnight. 'So, this is the new car,' she said, running a finger along the immaculate coachwork sheen of Sylvia's Porsche. 'Has he seen it yet?'

Sylvia shook her head. 'No.'

Molly smiled. 'Well, this will spur him on no end. I can see that my twenty pounds is even more secure because, darling, a man will do almost anything to get himself behind the wheel of a fast car. Do you think my sex life would improve if I sold the Morris Minor and got one of these?'

Sylvia laughed. 'You're so ideologically incorrect.'

'I'm not, I'm just jealous . . . By the way, is it true that they've given you your own TV show?'

'How did you know that?' Sylvia asked, aghast.

'Oh, you know me,' she hugged Sylvia, kissing her firmly on the mouth, 'super sleuth Kerr!'

'No, seriously, Molly, how do you know?'

'So, it *is* true, then.' Molly was already across the square to her car. 'Let's have lunch next week. Will you call me?' She was driving slowly away. 'Wednesday's good for me.'

Sylvia put one hand to her head, laughing, waving Molly away into the clear night.

It was a beautiful spring day. Sylvia felt annoyed with herself. For such a casual date she had gone to an awful lot of trouble, her bedroom littered with cast-off clothes she had tried and then had second thoughts about. She wanted to appear casual but chic. In the end she decided upon a blue denim midi skirt and a new (and expensive) white blouse. She felt neither casual nor chic. Vanny asked her where the barn dance was!

13

He was sitting at an outside table leaning over a script. 'Hello, there,' she said, sitting across the table from him. He looked up and smiled warmly before going into the pub to fetch some drinks and sandwiches. Sylvia watched the river and, closing her eyes, let the sun bathe her face hoping that it might reduce the death-like pallor she had gained from drinking with Molly the previous night. He returned in a while with their lunch.

'So,' he said after a rather nervous hesitation, 'how are you today?'

Sylvia began to wonder just how ill she looked. 'I'm fine, and you?'

'Fine.'

She smiled at him. 'Are you studying a script?'

He looked down at the curled pages. 'My agent has got me in to read for Marcus Kaine, the film director, he's casting for a new film.'

'You're reading for a part in his film? That's marvellous.'

'It's not likely that he'll give me a part but it will be interesting to meet him . . .'

'When is it?' she asked enthusiastically.

'Two days' time.'

'Are you nervous?'

He shook his head. 'I will be about ten minutes before I walk through his door.' He looked up and smiled at her.

'Well, that's marvellous,' she toasted his success with her orange drink, 'congratulations.'

He was silent for a long time. 'I'm glad you came,' he said finally. 'I wasn't sure if you would.'

'Why ever not?' She hadn't imagined he would display signs of nerves or lack of confidence. He hadn't appeared that way. 'You showed up.'

'I had to be in town, to see someone at the Garrick, I came on to Camden about an hour ago.'

'Well, I suppose this could almost qualify as my local, if I had one,' Sylvia replied, feeling a little disappointed at his attitude to their meeting, thinking of her room strewn with clothes. 'Why didn't you think I'd come?'

He shrugged. 'We come from a set of different circumstances, I suppose . . . I wasn't sure . . .'

'You seemed sure enough when you asked me.'

'Dutch courage . . . I was pretty tight yesterday.'

'You mean if you'd been stone-cold sober you wouldn't have spoken to me?' She smiled all the same.

'No, I don't mean that.' He laughed. 'I was watching you for a long time, I wanted to speak to you . . . I needed a few drinks to get some courage.'

'I see.' She took a bite from the small ham sandwich.

'So,' he said after another long pause, 'how did you enjoy yourself yesterday?'

'Fine.'

'You said you know Yolanda . . .'

'Through a mutual friend, we both knew Douglas Emmitt.'

'The artist, really?' He sounded impressed. 'Didn't she have a really heavy scene with him years ago?'

'Yes, I believe that they lived together for a number of years . . .'

He nodded. 'Yes, and you knew him, how was that?'

'I . . . I had to interview him once, for a magazine I was working on.' It sounded ridiculously coy and she felt embarrassed.

'He was supposed to be a pretty wild old boy. I remember that there was all this fuss after he died . . . Didn't he leave everything to some woman he'd only just met or something?'

15

Sylvia nodded. 'Yes, as a matter of fact it was me.'

He looked at her to see if it was a joke. 'Really?'

She smiled. 'You're right, he was a very wild old man with a reputation well founded in fact. I'm supposed to be sorting out his studio but I haven't even begun yet.' She moved some stray hair across her forehead. 'Do you know his work?'

David nodded. 'I have some post-card reproductions of the stuff he did in New York during the late fifties. They were all given weird names. I remember one, it wasn't really a painting at all, it was something to do with Central Park but there were all kinds of things stuck on to it, bits of cloth, bottles, newspapers, clothing.' He laughed. 'I've still got those pictures on my wall . . .' He looked at her. 'And you knew him.'

Sylvia nodded. 'That picture was *Central Park At Noon On Sunday*. She sounded like a tour guide.

'What do you call that kind of work?'

'It's really Assemblage or Junk Art. He was heavily into the likes of Jasper Johns . . . Robert Rauschenberg.' Sylvia stopped herself and laughed. 'I get carried away, I'm sorry . . .'

'No, really, I'm interested. Do you still work on the same magazine?'

'Yes, and I also do some work for *Arts Monthly*.'

'About paintings, art?'

'About whatever they want,' she replied. 'I did a piece on Yolanda a few issues ago . . . It covers anything that you could possibly consider might fit an "arts" type label, fashion, theatre, film, pop . . . I might even be interested in doing a piece on you.'

'On me?' He laughed. 'No one would be interested.'

Sylvia smiled. She wanted to know more about him.

* * *

16

They walked to her car, he was obviously rather taken aback by it. 'Can I give you a lift anywhere?'

'Do you like Joan Crawford?' he asked.

'Joan Crawford?' she smiled. 'She's okay . . .'

'She's a contemporary of Yolanda, they're showing *Mildred Pierce* this afternoon, I wondered if you might like to come along, might be useful research for you . . .'

'*Mildred Pierce*?' Her mind was cranking over, she wanted to go with him but ought to have been back at her office twenty minutes ago. 'As long as I can get to a telephone it will be all right, I suppose.'

'You'll go?' He sounded very pleased and surprised.

'I'll go.' Sylvia laughed. 'It had better be good, though.'

'It's the best, you'll love it.'

It was an arts-house, a comfortable little cinema which advertised a programme to encompass a wide variety of taste and genre. Every week-day afternoon for a month they were showing a season of Joan Crawford films.

'Do you think that Veda was really evil or just spoilt?' Sylvia asked him in the cinema coffee shop afterwards.

David shrugged. 'I felt sorry for that maid.'

Sylvia laughed. 'It must be a great responsibility for a woman to bring up a daughter. I would have hated it. I'm sure she would have ended up in a worse state than Veda!'

'Have you got any children?'

'Two boys.'

'How old?'

'Old. Charley will be seventeen and Peter fifteen this year.'

'Are you married or what?'

'My generation always did the "correct" thing. I was married for sixteen years.'

'Sixteen years! What happened?'

17

'Oh, I actually left him after fourteen years in 1972 on the grounds of terminal boredom.'

'That sounds very brittle. What was he like?'

'He was fine, really, won't hear a word said against him. I left university, was pregnant, got married . . . He is a barrister, *very* successful and married again now.'

'So, you're still friends?'

'You ask a lot of questions,' she sighed. 'Yes, we are quite friendly. Our different careers and a minority interest in one another's worlds made us grow apart.'

'What did you read at university?'

'English. Predictable, isn't it.'

'Did you meet one another at university?'

Sylvia nodded. 'Yes, but this is all past history and not particularly interesting.'

'I think it's fascinating.'

'Well, I really have to be going, you can have another instalment another time.'

David walked her to the car. 'I'm glad you came.'

Sylvia smiled. 'I enjoyed it. Can I give you a lift?'

He shook his head. 'That's okay, really.'

'Really?'

'If I rolled up in this my landlord would demand his back rent immediately.' He grinned. 'Very nice motor, though.'

Sylvia began to get in, then paused. 'What about dinner sometime?' She thought for a moment. 'What about this week-end?'

'This week-end?'

'Yes, this week-end, are you busy?'

'Where?'

'My house, I'll cook something.' She smiled. 'Don't worry, I'm capable.'

'Okay, when? What time?'

'Saturday, what about that?'

'Yes, that's fine, where do you live, though?'

'Camden Square.' Sylvia produced a notebook from her sack-like bag and scribbled down the address in red ink, handing it to him across the car top. 'There, can you find that?'

He nodded. 'Like I said, a different set of circumstances . . .' He watched her for a moment as though deciding something. 'What time, and do I have to dress?'

'Now, come on,' Sylvia warned. 'I think you're getting entirely the wrong opinion about me . . .'

He dug his hands deep into the pockets of his jeans. 'Let's hope not.' He grinned. 'About eight?'

'Come as early as you like, it's strictly informal.' As she drove away he remained at the kerbside, waving, standing there until she had turned the corner at the end of the road.

'I saw your car,' Richard said by way of explanation, brushing by Sylvia and walking into the lounge. 'I'm afraid it's trouble.'

'What's happened now?' Sylvia sounded exasperated, wondering if this was divine retribution for her afternoon of truancy.

'I've been calling your office all afternoon, they said you were out, couldn't tell me where.' He turned to her, his back against the elegant French window, the thin garden beyond. 'The headmaster has called me personally, I was with a client and it was rather difficult . . .'

'What's happened?' Sylvia asked again, annoyed with him already.

'Apparently Charley is refusing to co-operate with them.' Richard sat down in the old leather armchair next to the window and lit a cigarette. 'Hawser says that

Charley's place in the school is in jeopardy and you know what that will mean.' He expelled a long stream of acrid smoke into the room.

'That bloody school.' She glared at Richard. 'I really wish you wouldn't smoke in my house, the smell lasts for ever.'

Richard ignored her. 'Well, I can't say I relish the prospect of having him full-time, in any case, I could hardly expect Miranda to cope. I'm rarely in the country from one week to the next at the moment.' He looked at her. 'Did you know we were opening an office in Toronto?'

Sylvia took a deep breath. 'Wonderful. Do you really think I care about your bloody work?' She shook her head in disbelief. 'First you insist he goes to this rotten school when it was always entirely inappropriate to his needs, and now you seem surprised when he reacts against it . . .'

'Inappropriate?' he asked, bemused now.

'. . . And *now* you tell me that it's no good and you're washing your hands of any more responsibility!'

'Sylvia,' he said very calmly, 'there's little point in getting all worked up . . .'

'There's every point in getting angry, though.' She started to pace the large room. 'I knew it, I just knew it when I saw him last month, he looked ill . . . It's totally unbearable . . .'

'He was found drunk yesterday lunch-time, they found him staggering up the main driveway. You can hardly expect him to be treated with impunity.' He looked at her, his voice all reason and sanity. She could just imagine how he soothed those juries he held such sway over. 'What was it last time, discovered drinking with a bunch of his cronies late at night?'

Sylvia checked her response and sat down at the other

end of the room, as far away from him as it was possible to be, her arms folded tightly against her chest. 'Well, I don't want to spend one more fruitless afternoon being lectured by that damn headmaster. What does he expect us to do?'

'Hawser suggests that he repeat this year . . .'

'Never!' Sylvia was up on her feet again. 'And I suppose you just agreed to that. "Oh, yes, Headmaster, just put him down for an extra year. Oh, and here's a blank cheque." God, you really make me sick, it's the very last thing Charley needs, don't you see how much he hates that place?'

'I said that we'd consider it,' Richard said very calmly.

'There is nothing to consider, Richard, you only needed to say that it was quite out of the question.'

'Is it? I don't know, are you a teacher all of a sudden?'

'It's an absolute scandal. Apart from any other considerations it's probably one of the most expensive schools in the country and, as far as I'm concerned, the time he's spent there has been totally useless . . .'

'You'd have preferred the local comprehensive, I suppose . . .'

'Anything would be better for him and, yes, why not the local school, it certainly couldn't have done a worse job!'

'Well,' Richard began with a sigh, 'you obviously know best. You deal with it, I'm sick to death with the worry Charley has caused us, I can tell you. If it's not one thing it's another.'

'Yes, our wayward child must be a great source of embarrassment between you and Miranda, better to sweep these problems under the mat.'

'That was uncalled for,' he replied quietly, lighting another cigarette.

'What did you tell Hawser?'

'That I was due in Canada from this week-end and you'd call him to arrange a visit as soon as was possible.'

'Well, now, isn't that just bloody marvellous! And just what am I supposed to do with him? Strap him to a bed upstairs? Richard, I really think you may have failed to understand that I have a television show to get on air over the next few weeks. If you want me to do something you can damn well cancel your trip and help.' She was wildly angry and could quite easily have struck him hard across his sanctimonious face.

'It's quite out of the question. I can't just abandon an important business meeting because of some domestic problem. Don't be silly . . .'

'*I* have a career, *I* have important business commitments as well, my time is every bit as precious as yours. How dare you patronize me, you great shit!'

Richard glared at her through the smoke. 'You're quite impossible, why can you *never* behave in a reasonable way?'

'Why can't I let you off the hook, you mean. You're an absolute bastard.' They were both standing now, almost squaring up to one another in the centre of the room. 'You were the one who insisted that he go to the damned school, so you can fucking well sort the mess out now.'

Richard winced. 'Just so long as he's out of your hair, just as long as he doesn't interfere with your life and your men . . .'

Sylvia laughed in his face. 'God, but you're pathetic.' Her voice seethed with anger.

'Yes, well, this is all very good coming from a woman who walked out of the marital home. Charley's difficulties probably stem from all of that for all I know.' He turned

22

to leave but hesitated, looking back at her. 'Perhaps when you've calmed down you'll contact Headmaster Hawser.'

'Yes, that's right, Richard, just go, leave me to make everything better, as usual.'

He ignored her, slamming the front door after him as he left.

'So,' he said, hands deep into jeans pockets, 'this is it.' He looked around the lounge.

'Yes, this is Douglas Emmitt's house, with a major refurbishment. It's big, isn't it?'

David nodded. 'Did he do this picture of you?' He was standing in front of the large unfinished canvas that Sylvia had brought down from the ramshackle farmhouse after he died.

'I think it was supposed to have been a surprise. In a way I'm glad he never got around to completing it. I might have been rather shocked to see how he really perceived me.' Sylvia handed him a glass of wine. 'I hope you like chicken.'

He looked at her, smiling. 'I love it.'

'Tell me about your meeting with the film director,' she asked later as they ate, watching him across the dining-table through the guttering candle flame. 'Did it go well?'

'They're going to let me know.'

'Didn't he give you any idea?'

'Not really, said he liked my reading but there are probably another hundred-and-fifty people up for the part, some already have names, too.'

'Are all actors fatalistic?' She smiled. 'I suppose they are.'

'With most of the profession unemployed at any given time you don't have very much room to be optimistic.'

'But you must have a belief in your talent, your craft.'

23

He thought about that for a while. 'I don't have a completely cynical view of the business, if that's what you mean, but I don't have any belief about talent coming to the fore, that's a load of crap. I guess it's luck, mainly lucky chances.'

'What about the ability, though, the natural talent?'

'Well, there are better actors than me. I have some looks on my side.' He drained his glass and poured them some more wine. 'I probably have more ability than a lot.'

'What about goals?'

'The next part and then the part after that. It's hard to have too many goals. Sure, I'd like to be in films, if you can make it there that's where the big money can be made and then you can make some choices about the jobs you take.'

'I hope I get the chance to see you in something one day soon.' Sylvia felt calmer at last, she was taken by him, hooked. Sometimes when he spoke she found herself not really listening to the words but simply watching him. He was very beautiful and she wondered who else there was in this particular scene; another woman, another man? 'I suppose most of your friends must be in the business, too,' she said, fishing.

'Some are.' He was reading her thoughts now. 'I've worked hard to get a few breaks, it's necessary, but it leaves little time to maintain many friendships.' He smiled, his very blue eyes piercing her brain.

'Well, that sounds very dedicated,' she said, 'but what about recreation?'

'I run,' he laughed, 'and not from angry audiences. I'm *very* serious where my career is concerned, and I want whatever I can get out of it and to go as far as I can before my looks fade. I certainly don't want to be a fat, middle-

24

aged hack in some provincial company.' He pulled a face. 'I'd rather do anything than end up like that.' He smiled. 'End of speech.'

Sylvia laughed. 'Let's go through to the lounge.'

'I'll help with the clearing up,' he said.

She shook her head. 'No, leave it. Vanny will help me with it on Monday.'

'Vanny?' He looked interested.

'Vanny cleans for me,' she explained, 'I feel rather ashamed to admit.'

'Why be ashamed? I once spent a whole summer washing the dishes and cooking-pots in a hospital kitchen. Come on,' he began to collect up the plates, 'it won't take long.'

They dumped it all in the deep sink and Sylvia made them coffee whilst David sat at the scrubbed-pine kitchen table playing with a golf ball which had been resting on top of a ceramic tub full of pens and badges and general clutter.

'Do you play?' he asked as she placed two large cups and saucers on the table.

'Golf? No.' She took milk from the refrigerator. 'Sugar?'

'No, thanks. This is a nice room.'

'Yes, it's where I tend to spend most of my time. Wherever I happen to be in the house I always gravitate towards here.' She poured the coffee and sat opposite him watching the golf ball rolling between his strong hands across the worn wooden surface. 'Do you play?'

'Tennis, yes, golf, no.'

'One of the boys must have left it there. Peter plays it with his father from time to time.' She stirred in the milk.

David held the ball again, twisting it around, letting his

fingertips trace the dimples. 'It was a really great meal, thanks.'

Sylvia laughed, a little self-consciously. 'It was a very simple meal. I never have much time for cooking these days.'

'Because of the pressure of work for the magazine?'

She nodded. 'I'm also about to embark upon a TV arts thing. My own show, if you can believe such an idea.'

'That's great.' He grinned broadly. 'Maybe, when I'm famous, you'll have me on as a guest.' He laughed at that thought. 'You may have to run for a long time.' He kept watching her. 'That's *really* great, why didn't you tell me before?'

'It's early days yet, won't be on the air for ages and, besides, lots of things could go wrong.'

'"The Sylvia McLeod Show",' he said, holding his hands apart in mid-air as though gripping a sign.

'It won't be called that, it'll be something like "The Arts Hour", you know, very low key so as not to attract the wrong sort.' She giggled, feeling tipsy.

'So, you lied to me.'

'What?'

'Well, you are in the business.'

'Hardly. I'm not an actor, from the rehearsals I've done I'm not a presenter, either!'

'What do your kids think about it?' He rolled the ball across the table towards her. 'I expect they're excited.'

'Hardly.' She picked up the ball and held it, still warm from his hands. 'Peter isn't really interested in things like that and Charley . . . well, Charley isn't really interested in anything at the moment.' She smiled at him. 'Let's go through now, it'll be much more comfortable.'

'Right,' Sylvia said, tucking her legs under her as she crumpled into the sofa leather next to him, 'tell me about

26

yourself. Christensen, that sounds very Nordic, Scandinavian or something,' She poured them large glasses of brandy from Doug's "special" stock and was beginning to feel very warm and comfortable, and slightly out of control.

He nodded. 'I took my Dad's name although I never knew him . . . I was illegitimate, *am* illegitimate. He was a seaman and I was the result of a long affair he had with my mother. She died two years ago . . .' He looked at her. 'Sounds like a bit of a cliché to me.'

Sylvia shook her head. 'Do you know if he's still alive?'

He sipped his brandy. 'He was killed. My mother told me it was an accident at sea but I don't know. I have some photographs that she kept.' He looked distant for a moment. 'She always said I'd be famous, but I suppose every parent tells their kids that.'

'I never told my children that,' Sylvia said, a little sardonically.

'Anyway, that's it really, not much to tell, no sad stories, no bad memories. My mother was very strong, very stubborn, a little unbending, things were either right or wrong, black or white, no grey areas.'

'What did she think of you becoming an actor?'

'I think she was really appalled at the idea but she never said anything to me, she never attempted to stop me.'

Sylvia studied him closely. There was something else there, but for a moment she couldn't believe or quite understand what it was. She wanted to ask but was afraid of sounding foolish when she wanted to appear worldly and even sophisticated. Her briefs felt damp, she felt incredibly excited. They both moved towards one another on the squashy sofa, Sylvia still holding her brandy glass, and they kissed. She felt terribly relieved and much more

27

at ease, there was to be no death knell of rejection, no hurt pride.

He went downstairs afterwards to the kitchen. She thought he was leaving but then heard him clattering around in the kitchen. A little while later he reappeared with a tray of coffee and sandwiches.

'I'm very sorry about this,' he said. 'I always have to eat something after the first time with someone; must be to do with nervous energy or something.' He offered her a doorstep-size cheese sandwich oozing tomato ketchup which Sylvia declined laughing hysterically.

'My God, David, next time I'll make sure that there's a packed lunch-box under the pillow.'

He choked, laughing on his first bite.

Naked, he was far more beautiful than she had supposed. Not too heavily muscled, for she hated that, but enough to give him that fine 'V' shape she liked, broad shoulders and slim hips. He had footballer's legs; strongly built, muscled and hirsute, curling blond hair which covered his tummy and chest, too. She held him tightly and breathed him into her, soapy and carnal, sweaty and sweet. He rolled over in his half-sleep towards her and fell asleep in her embrace. He was that Angel in the darkness, over-whelming her with a sense of power, something which she possessed, something that breathed life back into her, handing back the excruciating pleasure and the release she craved. It was not love, then. She could only remember him inside her, his penis the only thing she cared about, never wanting it out of her as she fucked him on and on and on, screaming and shaking her head as though refusing to believe, her fingers biting into his hard flesh, riding him until he was spent, until the cords of his neck

28

stood out as though to explode and he called out as if in agony, and Sylvia never gave up until it was impossible to continue. They lay together for a long time, she could feel him wet against her skin. When he was deep asleep, which wasn't long, she eased herself out of his arms and masturbated away the slick, oiling desires he had released in her.

Sylvia got out of bed slowly, careful not to wake him. She showered, then dressed quickly. It was still very early as she eased the Porsche out of the square, driving the empty city streets towards the motorway. She had left a scrawled note for him, 'Had to leave at the crack of dawn to visit my son. See you soon. Please leave some indication! Love, Sylvia.'

She stopped at a motorway service to freshen up and have a bite to eat. She looked at her reflection in the washroom mirror, her long hair tied back in a pony tail, there was something different. She was sure she looked different although it wasn't a specific thing, something about her eyes perhaps, it seemed to emanate from them. She rummaged through her bag for a comb and make-up box and proceeded to rearrange her hair into a centre parting and bun which seemed to give her face more order. She stared at herself, brushing mascara on to her eyelashes and rolling a blood-red lipstick around her wide mouth, a startling contrast to her jet-black hair and perfect white skin. Someone had once described her as the embodiment of the English Rose, which she had always taken to imply some inherent quality of rusticity. However, today she could possibly understand what they meant, a thirty-eight-year-old English Rose! She smiled, it was quite a joke, her age and the fact that her mother was Russian. She threw everything back into her bag and took one more look, feeling very good indeed, very confident but wondering how long this sensation would last.

* * *

29

Ectonford School was in a dozy village of the same name in Northamptonshire, close to the border of Huntingdonshire. The main school building dated from the seventeenth century but there were more recent additions up to, and including, McLeod Hall, a teaching and library block built and equipped by Richard's father in the early sixties. The McLeod-Ectonford tradition seemed to stretch back into the mists of time, no McLeod male, so it seemed, ever went anywhere else! It was the law. Sylvia could almost feel the weight of this responsibility as she got out of her Porsche and looked up at the brown ironstone buildings set amidst perfect grounds. The boys were at church when she arrived but she was met by Charley's housemaster, a rather large, chummy sort of man with a vice-like handshake.

'Mrs McLeod,' he said, smiling wide.

'Mr Beavitt,' she replied, extracting herself from his grip.

'The boys are in church so that gives us a few moments of peace.' He guided the way up a clattering staircase to his small study which overlooked the playing fields at the back. The sash window was pulled up and a cool breeze pushed the crisp white net curtain to and fro. 'Well now, well now,' he began, settling her in a small armchair. 'What's all of this? What's going on with Charles?' He sat in the chair opposite, shuffling through a file of papers.

'I was hoping you could tell me that,' Sylvia said.

'Yes, indeed yes,' he nodded, sitting back to look at her. 'The headmaster has asked me to deal with this in the hope that we can iron out any problems.'

'I see,' but she really did not.

The door opened and in bustled Mrs Beavitt with a tray of coffee and fruit cake. Sylvia smiled at the grey-haired

30

woman and thanked her. Mrs Beavitt backed out of the overcrowded room clicking the door shut behind her.

'Shall I be mother?' Mr Beavitt asked.

Sylvia crossed her legs and smiled. She hated all such expressions, thoughtless words which kept the little woman in her place, a joke to be involved with such an unimportant domestic chore. She watched the steam rising from the golden-coloured liquid in the pretty tea cups.

'Milk?' he asked.

She tried to imagine him in a frilly apron, it made her grin. 'Thank you.'

'Sugar?'

'No, thank you.'

He handed her the cup and saucer.

'Thank you.'

'Cake?' He looked up from the tray, a quizzical expression on his face.

'No, thank you.'

'It's my wife's, you know, home baking and all that.'

'No, really, I'm sure it's delicious.'

'She'll be very disappointed.' He was already offering her a plate full.

'Well, perhaps just a tiny piece.'

He handed her a huge chunk on one of the delicate plates, watching until she had taken a bite then sitting back satisfied that hospitality had been done.

'Charles has been rather a problem of late, Mrs McLeod, this latest incident is one more in a long line of less important ones although let me say from the outset that Ectonford views all crimes seriously.'

'I see.' Sylvia attempted to balance the cake on her knee and drink the tea. 'What is the cause behind

Charley's reluctance to settle down this year, would you say?'

'In with a bad crowd,' he said sententiously.

'A bad crowd?' Sylvia couldn't imagine such a thing at Ectonford.

Beavitt nodded, flicking through his papers. 'Ah, yes, here we see it all, Dean Farrell-Lacey, Adrian Buckmaster, John Hayden . . .'

'But I don't quite understand; can't they be separated out, the ring-leader removed?'

'Charles *is* the ring-leader!'

'Oh.' Sylvia sat back and thought about that for a moment. 'You say that he's done other, less serious things, what were they?' She hardly dared ask.

'Missing his prep class, failing to give in his prep, missing some classes on his time-table, rudeness to members of cleaning and domestic staff, behaving foolishly and dangerously during fencing class.' He looked up from the list he was reading. 'It's unlike him, Mrs McLeod. I think he's got much worse over the last term, even though the *whole* academic year hasn't been very good.'

Sylvia nodded. 'I appreciate that we must treat this seriously, Mr Beavitt, but, surely, don't all teenage boys experiment with drink, don't they all get drunk from time to time?'

He smiled, rather sadly she thought. 'Well, not all, but a good percentage of them do. Never like Charles, though.' He sighed. 'I've never seen a boy in that state, not in my thirty years of teaching.'

'What do you propose doing about it?' she asked.

'Our usual practice is to withdraw privileges but, in the case of Charles, there are precious few left to take away.'

'Do you think it would be better for everyone if we

were to withdraw Charley from the school?' She would love to have seen Richard's face at such a suggestion.

Mr Beavitt looked appalled. 'Mrs McLeod, it's not the policy of this school to give up on one of its boys.'

'But, what if one of the boys gives up on it?'

He looked at her in disbelief, clearing his throat before continuing. 'I've arranged for Charles to miss Sunday lunch today as I thought you would expect to take him out. Normally this would be one of the privileges he could no longer enjoy but, in the circumstances, well, I think it could be beneficial.'

'Thank you.'

'Come, then,' he said, easing himself out of the comfortable armchair, 'I'll take you to him.'

Charley was waiting for them in the main entrance hall. He looked serious and, Sylvia thought, somewhat uncomfortable in his uniform.

'I suppose he's told you what an absolute disgrace I am,' Charley said as they drove away for lunch.

Sylvia slowed the car at the school gates and turned out into the narrow lane. 'He seems all right, just very concerned.'

'What about you and Dad, are you both *very* concerned?'

'Yes, of course, what do you expect?'

Charley looked straight ahead. 'Can't I just leave?' he asked at last.

Sylvia had no idea. 'You only have a bit longer to do, a year or so and you'll be at university.'

'Ah, yes, the next stage in the master plan.'

'Where do you want to eat?' Sylvia asked, ignoring that.

He shrugged.

'The Crown?' She remembered the hotel in the next

33

village. 'You haven't been thrown out of there recently I take it?'

He didn't reply.

They raced along the country lanes in silence until she pulled the Porsche on to the wide forecourt in front of The Crown Hotel. 'Come on, then,' she said climbing out, 'don't sulk.'

'Why didn't you go on the tennis coaching trip with Peter?' she asked over their meal.

'Loss of privileges,' he remarked sourly, looking up at her, 'like in prison.'

'Come on, Charley, for God's sake, Ectonford is hardly a prison.'

'You don't have to live there.'

'You used to like it.'

'When I was ten!'

'No, not when you were ten, until quite recently actually.'

'Well, I don't anymore.'

'I see.'

'Do you?'

'If you think that by behaving in this way you'll persuade your father to remove you from the school, then, let me assure you, there's absolutely no chance.'

He looked away, disgusted. 'McLeod Hall would crumble no doubt.'

Sylvia was forced to smile despite herself. 'Something like that.'

He looked at her and smiled as their eyes met. 'I'm sorry, Mum.'

'So you should be,' but she continued to grin all the same. 'Why do you do these things?'

'They're ridiculous, right?'

She nodded.

'I don't know, I just have to break away from that place, I've outgrown it all now, all that public school rubbish. I look around me and I see all these boys from the same background going in exactly the same direction. Nothing is ever going to change in this country as long as these places continue, do you know that?'

Sylvia nodded. 'You have a year left, don't put the rest of your life in jeopardy just because you're fed up with how things are now.'

'You mean attack from within, the way you do?'

'That's a nice idea, Charley, if only it were the case.'

'Isn't it the case, then?'

She shook her head. 'Not really.'

'Nice car,' he said as they emerged from the hotel into the warm afternoon sun. 'How do you like it?'

She handed him the keys. 'Fine, have a look at it yourself.' Sylvia crouched down by the open door explaining what everything did. 'As soon as you're seventeen we'll have to arrange some driving lessons for you.'

'Could I drive this?' For a moment he was all smiles, an excited teenager.

Sylvia nodded, laughing. 'Why not?' She let him start the engine before exchanging seats and driving them back to Ectonford. 'I don't want any more of this nonsense, Charley,' she warned him as they approached the school.

'Okay,' he agreed.

'In a matter of weeks it will be the summer holidays, *please*, just cool it until then.'

'All right.' Charley's voice had a slight edge to it now.

She parked the car in the Visitors' car-park and walked up to the main school building with him, the McLeod Hall was across pristine lawns to their right.

'I'll ring you next week,' he said. 'I think I get to use the telephone again by then.'

'You were always allowed to write, weren't you?'

He grinned at her.

Sylvia kissed him lightly on the cheek and briefly touched his back in an encouraging little pat.

'I really enjoyed my lunch, thank you.'

She removed a piece of snagged cotton from his coat pocket. 'I'm glad that Mother has some uses.'

'Mum,' Charley said as she was turning to walk back to her car.

Sylvia turned back to face him. 'Yes?'

His hands were in his blazer pockets, his head hanging down. 'I just . . . I wanted you to know . . . I'm sorry about all of this.'

She nodded. 'I know, Charley, I know,' she said, looking at him in his dark green blazer, like a man acting out the role of child now.

He waved and turned away, running back towards the school house.

Sylvia put a hand up to her mouth and her eyes filled with tears. She drove away quickly, the back wheels kicking up a spray of gravel, watching him running back in the rear-view mirror. She turned the powerful car into the lane but pulled up after half a mile, a jack-knife of emotion catching her, making it impossible to continue, leaning over the steering wheel sobbing. She should have hugged him close to her, it was her only coherent thought, she should have held him close and showed that she cared for him, that she loved him. After a while she sat up, reaching for a tissue to blow her nose and wipe her eyes. She took some deep breaths and slotted a cassette into the player, accelerating away to the sounds of Benny Goodman filling the car.

* * *

Sylvia went up to take another shower and looked at the crumpled bed sheets. It seemed like weeks, months, since she had left the house. David had left her a note in fine, clear handwriting. 'Sylvia, I've taken down your number and will call tomorrow, David.' She smiled to herself, tomorrow was too long, she needed him tonight.

Chapter 2

When David hadn't called after a week Sylvia had mentally shrugged and told herself to stop being ridiculous but, every time the telephone rang, she found herself quickly grabbing up the receiver. However much she immersed herself in work he simply would not go away. She rationalized by deciding that it was simply a reaction to having lived like a celibate for the last few months. Sylvia hated the feeling of being out of control with another person and she attempted to refuse it now. Vanny accused her of being irritable and she apologized, explaining it away by saying she felt unwell. In fact she did feel ill, she had not been sleeping properly and was working long hours to get the television show right.

It was Thursday and after eleven when she arrived back from the studio to discover him sitting on her top step at Camden Square.

'I lost your telephone number' he said by way of a greeting, standing up to allow her key to reach the lock.

Sylvia pushed the heavy door open and went inside without a word. David followed her through into the kitchen where she was filling a kettle for some tea. 'Do you make a habit of dropping in on people at this time of night?' she asked, turning to look at him, wanting him.

'I've been out there for hours,' he explained. 'Your neighbours have been giving me extremely odd looks!'

She smiled despite herself. 'You were lucky not to have been arrested, they're a very nervous lot around here.'

'I went through directory enquiries but you were

impossible to reach, they wouldn't give me your telephone number.'

Sylvia poured hot water into the teapot, warming it up ready for the tea leaves and boiling water. There was a certain therapeutic value in making tea and she enjoyed doing something vaguely domestic. 'Douglas was always ex-directory, I don't know why because he never answered the phone himself, he always had that answering machine thing.' She poured the warming water away and quickly made the tea, dumping the little house tea-cosy over the pot. They sat down at the old scrubbed table waiting for the tea to brew, Sylvia feeling as though a large snake was uncoiling itself in her stomach. She was rather infuriated at her reactions to this youth.

'We should be celebrating with something stronger than that, actually,' he said, watching Sylvia pour the tea. 'I've got that picture, they told me this evening.'

Sylvia held the pot in mid-pour and looked at him. 'But that's absolutely marvellous.' She smiled with pleasure. 'How fantastic.' She put the teapot down and, reaching across, took his hand, squeezing it hard. 'Why didn't you tell me when you arrived?'

'You were annoyed. I wasn't sure if I was being invited in or not.'

'It's been a long and difficult day . . .' She stopped herself. 'God, I sound *old*.'

'I have to go to the States,' he said very casually, 'New York and then Los Angeles.'

'When does filming start?' She hoped she hadn't sounded too anxious.

'I have six weeks before I have to leave.'

'Are you pleased with the part?'

'It's very showy. My agent said it could lead to other

things . . .' He smiled. 'Who cares, I get a free trip to America, a chance to see a bit of the world.'

'No,' Sylvia stated emphatically, 'this is for you, I can tell, they wouldn't take chances unless the risks were minimal.'

He toasted her with his teacup. 'To your success. I saw the TV ad for your show. I've told everyone I know you, they don't believe me, of course.' He smiled, he always smiled.

'I'm terrified about it,' she said. 'I feel sure that I'll fall flat on my face.'

'Nonsense, you'll be great.' He looked at her. 'I've missed you.'

'I missed you, too. I didn't know whether to expect you again.'

'What? Why not? I've been trying to reach you like crazy for days.'

'I'm glad.' She was flustered, falling into the same old traps, making the same mistakes as before. Even her smile was the same, the same phrases, the same man, younger and more beautiful this time but the same as before. Why, when she wanted security in a relationship, she went out of her way to court disaster she didn't know. Perhaps it was something to do with her libido. Perhaps it was simply a flaw in her personality. After all, hadn't she dumped Richard, Mr Security, and gone off in search of some mythical being, someone to make her whole again, to make her feel part of something. The snake in her stomach coiled and uncoiled itself with amazing rapidity. If things went any further with David, then she only had herself to blame when it all exploded in her face but, on the other hand, she couldn't resist him. To resist him now would mean unhappiness. The snake lurched, her mouth felt dry whilst the rest of her felt hot and clammy, she began to ache for him, rocking slightly to ease the tension. She rationalized her life in the seconds that remained. Richard had Miranda, didn't he? Douglas was dead. She was resigned to accept the consequences. She was a mature, liberated woman in control of her job and her life and she would not allow this 'youth' to take over, just pleasure her for a while. Sylvia didn't really believe any of this, in fact she felt out of control with her life, but it did serve to make the next mistake more acceptable. She would not get 'involved'. Sylvia smiled now, satisfied, and asked him if he was staying the night.

That was the night he told her he was in love with her. It was a long time after the heat of passion (how she loved these phrases) but he had told her all the same in that frank, serious way of his. How was she supposed to respond? She could almost hear Doug's crude laughter over her shoulder, which made her next comment all the more embarrassing. 'You don't have to say that, David.' She cringed inside.

'I know,' he replied. 'Don't you believe me?'

'You hardly know me.'

'Why should knowing you have anything to do with loving you?'

'Because I might be a first-class bitch,' Sylvia suggested.

'Are you?' he challenged.

'Quite possibly.'

There was a long silence in which she thought he might have fallen asleep. 'You don't have to tell me that you love me,' he said quietly in the dark.

Sylvia sighed a silent prayer of relief and didn't say anything. She was overwhelmed with sleep and could remember no more. She woke up late with David still fast asleep on his stomach, spread-eagled all over her bed.

* * *

'Call in sick,' David told her, sliding into the shower with her, swishing the curtain behind him.

'Don't be ridiculous.' She looked at his naked body in the steamy heat of the enclosed environment. They were facing each other and it was obvious that his intentions were not entirely honourable. 'Look,' she said, handing him the soap, 'I have my job and I must be there on time whether I'm ill or dying . . .'

'The show must go on,' he said, handing back the soap. 'Well, you know I understand that, but I'm in a real predicament . . .' He drew her to him, holding her close, guiding her hand down on to him.

Sylvia laughed. 'God, you have to be joking!'

He kissed her, the hot water tumbling over them, their hair slicked down, moving her hand in a comfortable rhythm until she established it by herself, placing his arms over her shoulders, the palms of his hands braced against the dribbling tiles.

Sylvia watched his shoulder muscles tense and bunch as she made him come on to her, biting into his hard flesh.

'What about you?' he asked, holding her.

She looked into his eyes as they kissed. 'I have to get going . . . *now*.'

He stepped back, holding up his hands in surrender. 'If work must come first . . .'

Sylvia picked up the soap and worked it rigorously, quickly over her skin, her words bubbling as she stood under the powerful jet of water. '. . . It must.'

Vanny came in as they were having a rushed breakfast, David wrapped in a towelling robe Sylvia had found.

'Morning,' Vanny said, looking at David and then scowling at Sylvia.

'Hello, Vanny.' Sylvia smiled. 'You're in early. I'd like

you to meet David.' She turned to David. 'David, this is Vanny Van Upp. He . . . he works in the house for me . . .'

'I *clean*,' Vanny said defensively. 'I'm the cleaning person around these parts.' He gave Sylvia the evil eye. 'I didn't catch the last name of your friend.'

'This is David Christensen, Vanny,' Sylvia replied, a fixed grin on her face.

'Pleased to meet you, I'm sure.' He walked over to the sink where he proceeded to make a loud and prolonged clattering, throwing pots and cutlery into the sink for washing up.

David got up and disappeared upstairs to dress. Sylvia took their breakfast things across to Vanny. 'What do you think?' she asked conspiratorially.

Vanny was pulling on his rubber gloves. 'Very nice, Mrs McLeod, but *very* young.' He turned to her and smiled sweetly. 'He the actor?'

Sylvia nodded.

Vanny shrugged. 'The film star?'

'He has appeared in films, yes . . .'

'Just be careful, be very careful,' Vanny warned like the old sage. 'They're like sailors, someone in every port.' He sounded grim.

'For God's sake, Vanny, don't be so bloody cheerful.'

'At least he's pretty, not like old Doug.'

'So, you approve?'

Vanny dunked his hands into the water and began to wash up with the aid of his mop. 'He'll do. This a last fling, then?'

Sylvia was appalled. 'No, it's not a last fling, it's not a fling of any sort.'

'What is it, then?' he asked, turning to her and

43

brandishing the dripping mop. 'Does he know about the two teenage sons etcetera, etcetera?'

'I think you're jealous. You are, you're jealous.'

Vanny laughed. 'Don't worry, he's not my sort.'

'Well, I don't want you to be rude to him,' Sylvia warned.

'Me? Rude? When have I ever been rude to any of your guests?' He sounded astonished.

'Molly. You're always rude to her.'

'She follows me around with a duster, a bit too pushy that one by far.'

Sylvia laughed. 'Yes, well, she's just a bit over anxious about my well-being!'

'Pushy,' Vanny repeated, returning to his washing up.

Sylvia turned to leave. 'My first real show today, Vanny, keep your fingers crossed.'

'I'll watch you. What time is it on?'

'At the week-end, we're recording some interviews today.'

'Oh.' Vanny didn't sound very interested then. 'Good luck.'

'Thank you,' she said, looking at the kitchen clock and rushing away.

David was standing in front of her mirror in his briefs as she went into the bedroom to gather up her things. She moved him out of the way to take one last look at herself. 'What do you think?' she asked.

He was sitting on the end of her bed pulling on his socks. 'You look great.'

Sylvia looked hard at herself. She was wearing a red midi outfit, a high-waisted skirt with full centre zip, and a short matching top. The dark blouse underneath was cut low and she had put some dangling chain jewellery on over it which she knew would cause problems later. 'What do you think?' she asked again, looking down at her dark tights as she slipped into black, low-heeled, chisel-toed shoes. 'Tell me.'

David was wriggling into his too-tight jeans. 'I told you, you look fine.'

'Do you like my hair parted in the middle like this and tied up?'

'It makes you look very intellectual, sophisticated, very beautiful.' He came across and kissed her gently on the lips. 'You'll be late,' he warned.

She took one more look at herself, tucking a strand of black hair behind her ear. 'Well, they'll probably change everything anyway.'

'Break a leg,' he said as she started to leave.

'Thanks, do they say that for TV shows?'

He shrugged. 'You look fabulous.'

'There's no need to go overboard!'

She rushed out of the house, tripping over Vanny as he pulled the vacuum cleaner across the hallway. 'Wish me luck,' she said, slamming out of the house and driving away like a woman in search of a speeding fine.

Sylvia walked from darkness on to the brightly lit set where the two chromium sit-up-and-beg interview chairs sat on thick shag pile. She looked at the backdrop, a panoramic view of London, with disgust.

'I thought we'd decided against this view.' She spoke to George, the Floor Manager, knowing that Edmund, sitting up in the gallery like a spider at the centre of his web, would hear. 'It's bloody awful, too distracting.'

George told her not to worry, but he was receiving a message from on high through his radio headphones, she could tell by the look of his eyes. 'Is she a fucking set designer now?' Edmund was asking him. 'Tell her to

concentrate on getting her part right, I'll decide the rest.'
George smiled. 'Edmund says that he'll have a word with
the designer.'

Sylvia took her seat and had her microphone attached.
More lights came up and make-up were soon on the set
dabbing at a shiny spot on her forehead. Sylvia had been
looking at herself on a monitor by her feet. 'What does it
look like?' she asked the girl.

'Fine, you look great,' she replied, moving quickly
away into the shadows.

Sylvia picked up her clipboard of questions, her first
'real' interviewee was renowned sculptress, Dame June
Skipworth, an ancient who was in the midst of rediscov-
ery. Sylvia met her for the first time as she shuffled on to
the set, guided by Trish, Edmund's personal assistant,
and George, who was talking at the old woman in a very
loud voice. Sylvia realized that the Dame was extremely
hard of hearing. She stood to meet the famous woman
who was now slumped into a chair. 'Hello, I'm Sylvia
McLeod.'

Dame June was wearing something akin to a pixy-hood
which was a little too large so that her small, wizened face
barely penetrated from under it into the light. 'Yes?' the
Dame asked.

Sylvia picked up a small gloved hand and shook it. 'I'm
Sylvia McLeod,' she said very loudly.

'Oh, yes.' She smiled vacantly into Sylvia's face. 'I shall
be ninety on Saturday,' she said.

Sylvia noticed with horror that the Dame's top set
dropped and moved about in her mouth when she spoke.
'How marvellous,' she said loudly, sitting down again.

'Have we begun?' the Dame asked, her teeth clicking.

'Not yet.' Sylvia articulated as loudly and as clearly as

possible. She looked into the darkness, searching about for George, but he was not to be seen.

'Who did you say you were?' the Dame asked, sucking at her wayward dentures.

'Sylvia *McLeod*.'

The old woman nodded, her pixy point bobbing about, causing Sylvia to gulp back a growing and hysterical desire to laugh.

'Okay, studio, quiet please,' George commanded, and the studio fell strangely silent, the atmosphere suddenly changing from noise and fuss to one of expectant silence, tense and focused now on to the one bright spot of light where Sylvia and her guest sat. They were running through the introduction now, the familiar music and the title graphics, the letters tumbling together to form 'THE ARTS PROGRAMME'. Sylvia was conscious of a red-eyed camera moving in towards her and of watching the fingers of a hand counting down the final seconds. The auto-cue began to move and Sylvia was reading her introduction.

'Hello, this is Sylvia McLeod and I'd like to welcome you to the first edition of "The Arts Programme". On this first programme in the series we meet Dame June Skipworth, a sculptress whose career stretches back over seventy years.'

'Is it now?' Dame June clicked from her chair.

Sylvia, smiling, continued with her introduction as the camera shot changed to Dame June under her pixy-hood, her little red nose pointing out from underneath it. She reminded Sylvia of one of the little animals in *Wind In The Willows*, but she completed her introduction and pressed ahead with the strange interview. 'Dame June, you knew Pablo Picasso and Georges Braque, Henri

47

Matisse, Albert Gleizes and many other modern artists . . .'

'Braque, did you say Braque?' she asked.

'Georges Braque,' Sylvia nodded, 'could you tell us something about him?'

'I didn't know Braque.' She looked vacantly at Sylvia. 'I believe I met him once, in Paris . . .'

Sylvia pressed on. The Dame was able to talk entertainingly, and at length, about Picasso and discussed her early work and its influences with clarity and an ease with belied her decrepitude. She spoke movingly of her work at the front in the First World War where she worked as a nurse.

'I enjoyed it,' Dame June said as she was unhooked from her microphone. 'What did you say your name was, dear?'

Sylvia took her hand, bending close to make her understand. 'Sylvia McLeod,' she said once again.

'Ah yes,' the hood nodded, almost as though it had a life of its own, 'and this is your own programme?'

'I present it,' Sylvia replied, still bent over.

'You did it very well, my dear, much better than those awful Americans who keep stopping you every few seconds for an advertisement about exterminating cockroaches, very Surrealist, I suppose . . .' She chuckled to herself.

Sylvia laughed.

'Was I all right?'

Sylvia grasped an arm and began to help the old woman on to her feet. 'It was fine.'

Edmund sat back into the old leather booth of his favourite pub and beamed at her. 'It was bloody good, darling, and you were *very* cool,' he said.

'She was a funny old thing . . .'

'Brain dead, really. She must be so used to working in television studios these days, she seemed to wake up quite suddenly and then went on to automatic pilot. I think she says exactly the same thing in every interview she gives . . . doesn't matter what the questions are!'

Sylvia smiled. 'Well, thank God it's over. Maybe we can have a live one next time.'

'We think it's a male dancer for you, one of those Russian defectors. You speak Russian, don't you?'

Sylvia looked at him and then realized it was a joke. 'He can speak English.'

'American, actually. You'll probably understand, though.'

'Did you see her hood?' Sylvia began to giggle.

'See it, darling, I was thinking of offering it its own show!' He looked at her, examining her face. 'Who's the lucky man, then, Sylvia?' he asked, taking another drink of beer.

'What makes you jump to that conclusion?' her smile giving her away.

'Well, darling, you have this kind of glow about you. You look terribly good and you came across in a *very* relaxed way. The camera *never* lies.'

'Why can't that be my natural professionalism?'

'Well, whatever, but this show lasts a whole season, do you think this current beau will stay the course?'

'No comment,' Sylvia said, leaning across to kiss his cheek before leaving.

'What was that in aid of?' he asked, smiling.

'Nothing,' Sylvia replied, 'absolutely nothing!'

She had smiled but Sylvia knew that it was wrong. Why should screwing around give her more confidence? Her high began to evaporate, she was doing it again, and this time it was on film, letting a man get the upper hand. She stopped the car and walked by the river for a while. She remembered that Doug had always told her to stop compromising herself and 'get on with the dance'. Of course, he had been the first to take advantage. The first time she ever met him he had been drunk, she had gone to interview him for the magazine at his house in Camden Square, now it was her house. She had disliked him from the very first moment. A drunken, boorish man, almost twenty years older than her, ill-mannered and smelly.

'I've heard about you,' he had bellowed, waving a finger at her. 'If you've come to do the same hatchet job on me as those other poor bastards, you can just get the hell out now and forget it.'

Douglas Emmitt had a reputation for being difficult. A famous artist, successful and bright, someone who did not suffer fools gladly. Sylvia had seen him once on a talk-show where he had been horrendously truculent, reducing the poor host to jelly in front of the viewing millions. It was this image that she carried with her, a fire-snorting dragon man with a shock of flecky black hair making mincemeat of all comers. Her research had dug up the basic facts: Douglas Emmitt, fifty-six years old (in 1973), Grammar School boy to Art College to International success. He had lived with Yolanda for over ten years but they never married. There were no dependants. He was known as a some-time drunk and all-time womanizer.

His work over recent years had become less prolific and he had all but disappeared from the scene when a retro-spective exhibition of his work was held to coincide with a series of new paintings which he had completed of the oil fields in Alberta. Sylvia had met him in the kitchen where he was balancing rather precariously on the draining-board washing his feet in the deep sink, his dirty, paint-splattered jeans rolled up to his knees. Sylvia had pushed open the door, having been let in and pointed in the right direction by a washed-out blonde who must have been all of eighteen and on her way out. She felt decidedly like Alice. 'I'm Sylvia McLeod,' she had introduced herself, looking at the scene with a mixture of horror and wonder. '*Artist's Choice*?'

It had been an inauspicious beginning. Once he had climbed down from the sink he tracked his way into the back sitting-room. It was full of empty bottles and cigarette burns in the furnishings. He cleared a space for her on the sofa by dumping a pile of soiled washing behind it. Sylvia sat whilst he prowled. He refused to answer most of her questions preferring to harangue her instead about the state of the world and his own angst in particular. She had left him with hardly anything usable and had sat up half the night rehashing her research notes. After writing the piece she forgot about it until, a few days after publication, she had received a call from Douglas Emmitt asking her to a private viewing of the Albertan Oil Scenes at Georges Eisenberg's Gallery.

He was wearing a crumpled cream-coloured suit, he had shaved, combed his curly hair and was sober. Douglas Emmitt was well preserved, some might say pickled, and looked, she decided, like an old boxer gone to seed. He was a very large man, strong-looking, bull-necked, and once, probably, rather handsome. He had very black eyes, she had noted them the other day when they had seemed to flash and spit fire at her, and large hands with thick, clumsy fingers that looked stumpy and faintly ridiculous.

'I was . . . difficult the other day, Mrs McLeod,' he began, 'and I apologize for that,' he said it defiantly, as

51

though it made no difference to him whether she accepted it or not.

'You were rude, Mr Emmitt,' Sylvia replied, but took the offered hand and squeezed it as firmly as she could.

He took her around the silent gallery. There were a score of canvases hanging at precise intervals along the hessian-backed wall. Each had a sudden, dazzling, almost garish, swirl of colour, bright yellows and orange, reds and turquoise. They were standing in front of a large canvas which, from the programme notes, she discovered was entitled 'Oil Well On Fire – 1971'.

'You have a rather prosaic way of naming your work,' Sylvia remarked with amusement.

He put his hands into the baggy jacket pockets and shrugged. 'Who cares . . . what does prosaic mean, anyway?'

Sylvia laughed and they walked on to the next picture in silence, her heels clicking noisily on the wooden floor. He was several paces behind, probably looking at her legs she thought as she had worn a mini-skirt suit, not too audacious though.

'You wrote in that piece that I saw art as being beautiful and worthy but not important.' He was standing back now, squinting at his painting. 'I don't really understand that . . . I don't even recall saying that.'

'You said it several times, repeating it over and over again.' She turned from the painting to look at him. 'I'll send you the cassette tape of the interview if you don't believe me.'

He didn't look at her. 'I believe you. Actually, I think that the reverse is true, sometimes art is sordid and disgusting and it's rarely worthy but it's always important.'

Sylvia didn't agree but declined to say anything. She turned instead to the next painting, an oil rig spouting crude oil entitled 'Oil Strike'. 'You didn't like the piece I take it.'

'On the contrary, you were very kind to me, I didn't deserve it at all.'

'No you didn't.' She walked on. 'How is the retrospective going?'

'Oh, my work is not what it was, that's for sure.'

'I once saw a picture of yours for sale in New York, must have been in 1958.'

'What were you doing in New York in 1958?' He had stopped to light a cigarette.' That was my pre-Pop Art days, it was all very daring and avant-garde,' he said in a gentle self-mocking way. 'I think it's like prehistoric days now, when one looks back . . .'

Sylvia smiled and felt a little sad for him. 'I wonder what you were up to in New York in '58.'

'Being *cool*, I suppose,' he answered. 'Just being cool and hanging loose around out there.'

'Historically, of course, it's a coincidence but it's rather intriguing all the same.'

'It's a long time ago that's for sure.' He blew a long trail of smoke out of the corner of his mouth.

'Not so long.'

'Getting on for fifteen years . . . Jesus, it's a life-time,' he complained, laughing heartily. 'I was a lot younger then.' He pointed a stubby finger at her then beat a fist against his chest. 'Inside I'm still a twenty-year-old, I guess.'

It had happened very gradually, she started to see him, perhaps once or twice every few weeks but on a continuing basis. It hadn't meant much to her, he wasn't as vile as she had at first thought and he could be very entertaining and amusing. They generally met somewhere for lunch or dinner, she never went to Camden Square and he never asked her. His studio was there and he was, he informed her, a pig when he was working. He had to go off to Spain for a month and it was only then that she realized how much she missed having him around. When he returned she was invited to spend a week-end at his old, ramshackle farmhouse which was, he said, his place of retreat and inspiration. She saw it first from the brow of a hill, nestling amidst tall pines and looking fabulous, something out of a fairy-tale. On closer inspection, however, she could see how the thatch resembled moth-eaten fur or a cat with advanced mange. It was a two-storey building, probably two hundred years old, and was shored up on one side by huge beams, like railway buffers, which pushed against the bowing north end of the tumble-down house. It had not received a coat of paint in decades and most of the woodwork was rotten, sunbaked and then attacked by frosts and rains and winters past. The window glass was opaque. The jungle of a garden outside was now in the process of crawling ubiquitously around and up and into the building. Sylvia had a mental picture of Miss Havisham amidst her wedding day ruin and decay sitting in some upstairs room covered in cobwebs.

It had turned out to be cold, rain swept over the week-end in a fine mist which gave way from time to time to a torrential downpour. They slept in a lumpy, creaking bed which felt damp. As she looked up Sylvia could trace cracks, like river tributaries on a map, roving across the ceiling and trailing down the walls, mingling with the black spider webs. Paint flaked off whenever it was touched. Douglas snored after making love to her, a half-hearted event which she hadn't enjoyed much, feeling, almost, that she really wasn't part of it. He tossed and turned in his fractured sleep, grunting muddled words. The mattress springs kept her awake, noisy and uncomfortable, and she had broken sleep and disturbing dreams. She finally got up at seven o'clock, having hardly slept, and went down the rickety staircase which had a length of rope instead of a banister rail. When she turned on the tap in the dirty kitchen the pipes exploded into life, banging and vibrating loudly enough to wake the dead. Needless to say, Douglas slept on. Sylvia attempted to make some breakfast and woke him up with a mug of black tea and matching toast, salvaged from the ancient gas stove.

Douglas went out in the pouring rain to sketch a copse of skeletal trees which stood high on a barrow across the fields at the back of the house. Sylvia made lunch on the gassy stove and lit the antique water heater for a proposed, and much needed, bath. Douglas came back, dripping oilskins creating pools of water wherever he stood, sometime after four-thirty, it was almost dark. Sylvia had built up a roaring fire in a last-ditch attempt to get warm and was curled up beside it in the sitting-room, the most comfortable place, reading yesterday's *Guardian*.

'It's bloody cold out,' he shouted from the kitchen. 'Are you all right?' He came into the room. 'Sorry I was so long. I met the old chap from the next farm, went over for a bite of lunch.'

Sylvia carried on reading.

He sat in the wing-chair opposite and rubbed his hands together in front of the flames. Rain crashed against the dirty windows and the tattered curtains blew back in the strong draught. 'I got some useful stuff down,' he said at last.

'How can you possibly work in the rain?' she asked from behind the newspaper.

'With great difficulty,' he chuckled.

'Doesn't the paper become soggy?'

'No, I sketch away quite happily under cover of some plastic sheeting.'

She glanced at him, lowering the paper to see if he was being stupid, he was quite straight-faced. 'How long did you stop for your lunch?'

'An hour or two, why?' He bent forward to move his heavy walking boots inside the ingle-nook closer to the heat.

'Oh, no reason. I saved you some lunch.'

'That's good,' he sighed, sitting back again and stretching out, toasting his feet. 'I'll have it in a bit.'

'I threw it out, you can't keep what I prepared.'

'What was it?' he asked, yawning.

Sylvia didn't reply. 'There's water dripping from the bathroom ceiling, it fell on to my back when I was in the bath earlier.'

'Oh, you managed to get some hot water, that's good.'

'It was barely warm, why don't you do something with this place, you know, bring it into the twentieth century?'

He smiled sleepily. 'It's all right. I ought to get rid of it really . . . Had it far too long now . . .'

Douglas snored noisily for the next two hours whilst Sylvia, exasperated, prepared herself some tea from the supply of food she had carried down with her from London in the wicker basket. The kitchen was damp and freezing, the wind howled around the house and she could hear a door or window banging on one of the derelict outhouses. She carried a tray through and huddled herself up in the armchair near the comforting fire, watching the flames. Sometimes she read a few lines from the book she had brought but, more often, she watched the licking flames and wondered what she was doing stuck out in the

56

wilds with a man she barely knew and with whom she was now sleeping and making, albeit unsatisfying, love.

She watched the flames and reviewed the events of her life, those which had led her to this present impasse, with a detachment that really appalled her. She attempted, at first, to catch the feelings of love she had certainly once had, had declared, for Richard but there was only numbness now. Charley and Peter were the only tangible reminders of it. Peter, brilliant and steady. Charley, causing her doubt and grief by his actions. Peter, who would follow in the footsteps of his ancestors. Charley, who would not, the product of some wayward gene probably from her side of the family, as the thought of Richard's family possessing anything so tedious was too far-fetched to countenance. She imagined some Russian ancestor of hers, framed against a cold wintry sky, standing on a vast steppe, probably on the run from Tsarist police, perhaps an assassin. Hadn't her mother, the great Natalia Fiodor, once told her about there being a romantic black sheep in the family? Sylvia wondered if that's what they were called in pre-revolutionary days – it was probably red sheep! Charley certainly had the looks of her maternal grandfather, Mikhail, sturdy, jet-black hair, like her own, and white skin . . . At least, Charley was sturdy, so, it was because of her that Charley had turned out to be bad, her family, her Russians, her fault. Peter looked exactly like his father, a Richard replica. Of course, she had known that he would from the first moment she looked at him. Richard staring back, even the curl of his lip when he yelped was the same. Nothing Russian about Peter, everything pure Richard except that as he grew he took on all the qualities she most admired in her own father, an inner calmness and a complete lack of malice. Peter was always very kind and loving. Whereas

Charley pulled away from bedtime kisses, as a child Peter always hugged her back, his strong little arms pulling her face down to his. Whilst Charley *was* naughty and malicious, Peter would for ever cover up for his elder brother's misdemeanours and, as they grew older, became the one who protected and looked after Charley. Sylvia never worried about Peter, whatever he was up to or wherever he was she didn't fret. When the boys went out sailing together it was always Charley she imagined drowning or doing something ridiculous.

As they grew up Peter became taller whilst Charley became stockier. Someone had dallied with a Cossack, she mused, or a serf. She remembered from a photograph that Grandfather Mikhail had been a nobleman but Sylvia had only ever seen a coarseness in his brooding features, that large head set upon a thick workman's neck, blue-black oily hair and a wicked grin set firm. No, either her mother had lied or the family were full of incorrigible males who had shot their seed into the peasant stock who served them and now she was paying the price for *their* debauchery.

It got her absolutely nowhere, of course, but always entertained her when powers of rationalization failed or deserted her. It always came down to family and guilt and motherhood. Sylvia had always wanted to hug both her children close to her and never let them escape but, instead, she pushed them out into the cold world. Boarding school at seven, it horrified her to look back and think about those tiny boys with their great trunks, like coffins, in which they transported their school things and their Teddy bears. She liked to think that she had rejected her past for Socialist ideals but, deep down, she knew that all the things from her history were too deeply ingrained for her to ever completely let go.

* * *

When they returned from the ramshackle farmhouse, Sylvia moved into Doug's place in Camden Square where she refused to clean and was constantly appalled at the things and the filth she found there. Through a succession of dreary, grey-looking women of various size, shape and age she met Vanny Van Upp who convinced her that he could manage the household routine. She hired him immediately and, after that, pursued her career whilst Doug painted for long hours each day and began to drink more heavily.

'Who's that long young man with the ruby-red hair?' Doug asked her one day a month or so later. 'I found him washing up.'

Sylvia stared at him over the women's page of the *Guardian*. 'For God's sake, Doug,' she winced, rolling her eyes up to the grease-splattered kitchen ceiling.

'Well,' he continued after a long pause, 'as long as he doesn't keep getting in my way, I don't mind.'

'That's very big of you,' Sylvia seethed, 'I mean considering that it's me who pays him to clean up after you.'

Doug shrugged his massive shoulders. 'I'm not that untidy, am I?' he asked, sounding confused.

She looked at him, he was grinning at her. Douglas had a lop-sided grin which never failed to win her over however angry she felt. He was still a ruggedly handsome man for all of his negative traits. It made her grin too despite her annoyance, he was like a great bear, something to cuddle up to and feel safe against. He was the most untidy, the most scruffily dressed man she had ever come across. His shirts were always untucked from his trousers, his collars were always sticking up, his hair always needed a good brushing. Sylvia viewed him like an extremely large twelve-year-old schoolboy and was constantly attempting to put some order into both his appearance and his life. 'You've dropped paint down the front of your new shirt,' she said.

He looked down and poked at the bright blue blobs on the red check material. 'Sorry,' he replied, still grinning.

'I thought we'd worked out a system. You promised that all your new shirts would be kept for when we went out, when *you* meet the public.'

'I never go out.' He laughed. 'I'm sorry, Sylvia I'm just a bum and you can't teach an old dog new tricks.'

She had decided to have a damn good try though. 'You are absolutely beyond redemption.'

He laughed out loud at that. 'You're right . . . quite correct.'

The morning of David's departure for New York Sylvia suddenly realized that it wasn't sickness but panic that was churning around in her stomach. They had spent almost the entire six weeks prior to his departure together, David having moved into her house. Sylvia had helped him move from his seedy bedsit in Plumstead. It was a large square room with a utility wardrobe and a small gas stove. He had furnished it with a double mattress and an old armchair. The disgusting wallpaper was almost obliterated by his posters. A smell of cooked cabbage seemed to permeate the entire house.

'Are you sure you want to take any of this?' Sylvia had asked.

'My books, my posters and my clothes . . .' He looked down at the rather grey sheets and the tatty blankets slung over the mattress. 'I think the rest can stay.'

A couple of boxes and his holdall was all it took to move him out, and they had piled it all into her spare bedroom where it all still lay.

He had gone out early for his morning run, a routine

which he had suffered for the entire six weeks because he wanted to be extra fit for his role. They ate a silent breakfast together after which she went up to help him pack, laying out some underwear, shirts, two pairs of jeans, a pair of training shoes, socks and a pullover, all of which she had bought him. David came out of the shower and dressed quickly, the taxi was due at eight o'clock. He packed everything into his canvas holdall and slung it over his shoulder; leaving almost exactly as he had arrived, blue jeans, leather jerkin, lumberjack shirt, tennis shoes and old crewneck jumper. He looked all of sixteen, the morning sun catching his blond hair turning it almost white. He kissed her very passionately as the taxi arrived, holding her so tightly she could barely breathe.

'I'm going to miss you like crazy,' he said, and left her standing in the quiet square, hugging her arms about herself and staring at the fast disappearing cab wondering if she would ever see or hear from David again.

Chapter 3

'He's only been gone a month and she seems really depressed.' Molly was busy at the sink preparing dinner, scrubbing some carrots clean. Jack sat at the kitchen table reading the daily papers. 'That's why I've asked her for the week-end, she's over tired . . .'

'I don't know why she ever left Richard, to be quite honest,' Jack said, turning over a page of *The Times*, 'and as for that damned artist . . .'

'Richard and Sylvia just grew apart, that's all.'

'I wonder sometimes if she actually knows what she wants.' He looked up at Molly. 'What about this latest man?'

Molly turned, leaning against the sink, carrot in hand. 'I'm not sure.' She looked thoughtful. 'If she's happy, though, that's the major consideration.'

'You said she's depressed a minute ago!'

John came into the kitchen, opening the fridge, searching for food. 'Is there anything to eat, Mum?'

Molly looked at her eldest son, twelve years old going on twenty-five, tall for his age and filling out. 'We'll be having a dinner with Sylvia in a while . . .'

'That's not for hours yet,' he whined.

Molly looked up at the clock. 'Just over an hour . . . What do you want?' she sighed. 'Make yourself a peanut butter sandwich but don't let anyone else see it, I don't want everyone in here.'

John grinned and started to prepare his pre-dinner snack.

'What's he like anyway, this actor?' Jack asked.

'David?' She glanced at John who was engrossed in his task. 'I've only met him twice, once over lunch and once briefly at her house.'

'What's your opinion? You disliked Richard and Douglas, how did your antenna react to David?'

'He seems very nice . . .'

'Not very descriptive.' Jack tut-tutted. 'An English teacher should do better than that. Come on.'

'Okay, he's really, really attractive, very young, blond hair, blue eyes, you know, the whole works.' She looked at John who was eating his sandwich listening to their conversation. 'Haven't you got any homework to occupy you?'

'It's Friday night, Mum,' John complained.

'I'm trying to talk to your father, God knows we get precious little time for that.'

'If you want me to leave just say,' John said in a very superior way.

'Right, *please* leave,' Molly demanded.

John shrugged and walked slowly across the kitchen with his sandwich and his glass of milk, he seemed to take an age to actually get out of the room.

'What's the age difference?' Jack enquired, turning to the sports pages.

Molly thought for a moment. 'David is early twenties to Sylvia's late thirties, I think she's thirty-eight.'

'How early twenties?' Jack asked.

'Early early,' Molly replied, lifting a saucepan down from its shelf and filling it with water.

'And, what do you think?' he asked bluntly

'It's nothing to do with me, she's a grown-up.'

'Well, for my sake, just hazard an opinion.'

'What do *you* think?'

'I think it's bloody ridiculous,' he said bluntly. 'Quite honestly, I don't know what Sylvia's up to . . .'

'Up to?' Molly moved her chopping board across to the sink and began to slice the carrots.

'She has this great new career which she's full of at the moment . . . In the space of three years she's left her husband, lived with a drunk, seen her son turn into a delinquent . . .'

'Charley didn't "turn" into anything, don't make it sound like her fault.'

'. . . And now she takes a lad almost young enough to be her son . . .'

'So, what are you saying, Jack, that she shouldn't have left Richard, the most boring man in the world, that she shouldn't have a decent career?'

'She seems to be making up for a lot of lost time, that's all.'

'That all sounds a little bit self-righteous to me,' Molly said, attacking a carrot with renewed vigour, cutting into it with real verve. 'She's a bright woman, why should she have to be stuck in a relationship she hates, which she finds stultifying?'

'Well, I can think of two good reasons,' Jack replied quietly.

'The boys were off her hands years before she left Richard,' Molly said, tipping the carrots into the sauce-pan. 'I admit she rather fell into a relationship with Douglas Emmitt but I hope this thing with David works out for her, I really do.'

'You don't sound very convinced about it.'

'I've only met him twice, what do I know?'

'You seem to remember exactly what he looks like, every detail.'

'For God's sake, Jack, he's stunning!'

'And he's in America.'

'Yes,' she said, exasperated. 'I hope you're not going to carry on like this when Sylvia arrives and, for God's sake, *please*, Jack, no politics this evening. I really couldn't stand another political argument.'

'She starts them,' he said defensively, childishly. 'I always find her strong Socialist leanings a bit hard to swallow, especially when you consider her background and her life-style.'

'Here we go again,' Molly said, looking in on the joint in the top oven. 'I think you're jealous, just because she's titled and comfortable . . .'

'Rich,' Jack interrupted, 'bloody wealthy I'd call it.'

'Well, I'm not about to argue with you now, it's so unproductive, you only get hypertensive.'

'I'm not arguing. I just don't see why you have to mother her all the time, whatever advice you give she always goes her own sweet way.'

'Because she's my friend. If it was a man we were talking about you'd be quite accepting of everything. If Richard had gone off with a teenage girl you'd be amused, impressed by it, probably even a bit jealous. Because Sylvia gets involved with a younger man you feel threatened.'

'Nonsense.'

'It isn't nonsense.' She finished basting the meat and closed the oven door. 'You've always perceived Sylvia as a threat.'

'That's nonsense, Molly, I've always perceived her as being rather selfish, this relentless pursuit of career at the expense of everything else.'

'Why isn't she allowed a career? If it was a man you'd think it odd if he didn't have one.'

'Because she has responsibilities to her children and, anyway, it's not as if she needs to work.'

'I work, and I have John-John, Irene, Paul and Jackie to look after . . .'

'That's different,' Jack said angrily.

'Why?' Molly demanded.

'Because you have long holidays and can work from home in terms of your preparation, and our children are different. We didn't pack them off to boarding school and get rid of them like Richard and Sylvia. They're more used to doing tasks around the house.'

'Also my mother just happens to live a few miles down the road and Mrs Blake comes in to clean four days . . . Don't let's forget how I exploit their labour in order that I can function at the university.'

'What's all this talk of exploitation? You pay Mrs Blake, and your mother, well . . . is your mother, for God's sake!'

Molly turned back to the sink and began to scrape the vegetable peelings together. 'Are you changing before dinner?' she asked without turning from her task.

Jack came up behind her and, holding her around the waist, kissed her neck. 'I'll shower and change and I promise that I'll be good.'

She turned into his arms and kissed his mouth. 'You, Jack Kerr, are a chauvinist.'

'I'll get Sylvia to liberate me,' he said, hugging her.

She pushed him away. 'Go and get changed, Sylvia will be here soon.'

'In the Porsche . . .'

'Yes, and then open the wine, make yourself useful for a change.'

'Yes,' he agreed, moving away from her.

'And check on the kids, Paul is supposed to be having a bath with Jackie, will you look in?'

'Yes,' he paused at the kitchen door, 'anything else?'

'Not for the moment,' she replied, emptying the peelings into the waste bin.

Sylvia arrived wearing her black hair long with jeans and a white, angora jumper. She looked very slim and incredibly youthful, Molly told her so as she greeted her friend, hugging her and kissing her cheek. 'Something must be agreeing with you,' Molly remarked, grinning slyly. They walked arm in arm into the house where Jack and the children were there to greet Sylvia. 'Doesn't she look well?' Molly asked Jack.

'Certainly does,' he said, greeting Sylvia with a kiss. 'How's our TV star? We saw your first programme . . .'

'Oh don't,' Sylvia laughed, 'they edited out the worst bits.'

'I thought it was very good,' Molly said, guiding her through into the sitting-room for drinks, 'looking forward to the next . . .'

'How is everyone?' Jack asked, handing Sylvia her usual neat Scotch. 'Peter and Charley?'

Sylvia took a sip. 'Peter's doing all right, seems to be turning into a fourteen-year-old swot. Charley's making progress, slow but sure they assure me.' She took another drink.

After dinner Jack disappeared with the children to put them into bed whilst Molly and Sylvia sat by the dining-room fire with their coffees.

'Heard from David?' Molly asked, stirring in some cream.

Sylvia nodded. 'I had a letter today, everything seems

to be going to plan, he thinks that there's another part in the offing.'

'Do you miss him?'

'Yes, really much more than I thought I was going to . . .' She looked at Molly.

'What is it?'

'You'll laugh.'

'No, I won't, what?'

'I think this is more than a fling.'

'So, what are you saying?'

Sylvia smiled. 'I have to admit I think I'm in love with him.' She spoke quietly. 'I know, it sounds ridiculous, doesn't it?'

'No, not at all,' Molly replied, matter of factly, 'as long as you're sure.'

'I've never felt about anyone the way I feel about David.'

'Not even Richard?' Molly sounded surprised.

Sylvia shook her head. 'Not if this feeling is love I didn't. It's ridiculous, the age difference is ridiculous, everything about it is – ' she paused, 'ridiculous!' She laughed.

'You're sure it's not just sex, aren't you,' Molly warned, 'he's very attractive.'

'I miss him so much. I know, we've only known one another for a matter of weeks . . . I imagine this is how one feels when a teenager. I never expected to experience this at nearly forty!'

'Stop it, Sylvia, don't be ageist, anyway, you're not nearly forty.'

'Thirty-eight,' Sylvia said.

'You don't look anything like, look at you, you could pass for early twenties.'

'Ah, yes, but what about in ten years' time?'

'The same, be positive, for God's sake, if you're both in love . . . What the hell . . . Perhaps this will end in marriage,' Molly suggested.

Sylvia looked horrified. 'Marriage? My God, there's no chance of that, I'll never marry again, couldn't go through that again.'

'What if David wanted you to?'

'There is absolutely no way I would ever marry again.' She looked at Molly's doubtful face. 'I *mean* it.'

Molly shrugged. 'When are you seeing one another?'

'God knows. I'm stuck in London and, if he gets this other film, he'll stay in California.'

'Have you told your mother?'

'No, not yet, I know exactly what she'll say about it, though, nab him whilst you have the chance, it's what she always says.'

'Well, maybe you shouldn't think about what will happen, just enjoy it.'

'If I ever see him again.'

Molly smiled. 'Yes, that's right, be positive, won't you.'

Sylvia reached across and squeezed her friend's hand. 'I *want* him, Molly, I can't explain it, I'm completely out of control with it.'

Molly looked into her eyes. 'Then it has to be love, Sylvia, and you have to make sure this time.'

'But how?' Sylvia wailed.

'You have to be strong and you don't have to rush.'

'There's a fifteen-year age difference,' Sylvia sounded horrified at this fact. 'I want him now, not when I'm sixty!'

'Sylvia, you're a mature woman of the world, you know the score.'

'I don't, I don't know the score. If I knew the score I

wouldn't be involved with someone practically young enough to be my own son.'

'Well, if you feel like that, then, you should end it now. If you don't believe in the relationship you can hardly be shocked if it doesn't fulfil your expectations.'

'There he is in Hollywood, surrounded by all that machine, they won't want him to be seen with me . . .'

'For God's sake, Sylvia, I can't stand to hear much more of this. Do it or don't do it, but don't get hysterical about it.'

'I can't help it.'

'I know,' Molly laughed, 'perhaps you should have a talk with Irene, she's all of thirteen, her emotional condition may be more in tune with your own. They tell boys to take cold baths, don't they.'

'You think it's a joke,' Sylvia complained.

'I don't, I just hope you're not going to be hurt.'

'You don't like him?'

'I don't *know* him, Sylvia, be sensible, I've only met him twice . . .'

'You sound like my mother,' Sylvia sulked. 'I want you to support me . . .'

'Not my blessing, surely. What difference does it make what I think?'

'You're my best friend, I want you to like him, too.'

'I will like him, I think he looks very handsome. Now, there's a start.'

'But I don't want it just to be a physical thing, that's how I started with Richard.'

'Sylvia, stop it, you're making my head spin. He's not the same as Richard, no one is the same as Richard!'

Sylvia smiled warmly. 'Thank you.'

'That's all right, I haven't done anything.'

'You have, you think it's all right, feasible.'

Molly considered that an odd word to use in the circumstances. 'You'd better see him quickly, before you have a complete breakdown.'

Sylvia laughed. 'It's ridiculous, isn't it?'

They all settled down to watch a late-night film but Sylvia's mind seemed to be spinning with thoughts until the television became a meaningless accompaniment to what was going on inside her own head. She always remembered things at odd times, things that came into her mind and disturbed her, even events that had taken place many years before. Such things still served to embarrass or upset her or make her feel guilty. Things that she had said or done, things she had failed to recognize, people she had let down. She still felt guilty about leaving Richard, although she knew she could never have continued living with him. She felt guilty about Douglas. Most of all she felt guilty about Charley. Often these quite debilitating thoughts came into her head just before an important interview or just as the show was due to go on air. She wondered if it was merely nerves which drove these things into her mind; after all, other people twitched or became sick. But she didn't think it was nerves because even when she sat at home reading or doing a little work these ideas invaded her thoughts. She had a recurring dream, too. She was on the beach beneath her summer house in Norfolk and Charley would be running backwards, away from her along the sands. He would always say something but she could never remember what it was and his face would become blurred. She could never catch him and then she would wake up with a start, her heart pounding and the bed sheets drenched with sweat. It was at these times that she would wonder how pretty, intelligent Sylvia Wessley-Carroux, the only child of a peer of the realm, could end up as McLeod with her life crashing in pieces all around her.

In 1955 she had been so bloody gorgeous, even though she did say it herself. Academically bright, an accomplished tennis player, physically beautiful, all of this and a background that counted for something then. She, of course, had her tongue held firmly in her cheek when she considered all of this but, for the most part, it was true. In later years she thanked God for her parents. She was glad that they expected her to attend university, that they would not countenance her wasting valuable time at Swiss Finishing Schools or doing the rounds of Coming-Out Balls, husband-shopping her mother called it. No, in 1955, Sylvia was busily engaged in scholarship and enjoying a first year at university where, after one term of Molly Gardiner, a spunky little creature from 'up North', she had joined the Labour Party and proclaimed herself to be a Socialist. In fact, it was one of the few things that remained with her, she was still a member and, if anything, her conviction had increased in later years, whereas Molly's seemed to have floundered amidst her children and her slip-shod husband. Richard had always called her his 'red in the bed', which he found terribly amusing and, no matter how many times he said it, roared with laughter. Sylvia winced at the memory, he was so bloody humourless.

Molly was her best friend at university and it was because of her that Sylvia had met Richard. They sat one hot, sunny day in the summer term watching him playing tennis. Sylvia was reading a book but Molly was interested in the men. 'That's the one,' she announced, nudging and pointing Richard out.

'For God's sake,' Sylvia looked up, '*you* call them all

public school virgins.' She laughed. 'What are you going to do with him?' She looked a little closer. 'Who is he anyway?'

'He's the friend of a friend who's going to fix my car for the price of a free meal and a look at an essay.'

'How do you know he can fix cars?' Sylvia asked doubtfully.

'He says he can, and if he doesn't he won't get any food or any essay.'

'It's immoral,' Sylvia said.

'Rubbish, it's exploitation, it's bloody marvellous.'

'What does he do here?'

'Plays sport, gets drunk a lot. His father is a super rich barrister, your father probably belongs to the same clubs,' she said, teasing her friend.

'My father doesn't have time for clubs. Why didn't you tell me he was coming?'

'What difference does it make?'

Sylvia grabbed up her books and began to run. 'What time is dinner?' she called, dashing away.

'Eightish . . . Where are you going?'

Sylvia tugged at one of her bunches. 'Wash my hair . . .' She disappeared down the grassy bank.

Molly lived off campus in a sprawling flat, the top half of a Victorian eye-sore which she rented for next to nothing, probably because of its hideousness. She was always in the process of 'fixing' it, although Sylvia was never aware of any real changes. It was spectacularly untidy and always smelt vaguely of dustbins and spilt beer. Sylvia arrived early with a bottle of cheap wine and a bunch of flowers to find Richard hard at work under the car bonnet.

'Molly in?' she asked in a loud voice.

He eased himself out, his face and arms streaked with engine oil and grime. 'What?'

'She said you were going to tinker with her car, is she up there?' Sylvia pointed with the bunch of flowers, jerking them upwards.

'I'm not tinkering,' he stood up and wiped his hands on a piece of oily rag, 'I'm fixing the old heap.'

Sylvia listened to the lazy, English public school accent and immediately disliked everything about him. 'I'm Sylvia Wessley-Carroux by the way.' She announced it in clipped county tones with an accent like Windsor soup.

'Richard McLeod,' he replied stiffly, returning to his chore and ducking beneath the bonnet once again.

'You're right,' Sylvia said, walking into Molly's cluttered flat without bothering to knock, 'he's typical of his class but rather attractive all the same, if a bit oily!'

Molly was cooking up something in a frothing saucepan which smelt disgusting, it turned out to be knickers and handerchiefs, she didn't look up. 'Too good-looking but at least you have something in common with one another.'

'How sweet, you mean you think I'm good-looking as well?' Sylvia oozed.

'No, you're typical of your class.'

Sylvia laughed. 'Is he staying for dinner?' she asked, giving Molly a meaningful look.

Molly turned around holding a large wooden spoon in front of her from which dangled a lethal pair of steaming, greyish-looking knickers. 'Now don't start, Carroux. Besides, Bill's coming back later tonight.' She examined the knickers in the light and then returned them to the bubbling saucepan.

'Ah, yes, Bill, connubial bliss with your philosopher.'

'Hardly connubial, darling, never that.'

'How is he?'

'Philosophical, of course.' Molly turned to face her friend. 'If you want to help you could lay the table.'

'I think I'd rather lay our friend outside.'

'Yes, I thought you'd soon be wanting to get your hands on to his dipstick!' Molly said, throwing a blue tablecloth at Sylvia.

'For God's sake,' Sylvia giggled, 'don't be so forward.'

'If you want to do that, get him out of here before Bill arrives, he'll insist upon everyone staying up half the night listening to jazz records and boozing till dawn.'

'What do you think?' Sylvia asked, throwing the blue cloth across the kitchen table, straightening out the wrinkles and smoothing it flat.

'I don't know, what do you think? I'm just going to feed him, show him the essay, *if* the car is fixed, pat him on his head and send him back from whence he came.'

'So, you wouldn't think I'm being stupid, then?' Sylvia asked.

'Carroux, I don't care, just be sensible and make sure he uses something. You'd better take some of Bill's things just in case.'

Sylvia pulled a face. 'I couldn't do that, I mean, it's hardly very romantic, hardly very subtle to suddenly produce a *thing* – a condom out of my bag, he'll think I'm a whore.'

'Well,' Molly said reasonably, 'better that, lass, than the consequences. In any case, get this idea of romance out of your head, it's sex, dear heart, pure, plain old sex. You're not Doris Day, and he's no Rock Hudson, this is boring old England in 1955.'

'That's so cold,' Sylvia complained, 'your view is so cold.'

'Look, you have to stop dressing it up with all these

romantic clichés, it's only romantic when you don't have to pay the price.'

'How awfully cynical you are.' She thought for a moment. 'Do you think he knows what to do?'

Molly shook her head. 'It's doubtful. You'll probably have to be good enough for two.'

Sylvia frowned. 'I bet he won't come back with me anyway.'

'I'll suggest that he takes the car for a trial run, he can give you a lift back and I'll pick up the keys from you tomorrow,' she grinned with satisfaction at her plan, 'how's that?'

Sylvia didn't reply but busied herself setting the table and arranging the flowers she had brought.

Molly cooked something vegetarian, wholesome and delicious. Richard said little over dinner whilst Molly gave her opinion about almost everything. Afterwards, Sylvia watched as Molly went through the essay with him. She was sitting in the bumpy old armchair watching them on the lumpy sofa, the essay spread out between them, their heads almost touching. Sylvia felt tired. She looked at Richard: he was big, muscular, very blond, Teutonic she thought. His hair was cut short but had a quiffy bit at the front which kept falling forwards and which he kept brushing back. She found it very appealing. Blue jeans, white shirt, black slip-ons, he looked all right, if only he would behave in a reasonable way.

'Well,' Sylvia said at last, 'I have an early class in the morning.'

Richard immediately offered to walk her back before Molly could launch into her prepared story.

'Take the car,' Molly said very casually, 'I can pick up the keys from Sylvia in the morning. You can give it a trial run.'

* * *

'Is she always like that?' Richard asked as they drove away, the engine spluttering.

'Like what?' Sylvia asked, a warning edge to her voice.

'So aggressive, self-opinionated, so terribly left-wing.'

'You're just peeved because you had to work hard to earn your dinner and your essay crib.' She was watching the houses out of the window. 'I could be a rabid Marxist for all you know.'

'You're obviously not, though,' he glanced over at her, 'are you?'

'Yes,' she claimed defiantly, feeling angry that he should attack her best friend.

'What shall I do with the keys?' he asked as he pulled the Morris up outside the women's residences.

'What do you want to do with them?' she asked, turning to face him.

'I'm sorry?' He looked confused, as though he didn't understand.

'Do you like fresh coffee?' Sylvia asked, smiling at him.

'Yes, I do as a matter of fact,' he said cautiously, suspecting a trick.

She opened her door feeling very conspiratorial. 'Second floor, then. Park the car over there, under the trees and I'll see you in a minute.'

Years later she would claim that he had been slow to respond, that she had practically forced him to stay that first night with her. He, of course, for ever denied that, he claimed that he had been playing hard to get, enjoying a game with her. Sylvia used to laugh at that. She remembered him as a methodical, perhaps even dutiful lover. He was very muscular, extremely powerful, something which she had always been unsettled by, even as she desired him. She had not lost her virginity with Richard but she did lose a big part of her self, her identity, to him, that part which she had always been so very careful to protect. It would be dishonest to say that she never loved him but she could now never recall how that felt; all these years later it was difficult to remember and it worried her that she could not.

Go back twenty or more years, Sylvia sitting high on the top step, her arms close around her knees holding a flared skirt tightly, as tightly as the stiffened petticoat would allow. There she sat, on the top step, and watched the lawn sprinker droplets catching the evening sunlight and listening to the metallic whir, whir, whirring noise from the contraption. It was a warm, scented evening, right slap bang in the middle of June and Sylvia was waiting for Richard to come and pick her up in his shining second-hand Ford which shimmered under the weight of its brilliant chromium plate, pristine and sparkling against that evening sun. She *was* in love then, she was quite sure . . . Or in love with the idea.

Go back seventeen years. Sylvia sitting high on the top step her arms close around her baby, sitting and watching leaves which skittered across the autumn blown lawn. She thought about Richard and looked down into the dark eyes of Charley. She waited for Richard to arrive home from his law practice (his father's law practice to be precise) in their cramped saloon car, practical and new. Sylvia – Housewife. Richard – Lawyer. No more illicit thrills in the back seat of a second-hand Ford. (She suddenly remembered her hand against the dampness of Richard's muscular back and on the nape of his neck, where the hair was short and spiky and prickled to the touch, and that horny smell of his that drove her wild.) Charley suckled noisily, insatiable, instinctive and always hungry, a roly-poly fourteen pounds of over-ready baby.

Sylvia yawned and surveyed the gorgeous afternoon whilst remembering the hot, dusty paths of her youth.

A while after once the boys were off her hands and the new, large-status Hampstead house was empty all day, Sylvia went back to engaging her brain, understanding that advanced brain death was drawing nearer with every passing day, and took up the offer from the friend of a friend in publishing to write for *Artist's Choice* which Richard referred to as '. . . a little job to take her out of the house now and again . . .' When, after a few months, she went full-time, he called it '. . . rather inconvenient at times . . .', and when she began to earn almost as much as him from her free-lance work and television and radio appearances he ceased to mention it at all. It wasn't because of this that Sylvia left Richard in the March of 1972, in fact she had been thinking about leaving him ever since the previous year, when Peter went off to boarding school. They had been married for over thirteen years by then and the future looked ominous to her. Just what, exactly, were they doing together. She took to looking at him, seeing him in new ways, wondering about him, what he was thinking about, or what he *wasn't* thinking about. She understood that they had become that sad cliché which she had so often despised in others, married strangers.

Richard bored her, that was the real problem, the absolute truth, he was staid, unimaginative, settled and satisfied. She would look at his sleek, expensive head and want to shake him hard, to try to recapture something of the tousle-haired boy she had fallen in love with one summer all those centuries ago. She packed up and found herself a small flat. Richard insisted he would never divorce her but she knew he would. The children were held in joint custody but she refused anything else even though he offered it, he was a senior partner in the family law firm by that time. The boys took it very calmly, they would see as much of their father as they had before and never really discussed it much, except to complain that Sylvia's flat was too small and didn't have a garden. 'Most of our friends are divorced,' Peter announced like a cynic at a wedding, making her roar with laughter.

After their divorce she saw much more of Richard than in the previous five years put together. He was always taking her out to dinner and sending her gifts. He would often get despondent after they made love (this had also improved considerably since the separation) looking doe-eyed at her and talking vaguely about '. . . another go . . .'. One day he had arrived at her flat late and without any warning. They chatted about superficial events concerning their day and then went to bed where he fucked her like it was some kind of an apology and, afterwards, as they lay there, she clutching the crumpled bedding about her, he told her, quietly, that he was getting married again. Sylvia blinked, watching him dress, his sexy little arse encased in his tight, white, cotton briefs, always the same brand, same size, same colour (he had a thing about never wearing anything but white underpants, something to do, she supposed, with him not wishing to suffer embarrassment after a major road traffic accident!). God knows how many pairs she had purchased for him over the years – she attempted a quick mental sum to work it out. She watched until all of Richard's beautifully careless muscularity had been hidden by his careful and expensively cut clothes.

'You might have told me first,' she said at last.

He was sitting on the end of her bed. 'I'm sorry,' he mumbled.

'Well, you can stay the night, or would that be too much of a compromise for you?'

He didn't answer her.

'Who is it?' she asked, already knowing; Miranda Blanke, that bloody woman.

'Miranda,' he replied sheepishly, turning to look at her. 'It will be sometime next month.'

'Congratulations,' Sylvia said, without a moment's hesitation. 'Does that mean you won't be sleeping here any more?'

'Sylvia, *please*.'

'No, really, I'm serious, Richard. Don't I have the right to know that kind of information?' She laughed. 'Well, I never left you for anyone else, I was always faithful to you, whatever that means. I certainly thought that I was in love with you once.' She breathed out. 'Miranda Blanke?' and she waved a finger at him, as though to a naughty school boy. 'Will this be her second or third time?'

'Second,' he replied, rather more sullenly. 'I don't have to seek your approval, you know.'

'So why bother to even tell me about it, who gives a good fuck.'

'I can't wait any longer, Sylvia, I need to be with someone, to be married.' He shrugged. 'I have to experience continuity, I'm just no good at having affairs. Miranda says that she loves me and I have always got along with her . . .'

Sylvia's laughter interrupted this explanation. 'You need a mother,' she said. 'Miranda will eat you up and spit you out.' She looked at him seriously. 'Does she ask for any children? She's not having mine.'

'Sylvia, please stop this.' He looked very depressed. 'If

81

I'd thought for one moment there was any chance for us . . . After all, it was you who walked out . . .'

'There's no chance for us, there hasn't been for years, probably not for most of our time together, besides, I don't want to be a wife. Since we split don't you think that the illicit nature of our relationship has brought out the best in us? You've been so different these past months. Why weren't you like this when we were together?'

'We were still married for part of the time, how can it be called illicit?'

'You know what I mean.'

He kept looking at her. 'What will you do now?'

'Oh, I expect I'll become a recluse, wear floppy hats and dark glasses, continuing as before, sadder but wiser, a Garboesque tragedienne, ' she finished dramatically, grinning at him. 'What do you expect me to do, kill myself?'

'Trust you to make a joke out of everything. I sometimes wonder if you ever loved me at all.'

'This has nothing to do with love, it has everything to do with us being grown up now, and with me having responsibility for my own life.'

'You make me sound such a martinet. I didn't prevent you from doing what you wanted.'

'Yes, you did,' she said firmly. 'You didn't lock me in a room but you did put pressure on me when the boys were small. I didn't have to stay at home, they had a nanny . . . my only function was to appear at your side, the dutiful wife . . .'

'You didn't say anything then.'

'I did, you just weren't listening. Face the facts, you were never prepared to make the compromises.' She spoke quietly, calmly, with no anger in her voice. 'You have the same values as your father and as his father, you don't have to beat me up or threaten me to be chauvinistic, your general attitude to me, to all women, is enough. I'm probably brighter than you academically, I'm more practical than you and yet I had to play the role of housewife whilst you muscled your way into the city every day to practise law, the wonderful, providing husband and father bit.' She climbed off the bed, dragging an old towelling robe around herself, sitting down opposite him.

'Do you hate me?' he asked quietly.

'Look, we were children when we married, we have simply grown up and apart. I will always be a part of something you once had, the boys will maintain some kind of bond, I suppose. God knows, I don't want to be completely estranged from you. I hope that you might have some kind thoughts about me, especially after a few months of Miranda!' She couldn't resist twisting the knife in a little more but she laughed to take the edge off her words.

He stood up from the bed. 'I'll call you in a few days' time.'

'Have you told the boys yet?'

'Not yet.'

'Better tell them soon, and don't forget to invite them to the wedding.'

'It will be very low key, a registry office and a small reception afterwards, I expect.'

Sylvia grinned. 'Send me a piece of cake, won't you.'

He looked at her from the doorway and then left quickly.

She flopped back on to the bed and wondered if she had just made the worst mistake of her life.

* * *

Before her finals, and when she was overwhelmed with desire for Richard, she stole away with Molly in the battered old Morris to her parents' beach house in Norfolk. For ten days they stayed there, like nuns, up early, silent, working, hunched over some text or note book, eating, walking the sands but seemingly lost to one another in their solitary study. The days were planned, a walk after lunch, back at work until four when they had tea, back to work until it was time for one or the other to prepare dinner. Everything planned and meticulous. After coffee another walk and back to work until midnight or until sleep caught up with them.

They worked like this until one afternoon, after a particularly concentrated effort, a day when her head ached from reading the recommended texts and the words blurred in front of her eyes, Sylvia stretched and looked out of the window at the roaring spring tide. 'I think that it's time to go back,' she said.

Molly looked up from her own revision and sounded extremely relieved. 'I'm all for that plan, Carroux.'

They packed and drove back that evening. Neither said very much until they were close to the university again and the strange pull of the sea had lessened its grip on their tongues.

'Did you cover everything?' Molly asked over coffee in Sylvia's room.

Sylvia shrugged. 'I'm not doing anymore, my first paper is in twenty-four hours' time . . . My poor brain cells will short-circuit if I read one more sentence!'

Molly smiled. 'My brain feels puddled!'

Sylvia took down the notes that Richard had pinned all over her door asking where she was. 'Can I stay at your place tonight?' she asked Molly.

'What about him?' she asked, pointing to the pile of note paper.

'I don't want to see him until after the first examination.'

Molly pulled a face and began to collect her things together. 'Come on then, Carroux, let's get started before love's sweet dream comes bounding up the stairs for you.'

Richard was pounding down the grass running track. It was almost dusk and Sylvia had been watching him for a long time before walking over the smooth, damp grass of the high bank which sloped gradually down to the track arena. She sat down next to his kit bag, tucking her light jacket under her and, pulling her knees up, rested her chin on her hands. Richard saw her and broke off, running out of the curve in a straight line towards her, standing, bent over, hands on hips, breathing hard. 'Hello,' he gasped, 'you came back, then.'

Sylvia looked up at him, running spikes, shorts, tanned skin, all of that prime muscle just ready for her. 'I went to the coast,' she began, 'to get my revision done. I went with Molly. My first paper was today.'

'You didn't say anything.' He pulled his track-suit top on. 'I couldn't find out what had happened, no one knew, why didn't you tell me?'

'I wanted to work. You would have persuaded me not to go.'

He shrugged. 'Did you get the work done?' He sounded hurt.

'Yes.'

'I had revision as well, you know.' He sat down on the grass next to her, taking off his running shoes. 'I could have worked with you.'

'You would have been a distraction, we wouldn't have got anything done.'

'Why did you go with Molly?'

'Molly works.'

'I missed you,' he said softly as the dusk gathered around them.

'We can spend some time together when the finals are over,' she said.

'I have to go home, then. I haven't been near them for a whole term, I've been with you.' It was very close to an accusation.

'I'm sorry if you think I've been keeping you from your family,' she replied coldly.

'I didn't mean that, stop twisting my words.' He was staring down at the grass, pulling little clumps up and examining them between his thick fingers.

'We can spend some time together when you've been home.'

'I'm crewing a boat for my brother then,' he replied.

She remembered and nodded to herself. 'Ah, yes, sailing around the Caribbean all summer, you'll get a superb tan.'

'Sylvia, I told you about this months ago.' He turned to look at her in the half-light, listening to the voices of people as they walked along the bank above them.

'I know, I know you told me.' She buried her face in her hands. 'Can't you simply not go?' she asked, her voice muffled through flesh and material.

'I *can't* do that, besides, I want to go and I've promised William.'

'And a promise is a promise, right?' She turned to him. 'Boy Scout's honour, the old-school tie, and all of that.' She stopped and got up suddenly. 'And what about me, what am I supposed to do?'

'I *have* to go,' Richard insisted.

'Why can't he afford to hire proper crew members?' she asked nastily, feeling ridiculous for being such a petulant little bitch.

'I am a proper crew member,' he replied very defensively, full of hurt feelings and damaged pride. 'I'm a very good sailor in fact.'

'Then why not tell the whole truth, why not say you'd really prefer to go instead of all this stupid play acting?'

'Why shouldn't I want to go?' He began to raise his voice. 'I'd have to be pretty stupid not to want a summer in the Caribbean, after all, it's not as though we're engaged or anything!'

'Well, far be it from me to attempt to tie you down. Marriage is the last thing I have on my mind if that's what you're worried about.' She turned and walked away, stumbling a little, her ridiculous high heels stabbing into the earth as she climbed the bank. He called her, running to catch up, grabbing her arm and stopping her from going any further. 'Just leave me alone,' she snarled, almost crying with frustration and powerlessness, 'get your hands off me.'

'I don't want to argue with you, this is stupid, I was looking forward to being with you. I don't know why you wanted to be with Molly rather than me, you knew that this would be one of the last chances we had before the summer . . .' He ran out of words and they stood silently for a long time.

'Richard . . .' she began, but then thought better of it.

'What is it?' he asked.

'You should go and take a shower, you'll catch a cold. I'll be in my room later on if you want to see me.'

Richard released her arm. 'Are you sure you want to?'

She began to move away from him. 'I'll be in my room.'

* * *

Sylvia hung around the university until the results were posted and she got her First. She felt no great pleasure at this fact. Molly went off to Israel for a summer as a kibbutznik and Sylvia went home after seeing Richard one last time before he flew out of her life. It was raining and the small railway station was chilly, dirty and depressing. They didn't touch and barely spoke, both were lost in their own thoughts. The train rumbled to a halt and he put his cases on board before coming back to say goodbye.

'I hope all goes well for you,' she said. 'Send me a letter or a post-card.'

He nodded and looked down at his large feet. 'You could always meet up with me in the States at the end of August,' he suggested.

'How could I?' she asked, exasperated with him now for making such a suggestion, it was impossible.

'Why can't you?'

'I couldn't, that's all.'

'I don't really see why not.' He looked anxiously along the platform towards the guard who was already placing the whistle between his teeth. 'Promise me that you'll think about it, just consider it.' The whistle blew and the flag waved and the train began to shunt slowly away. 'I want you to promise me, Sylvia.'

'The train . . .' she said hopelessly.

'*Promise* me,' he demanded.

She nodded. 'All right, but go now . . . You'll miss the train . . .'

He raced along the platform and scrambled inside leaving her feeling everything and nothing. He hadn't kissed her, and she wasn't sure if she even desired him to until it had been too late. She watched the train curving and banking steeply on the rails until it was a long way distant.

Sylvia's own train arrived a little while later and she left behind her all of the last three years of her life without a second glance or thought. She wondered how her parents would react to her news, a first-class honours degree, something of which to be proud. She wondered, too, how the news of her pregnancy would be received, it would be more difficult to explain. Sylvia watched the passing countryside through the misty, dribbling train windows.

Summer rolled on into a wilting glare which burnt up the farm vegetation and reduced Sylvia to soporific inactivity. She swam in the ornamental lake in the warm evenings and practised her tennis shots against the dark green practice-wall in the mornings. She walked the dogs and had long talks with the gardener about the roses and the burnt lawns. Sylvia always remembered that summer, not so much for the fact that she was carrying Charley, although that thought would always be with her, but rather for her feelings of being quite adrift. Her parents were very understanding but they would only be there for a short while before they went off to Europe, her mother for a series of summer concerts, her father attending conferences and lecturing on International Affairs. Richard sent her a card after three weeks, 'See you in August?' was all it asked, 'Love, Richard.'

Neither of them seemed particularly shocked by her news, she had told them straight away. They were terribly preoccupied people anyway, always very busy with their own lives and separate careers. Her mother practised every afternoon until five o'clock in preparation for a nine-city concert tour. Natalia Fiodor, internationally acclaimed pianist, reputation and technique second to none. Her father, Charles Carroux, was a Professor of International Law with a reputation in Europe and North America, where they both lived for half of the year or more. Sylvia sat out with them on their last night in the country, it was extremely warm and they sat talking and working whilst Sylvia pretended to read.

'Why don't you go out and meet Richard?' her mother suggested, putting down a sheaf of manuscript papers at last. 'You could easily stay in the New York apartment, it's just sitting there, closed up and unused, what a waste.'

'I can't face him. I'll have to tell him and he'll jump back on to his brother's boat and sail off into the Atlantic.'

'Well, Sylvia, I think you're being rather inconsiderate. Richard should know.'

Sylvia looked up from her book at her mother. 'I haven't the money for the fare,' she said.

'Would you go if you did?' her mother asked.

'I may.'

'You should go, you should tell him that you're expecting his child and, then, if he jumps back on to that boat, as you insist that he will, at least you'll know that you're not giving up very much.' Natalia Fiodor gave her daughter a stern look.

'I don't want to make him feel obliged to do anything . . .'

'For God's sake, Sylvia, don't be so wreckless with other people's feelings, how can you not have told him yet?'

Sylvia stared down at the flag-stones beneath her bare feet, the stone felt warm and comfortable as she rubbed her toes along the rough surfaces. 'What if he wants to marry me? What then? I'm not going through some ghastly white charade with him!'

'Who wants you to?' her mother asked. 'I don't want

you to, if you want to have this baby by yourself, well, that's up to you, but Richard should know.' She turned to her husband. 'Charles, please tell Sylvia that I'm correct.'

Her father looked up. 'Go out for a holiday, it'll be our treat for doing so terribly well at university. Don't *worry*, darling,' he told her, as though she had just lost her purse.

She went. In the end she felt as though she was being forcibly exiled. She spent a week in New York where she was escorted around by some family friends who insisted upon her meeting every eligible bachelor in town. Sylvia found all of this very amusing in the circumstances and 'did' Broadway with them and the art galleries and endless rounds of cocktail parties full of the most excruciating people she had met in a long time. Someone offered her the use of a house near Boston as they were about to 'do' Europe. As this took her one step closer to Richard she agreed and escaped the muggy heat of the city and her mother's creepy old apartment very early one Sunday morning. She drove herself in Natalia Fiodor's vast American car, the big windscreen wipers slapping away at the morning mist. She was suddenly in the middle of an adventure and started to enjoy this brief moment of freedom.

Richard looked different, older, sunbleached, his skin darkly tanned, his hair almost white, longer, raggedy and curling. He looked much bigger.

'I came, then,' she said, standing on that dripping dock in the early morning with the sea fog still rolling back across the quiet water.

He dropped his bag on to the planking and came across to her. 'Sylvia,' he laughed, delighted and surprised, kissing her hard on the lips.

He smelt different too, of the sea and musty, his beard

stubble rough against her cheek. Sylvia held on to him then as though her very life depended upon it. 'I had to come here, to let you know something,' she began.

He put his head to one side and smiled quizzically. 'Tell me, then.'

'Before I do, I want you to promise me that . . .'

'Tell me,' he insisted.

Sylvia looked up into his eyes. 'I'm pregnant.' She bit into her bottom lip, watching him carefully. 'You're going to be a father.' Richard's mouth had fallen open and he looked pale underneath his tan. 'Don't throw up,' she said, adopting the local vernacular as her hysteria grew.

Weeks later they were married, a huge white affair with eight hundred guests, a vast tiered cake complete with a little bride and groom standing on the top, a honeymoon in the South of France and a little house to come back to close to Richard's work. Sylvia was pregnant and deliriously happy.

She looked up at the television screen, blank now, the film being long over. Molly and Jack were fast asleep in their respective armchairs. Sylvia went over to the television set and switched it off, that story had finished.

Molly stirred from her sleep. 'My God, what time is it?'

'Late,' Sylvia replied, 'it's very late.'

'Was it any good?'

'I didn't really see it.'

'Did you fall asleep, too?' Molly eased herself out of the chair, touching Jack on the shoulder to wake him. 'Time for bed.'

Sylvia yawned. 'I'm sure we never used to get this tired, I feel decidedly geriatric these days.'

'Time and tide,' Molly replied. 'Your room's ready. Are you sure you can make it up the stairs?'

Sylvia nodded. 'Thank you, I'll make an attempt.'

'I have to go into Colchester tomorrow, want to come?' Molly asked, kicking Jack's outstretched foot in another attempt to rouse him for bed.

'As long as it's not too early,' Sylvia replied. 'Goodnight.' Molly was still persuading Jack out of his comfortable resting place as she retired for the night.

They crossed Colchester High Street and entered the fake beams and coach lamp atmosphere of 'The Tudor Café' where they sat in a corner and ordered coffee and cream cakes.

'I always break my diet at week-ends,' Molly explained, fresh cream at the corners of her mouth making her look a bit rabid.

'I don't know why you bother,' Sylvia replied.

'Jack complains if I get too fat, you know he has this thing about being with a teenager with flat stomach and full breasts . . . I don't think he can come to terms with my post maternity padding.'

'Women are supposed to be round,' Sylvia said in defence of her friend. 'I bet he hasn't got a flat stomach, anyway. You ought to tell him what you fancy . . . fucking cheek!'

'Well, you're all right, love, you get these beautiful young men lusting after you.'

'I expect you do as well, all those marvellous male students, thirsting for knowledge . . . In any case you wouldn't want that,' she looked at Molly carefully, 'would you?'

'I don't know, I don't suppose so . . . I feel I've reached *that* age, you know, where you look backwards to when you were young, look forward and all you see is an image of encroaching disaster – old age.'

'For God's sake, Molly, come on, you'll have us both jumping into the Colne!'

'Being with David, though, it must make all of that seem a long way away.'

Sylvia thought about that. 'In a way it makes it seem all the more obvious.' She paused. 'Oh, I don't know, I hardly think of us as having a *future*.' She said the word with a certain amount of disbelief. 'I'm not exactly over the hill but he is *very* young and I find I can't let go, even if I was inclined to do so.'

Molly nodded. 'Don't you have any plans to meet?'

Sylvia shook her head. 'It's not possible at the moment, even if he were free I have this TV thing to work on . . . I'm filming a feminist theatre collective next week, did I tell you?'

Molly shook her head. 'In London?'

'Yes. I had to argue with this bloody director to get them on the programme, honestly, they just want to fill the screen with ancient luminary types like Dame June . . .'

Molly started to laugh. 'Her of the pixy hat!'

Sylvia giggled and finished off her cake, picking up her coffee cup and proposing a toast. 'Here's to middle age.'

'Oh don't,' Molly said, clinking her cup against her friend's, 'here's to you and David.'

Sylvia looked into Molly's eyes and smiled. 'To you and me . . .'

Everyone was outside in the large garden when they arrived back at the cottage. Irene and John were playing on a large climbing frame that Jack had constructed. Paul was digging in his vegetable plot whilst Jackie, the youngest, was helping his father clean the Volvo estate.

'They all have the Protestant work ethic, apart from Irene and John,' Molly said as they carried the bags into the house from the Porsche. 'I think they must have conspired in the womb to be more difficult.'

'They help, your kids are very good, not like mine, Charley and Peter never lift a finger to help.'

'But, darling, you have the wonderful Vanny!'

'Don't start, Molly, Vanny's all right.'

'Is he still with his hairdresser?' Molly asked, starting to unpack the bags and putting the shopping away.

'Yes, Frank keeps colouring Vanny's hair, I sometimes come down in the morning and wonder who it is at the sink!'

'I have Mrs Blake . . . Jack would never be able to cope with the likes of Vanny.'

'Nonsense,' Sylvia replied, stacking tins of beans into a top cupboard. 'Vanny's fine, I don't know what I'd do without him sometimes, he was an absolute tower of strength to me after Douglas died.'

Molly nodded. 'Can't clean to save his life, though.'

Sylvia ignored that. 'Let's take the kids to Manningtree after lunch to feed the swans and look at the boats.'

'All right, but you know they'll all want to go in that bloody car of yours.'

Sylvia laughed. 'We can take two cars, some can come with me on the way there and we'll make a change over for the return journey.'

'You're a real sucker for punishment, aren't you. Those kids of mine are wild animals, you'll get muddy boots all over your clean leather seats.'

'Love it,' Sylvia replied, dumping a small sack of carrots on to the vegetable rack, 'what's a bit of mud between friends.'

'Jasper will have to come as well,' Molly warned.

Sylvia had forgotten about their large, lumbering yellow Labrador. 'Right, but in *your* car, mud is one thing, slobbering old dogs are another.'

Jack was way along the harbour taking photographs of the boats, the kids were throwing lumps of stale bread into the water at the swans. Molly and Sylvia rested against the upturned hulk of a clinker-built fishing boat.

'If you could articulate your feelings for David how would you describe them?' Molly asked, shading her eyes against the bright sun and watching her offspring.

Sylvia thought for a moment, her eyes closed against the sunlight, leaning back and allowing it to warm her face. 'In a way it's like breathing again,' she clicked her tongue, 'like letting your breath out after holding it in for a long, long, time. Does that sound silly?'

'Not at all, it sounds to me as though you're really in love.'

Sylvia moved away then, down to where the children were playing and, dipping her hand into the big brown paper bag full of scraps, began bombarding the swans with food. The water sparkled in the afternoon sun and the beautiful birds dribbled water from their bills as they retrieved the soggy bread. She watched a boat with blue sails turning into the stiff sea breeze and listened to the gulls above her as they soared away. It was a moment of peace before reality had an opportunity to strike hard again.

Chapter 4

Sylvia looked at a picture of David as the plane came in to land at Los Angeles International but, in the flesh, tanned now so that the whites of his eyes looked whiter and his eyes bluer, she felt overwhelmed by him. He was living in a rented bungalow at the Chateau Marmont on Sunset Boulevard and, having just finished one film, was preparing for the next. He drove her himself in a rented Ford sports car, very flashy, very red. He looked at her, they had been apart for two months. She lay down next to him freshly showered, the cool crisp linen against her skin, she was white against the dark brown of his skin. He had pulled the blinds shut and the room was dim with just the faint sound of the outside world filtering through to them.

'Miss me?' he asked, a hand brushing against her shoulder.

She kissed him for a long time, she had missed being with him much more than she had ever imagined. They made love almost immediately, she had thought that they might have talked, exchanged a few pleasantries but it no longer mattered, he was there, behind her at first, hands on her breasts, penis in her slick vagina, rolling over after a time, his face coming up close, so angelic in lust just before the contorted rage of love and release came near. David loved to fuck her like this, until she came, clinging on until the last drop, no pretence that afternoon as he charged on in full flight, thrusting at her. 'Jesus!' one of them gasped, and he began to move harder until he was there as well, coming, on and on, still hard inside her but now, like two wet rag dolls, their bodies breathing in heavy unison, his heart pumping, pumping, pumping. Finally they eased apart and he lay spread-eagled, one arm across his eyes, unspeaking as Sylvia flicked on the bedside lamp and left him for the bathroom before coming back quickly to his side.

'That must be the reason,' she said as he looked up at her.

'What reason?' he asked, rubbing at her back.

'You know the reason, *any* reason.'

'Wasn't it like this with Richard or Douglas?'

'Typical of you to want a size of penis competition,' she said, breaking the spell.

'What?'

She reached over and pressed a finger firmly against his lips. 'Don't say anything, just lay there and look beautiful.' In a while she could hear his deep regular breathing and knew he was out for the count. She took a cup of freshly made coffee out on to their terrace and watched the palms swaying against the sky, listening to the sounds of the street close by. Being in love, she thought, being in love, the definition of that trite little phrase was becoming clearer to her, it was her own definition. It had to be *this* time that she would remember, loving him to the point of death, there was no limit now and it made her sure, for that moment at least and, comforted within that feeling and rocking within its warmth, she relaxed into her feelings of happiness and desire.

The next morning they sat out by the blue pool side surrounded by fake green nylon tufty grass and the real tall swaying palms. It was a drop of Hollywood, a tiny speck of what unreality was *really* like and she found it grotesque and fascinating at the same time. Sylvia looked around her at the rich, rich bodies as they gently fried in the hot sun. The aged bodies bulged whilst the young ones preened and bronzed, playing in and out of the sparklingly clear waters. A police helicopter crossed over the cloudless sky and outside, on the Boulevard, wailing sirens screamed up and down, heard distantly above the splashing pool and the cunning music which surrounded them drifting down from the hidden speakers high up in the palms lulling them into the Hollywood haze.

Later in the day they left their perfect sanctuary and walked the Boulevard, jumping the stars to the Chinese Theatre. Here they saw the paw- and footprints of everyone they had ever heard about, Monroe, Gable, Crawford, Bogart, Lassie and Trigger. Sylvia wondered if David's handprints would ever be placed in slabs of concrete outside the Chinese Theatre! One gorgeous evening he took her through the studio gates to the silent sound stage where he had filmed.

'So,' she said, walking slow, measured steps across the enormous hangar-like stage which echoed in the still, humid atmosphere, 'this is where it all begins.' She looked over towards him.

David grinned, hands in pockets. 'I can hardly think about it.'

'Does it bother you, then?' She walked back to him. 'The idea of this kind of success, I mean.'

'I haven't got it yet,' he reminded her quietly.

'You will,' she said, remembering the vast billboard sign on the drive in from the airport, a huge picture of him advertising the film, his name spelt out in large lights.

'Come on,' David said, 'we can drive to Malibu and swim in a real ocean before dark.'

Sylvia considered the colours of LA as they drove on towards the Pacific. The dusk had the quality of electric neon, stark blues and greens and reds, banding orange sky, purple and oozing crimson at the horizon line. The hills outlined sharp and black, the cutting edge of the palms crisp against all of this saturated colour. It had the quality of a dream for her and proved a perfect backdrop to the life they lived out here, everything reflected and reflecting, everything shiny and defined, new and keen. It was an odd contrast to Norfolk where the colours were of nature, the grey of flint, the muted yellows and greens of the beach and the high northern light, expanses of open sky which went on and on over an empty, flat landscape where sea and sky would merge, cold and awesome. California, hot and dry and burning with all that one could desire, all that one could manage, another world, the odd sort of place that David now called his home. Could she ever be a part of this? Sylvia closed her eyes to consider the idea, shutting out the crowded present to consider her future.

David ran along the honey sand beach in the late evening. He had parked the car on the sands and ran gracefully away, legs, arms, torso all together in one oiled action. She smiled and watched him objectively, the all American blond bombshell, tight silky running shorts and smooth rounded muscularity, his skin burnished from Californian exposure, all of this immaculate manhood for her to contemplate and have.

She sat down on the sand watching gentle waves ripple, washing up on to the beach. She watched until David finally jogged back stripping off his shorts to reveal skimpy swimming briefs before running into water which the sun had now turned to blood. He came back after a short while to fetch her and she joined him in the water, shrugging off her dress to the sands. He dove into the surf emerging into her arms. Sylvia was breathing hard, feeling him, fingers biting into his firm flesh, falling backwards

100

into the dark ocean, his laughter under her submerged in the water.

'Are you in love with me?' he asked, his hands moving across her breasts.

Sylvia held her head back for a moment and laughed, expunged of all guilt and opening herself up to him, pressing herself against him, open-mouthed to kiss and to possess, darting, pushing tongues, salty and warm against the pushing ocean and rushing tide of carnality and expertise. 'I love you,' she breathed, a quick gasp, an intake of sharp breath as he slid her briefs down, pushing herself on to him as they washed up at the water's edge, his warming tongue inside her. 'My God,' she breathed and felt herself to be on the edge of time drifting with the swell as the water lifted their bodies slightly and darkness began to surround them, black water now, slipping up against them, running over and falling back gently.

The first few days proved to be an awkward period for Sylvia for, in reality, they barely knew one another. A few weeks together, a protestation of love, a separation. They seemed to have picked up their relationship from where it had been left but everything was changed. He was in America now a film star and in Britain she was over her head, immersed in a frantic work schedule for 'The Arts Programme' which might or might not make her a personality, albeit a minor one by the scale of things in California, a Lilliputian to the Gulliver of his success.

She remembered preparing for this trip, her feelings had been confused, she wanted to see him, to be with him, but she doubted the wisdom of her actions. She felt out of control with him, not that he made any specific demands on her, but she felt sure that, if he were to, she might not necessarily refuse him. It seemed like a dangerous situation to her, one she wasn't sure quite how to resolve. She had always wanted to be with him but now it was as though she had to re-learn, re-know him.

They were as friendly and close as before and their sex was just as before, born out of their lustful desires for one another but, out of London, away from her house, her own life, her own bed, she was slightly uncomfortable and not a little lost lying in a strange land with him. However, by the end of the first week she was starting to feel a little better. He was, as he had appeared to her at first, an open character, no malice, very even-natured, capable of passion and humour, capable of anger. He was, he said, at ease with her, he told her that he loved her and that she had to believe it.

'When can I meet your kids?' he asked one beautiful morning as they sat around the pool.

She felt surprised. 'Charley and Peter?' She put down the paper which she had been reading.

'Unless there are more!' he replied cheekily.

Sylvia ignored that. 'Well, I suppose when you, and they, are in London.'

'Do you want me to meet them?' he asked directly.

'I've never really thought about it . . . You make it sound so formal.'

'You mean permanent.'

'Yes,' she thought for a moment, 'I suppose that's certainly part of it.'

'So?'

'So?' Sylvia looked at him. 'They're away at school . . . Perhaps a week-end. God knows, I can't be expected to arrange things for you in England whilst you're still out here.'

'It's only a temporary arrangement, though.'

'What is?'

'Me living here.'

'You're coming home, then?'

He smiled. 'Who knows?' flicking a sweet paper across, teasing her.

She returned to her paper.

'I don't know, Sylvia.'

'We're having some problems with Charley,' she admitted, shrugging. 'I don't know, either.'

'Aren't things any better on that score?'

Sylvia shook her head. 'He absolutely hates the school and Richard insists that he remain there no matter what.'

'What do you think?'

'I think that Charley ought to be just a little more responsible . . .'

'He's just a kid . . .'

'He was seventeen this summer, it's old enough to know what's what.'

'Maybe he just doesn't like boarding school.'

'That's quite obvious but it's more than that.'

'More?'

Sylvia nodded. 'Yes, I don't know what it is but all this fuss over a school at which he only has a bit longer to spend is . . . is irrational.' She turned to David. 'A few more months at Ectonford and then on to university.'

'Things are very worked out in your kids' lives, aren't they?' It was almost a criticism.

'You'd think it might have helped him to settle.'

'Why is he so troubled, then?' David asked simply.

'I don't know, I'm *hoping* that it's just a phase he's going through.'

'What does Richard have to say about this?'

'Richard sees everything as a personal attack. He's sent Charley on a summer school to catch up on his year's work.'

'Poor kid.'

Sylvia felt it odd that they should be discussing Charley, she wasn't entirely sure if it was what she wanted; David was her escape route from all the problems associated with family. She looked at him but made no reply.

One of her final acts that summer in California was to see him on the screen for the first time. He took her to a sneak-preview of his first film. Sylvia had no idea that such things still happened. She had found the film rather uninteresting, an all-action space adventure in which he, of course, was the all-action space hero fighting, and winning, against the most villainous villains imaginable. However, when it came to him, his first close-up, she had held her breath as his face filled the screen. It was then that she really knew everything was his. They said the camera either liked you or it didn't and, if it didn't, then, you forgot about a career in films. It obviously adored him, it seemed to enhance everything about him, it made him breathtaking.

'A star is born,' she said in the car on the way back to the Chateau.

David laughed. 'You hated it, I could tell, you kept squirming about in your seat.'

'Nonsense.'

'Did you enjoy it?' he asked, turning to her.

'It was different.'

He grinned and sat back. 'I knew it, you *loathed* it.'

'I thought you were fabulous, though,' she said, linking her arm through his and resting her head on to his shoulder. She could feel him shaking with laughter.

Later he drove her to the International airport in the red Ford, parking it carefully and waiting with her until she had to go through into the departure lounge.

'Well, what do you think of it all?' he asked as she prepared to leave him.

Sylvia sighed. 'I think you've made it, kid!'

He kissed her. 'I'll be with you at Christmas.'

'Oh, so *soon*?'

He took her hand and squeezed it. 'You've no need to be sarcastic.'

'Well, for God's sake, Christmas!'

'Christmas.' He nodded his head. 'The film will be opening in London by then . . .'

'Great, I'll get your room ready as soon as I arrive home.'

'My room?'

She looked away.

'It won't always be like this, Sylvia,' he encouraged.

'No, it'll be worse.' She turned back to him. 'Of course it'll always be like this.'

'So, come and live out here with me. Move out to California, let's get married . . .' He was smiling at her.

Sylvia looked pained. 'I have to go, I'll miss my flight.'

'Come here,' he said, kissing her for an age and then taking her by the hand, walking her to the passport control.

'I'll ring you when I get back to London.' She shifted the bundle of magazines and books he had bought for her under her other arm. She looked up into his eyes and, kissing him on the lips, quickly left.

Chapter 5

The weeks before Christmas passed slowly for Sylvia in London. She thought back to her time with David that summer. She missed him terribly but, for the most part, was submerged under a deluge of work. The programme took up so much of her time and energy that Sylvia was often too exhausted for anything other than sleep. Looking back she was often thankful for this period because it left her little time to mope over her separation from David.

The boys were with her before David arrived. Neither seemed particularly interested about David's impending arrival. Charley was too preoccupied with himself, often locked away in his room for hours or out a lot to meet friends. Peter watched too much television, slept in late and ate junk food behind her back with Vanny as accomplice number one.

'Why do we have to spend Christmas at Hampstead?' Charley wanted to know, standing over her as she squatted on the sitting-room floor wrapping presents.

'You don't have to go,' Sylvia replied without bothering to look up from the task in hand.

'You don't want us here with you and the actor, do you?' he asked nastily.

Sylvia bit off a piece of sticky tape and slapped it across the end of the parcel. 'I thought you were going out with Vanny and Peter to help with the shopping,' she looked up at him, 'you *said* you'd help.'

He turned to go but held back for a moment, 'Do you

care what I do?' he asked before leaving abruptly, slamming the door behind him without bothering to wait for an answer. Sylvia sat back, reaching over for the next present to wrap, continuing with the Christmas tasks she loathed.

Charley arrived back with Vanny and Peter before lunch-time. She was busy in her study by then, scribbling cards that should have been sent a week ago, tired of Christmas, wanting only to be with David and forget about the rest.

'All right?' Vanny asked, sticking his head around the door.

She looked up and nodded, smiling. 'What's for lunch?'

'Your offspring want burgers . . . it's burgers!'

Charley pushed into the room and sat down opposite her on the cluttered sofa. 'What are you doing?' he asked.

'What does it look like?'

'You want burgers, then?' Vanny asked, his eyes widening, knowingly.

Sylvia smiled. 'Cheese sandwich?' she suggested, responding to Vanny's look.

Vanny grinned and his head disappeared abruptly.

'What are you doing?' Charley asked again.

'Signing cards from us all, writing happy little Christmas messages . . . spreading joy!' She looked up at him before opening another ghastly card.

Charley sighed.

'Don't do that,' she said through clenched teeth, 'don't come in here and impose your frustrations on to me.' Sylvia snapped her pen down and addressed him. 'Look, this is my time, Charley, I have things to do, things to get out, Christmas doesn't just happen.'

'Why do we have to spend Christmas at Hampstead with Dad and that woman?'

Sylvia pushed her hands back through her long hair. '*One* day, you're spending one whole day with your father who, incidentally, you hardly ever see and with Miranda, who isn't the wicked witch of the west!'

'You don't like her,' he accused.

'That's not true, she's perfectly all right.'

'Why Christmas Day?'

'Because you spent Christmas with me last year and you moaned for the whole day – and it's part of the agreement we reached.'

'Not with us.'

'I'm sorry?' she asked confused.

'No one ever reached any agreement with us about who we spend time with.'

'Well, he's your father, Charley, and he wants to spend some time with you and Peter.'

'What if I want to stay here?'

'Then stay,' she answered simply.

'You won't say anything? You won't mind?'

'I don't mind, darling, but you *will* have to explain to your father just why you aren't going, it's only polite that you should. You have to let them know you're not going.'

'What about Peter?'

'What about Peter?' Sylvia asked.

'Will he still have to go?'

'Peter has exactly the same choices as you. Now, go and find something to do, go and annoy Vanny for a while.'

David arrived on Christmas Eve, she had just finished watching him on an early evening talk show and then he was with her. The house was quiet for a moment, the boys were upstairs watching a film on their television.

'Hello,' he said, grinning at her.

'Hello, you,' she smiled, reaching up to kiss him, there were traces of television make-up at his hair-line. She took his arm and they went into the sitting-room where there was a pretty Christmas tree with presents piled up underneath it. 'I was just watching you,' she said, sitting down next to him on the comfortable sofa.

'It's the last one,' David breathed, 'I'm free until after the festivities,' he smiled, 'thank God.'

Sylvia got up to pour them both a drink. He had been in the country for several days but they had not seen one another, although she had been able to watch his progress on all the TV shows promoting his film. It had been a frustrating experience for Sylvia but he had telephoned her every day, a few minutes of fractured conversation in between the different appearances he was making.

'How are you?' he asked, taking the glass of whisky.

'Okay. The boys are off to their father's first thing in the morning. Charley doesn't want to go, of course, but I persuaded him in the end.'

'I have a present for each of them,' he looked over at the Christmas tree, 'do they have a pile each?'

Sylvia nodded. 'You really shouldn't buy them gifts . . . they haven't got you anything.'

David laughed. 'For God's sake, Sylvia, I don't care. I'll just bribe them to like me, it can't hurt.' He reached down over the side of the sofa into his holdall, fumbling around inside until he had found the two slim packages. 'Watches,' he explained, holding them aloft.

'You really shouldn't.'

'Nonsense.' He went over to the tree and, finding their respective piles, placed the packages on to them. 'Nice tree,' he remarked coming back to her.

'Vanny and the boys did it.'

'Artistic.'

'Yes, well, pretty anyway.'

'Yes,' he nodded his agreement.

She looked at him. 'For God's sake,' she said, before reaching over and kissing him again. A door slammed upstairs which made them break apart as the boys came thundering down the stairs. Charley was the first one through the sitting-room door closely followed by Peter. They hadn't realized that David was in the house and both looked slightly taken aback. Sylvia smiled, sitting forward and adjusting her blouse. 'Well, that's shut you two up for a moment, hasn't it?' She turned to David. 'These are my sons,' she said, introducing them in turn.

David stood up and shook hands with them, it was very formal and slightly uncomfortable.

'Mum said that you were just on TV.' Peter was the first to speak.

David smiled. 'I've come straight from the BBC to your house.'

'You promised us a drink when David arrived,' Charley reminded her.

'Did I?'

'You know you did,' Charley was insistent.

'In a moment of weakness no doubt.'

'You promised.'

Sylvia gave in. 'Help yourself, then.'

'Can I have one?' Peter asked.

'You can't drink, you're too young,' Charley replied immediately.

'So are you!' Sylvia reminded him. 'You can have a *drop* of something,' she told Peter, 'as it's Christmas.' She looked at David and smiled encouragingly.

The evening passed quickly. The boys were intrigued to know about David and his work, they wanted to know about how films were made. Even Charley seemed to forget about his adolescent superiority and sat on the hearth rug listening intently. Sylvia breathed easily, she had not really known how it would go, she imagined Charley being beastly but, then, it occurred to her that he and David were not so distant in age and David certainly only looked like a teenager! She wondered what they must think of her and David. So far, so good, she thought to herself but there was still plenty of time for Charley to turn nasty!

'Well,' David said as they lay together that night, 'It didn't go too badly. What do you think?'

'I think it went very well, even Charley was on his best behaviour. You must have impressed him.'

'Of course,' David joked, 'I'm a very impressive person.'

Sylvia reached over and pinched his side. 'Big-headed, too. Charley must have recognized a kindred spirit.'

'Ow!' David said. 'Don't bruise my ego after I've done such a good job with your kids.'

'What did you think of them?'

'Charley looks like you . . . Peter, I assume, is like his father.'

'What about personalities?'

'I hardly know them but they seem very much as you described. Peter seems a very bright kid, Charley very thoughtful.'

'Devious.'

'Thoughtful.'

'They liked you,' she said.

'Of course!'

Sylvia laughed in the darkness. 'I bet it's Christmas now.'

'Good, shall we open our presents?'

'No,' she sounded shocked, 'it's family tradition not to open them until after breakfast.'

'How boring.'

'Not at all, it's more exciting.'

'What have you got me?' he asked.

'Wait and see.'

David was silent for a while. 'What time are they going to Richard's house?'

'Oh, he'll be here at the crack of dawn.'

'Do I get to meet him?'

'If you want to . . . do you want to?'

'Not particularly.'

'Then don't, it's not compulsory. We'll just have a calm day together.'

'Great,' he said, turning on his side and slipping his arm around her waist, kissing the back of her neck before drifting into sleep.

After Christmas she was left alone. David had flown back out of her life once again. Whilst the boys remained at home she made the best of it. Charley lost the watch David had given him which caused an awful row.

'How could you be so careless?' she asked.

'I lost it, okay? Don't keep going on about it.' He looked at her coldly.

'Where was the last place you remember seeing it?'

'I don't remember.'

'You're absolutely hopeless.'

'Look, I know that he's your boyfriend but there's no need to keep going on and on about it.'

'That has nothing to do with it. Everything is a case of easy come, easy go as far as you're concerned.'

'Yes, well, maybe that's just a product of my broken home,' he sneered.

112

Sylvia held herself in. 'I want you to have a jolly good look for it. Did you leave it at your father's house?'

'I've looked around for it; no, it isn't at Hampstead; yes, I have turned my bedroom upside down.'

'Then look again,' Sylvia snapped angrily.

He stared at her but made no reply and Sylvia left the house for her office knowing that they would never see the watch again. When she told David he told her not to worry but she did, she worried because she was no longer very sure about Charley, no longer certain what was happening to him, concerned that he told her lies about where he was, where he was going, what he was up to.

It was after the boys had returned to Ectonford that she began to discover things missing from around the house, small things, a silver snuff box, one that her mother had given her, Georgian and rather nice, rather expensive. A pair of binoculars which had hung on the hall-stand for years, even a tiny oil painting from the guest room. She told Richard.

'You think it's Charley?' he asked looking concerned. 'Are you sure it isn't that cleaning boy of yours?'

'Vanny?' Sylvia sounded amazed. 'For God's sake,' she said dismissively, 'I *know* it isn't anything to do with Vanny.'

'Perhaps you've had a thief in, then?'

'No, these things have disappeared over the last month or so, that's why I've only just begun to notice. And there's the watch that David gave to him . . .'

'That was a ridiculously expensive gift.'

'He says he lost that,' she continued, ignoring Richard's jibe.

'So, what are you saying? That Charley's selling these items? For what?'

113

Sylvia shrugged. 'Debts, drink, drugs?' It was the first time she had said the word, it made her feel frightened.

'Drugs?' Richard sounded unconvinced. 'Be serious, Sylvia, on what grounds?'

'He's changed, he's changed a lot over the last few years . . .'

'Puberty, the old sap beginning to rise and all of that.'

'No, it's more than that, haven't you noticed the changes in him? His life seems to have come to a full stop, this general malaise seems to be in every area of his life.'

'Are you serious?' Richard sounded concerned.

Sylvia nodded. 'Yes, absolutely.'

'What do we do about it?'

'Alert the school? I don't know.'

'He's been back there for almost two months now and we haven't heard anything negative. He seems to have settled down again. You're worrying too much, perhaps everything will be all right.' He seemed to be seeking her assurance that, indeed, everything would be all right and when that wasn't forthcoming he continued. 'Yes, I'm sure it will, aren't you?'

'Perhaps.'

'You always look on the black side, Sylvia. Have you asked Vanny if he's moved the things you think are missing?'

'Yes, of course,' she snapped, 'you don't think I want Charley to have taken them, do you?' She stood up and walked to the window. 'I think you imagine I derive some kind of neurotic pleasure from all of this.'

'Not at all, I think you worry *too* much. Charley has gone through a period of rebellion, it's really quite natural.'

Sylvia was unconvinced by this analysis but, for once,

preferred to try to accept Richard's idea. Clutching at straws her mother would have called it, clutching at straws.

The day it happened was stamped upon her memory as though with a glowing branding-iron. Charley was expelled from school for dealing in a variety of illicit substances, far too numerous for her to take in then. Richard drove all the way at ninety miles an hour, screeching to a halt outside the main school building where they were immediately greeted by the headmaster. Sylvia stared at Richard's car, noticing with some irritation the flashes of mud on the wheel arches and along the bottom of the doors. Charley was waiting for them, packed up and ready to go, in his room. The school was attempting to erase the whole matter from the collective mind in as short a time as possible. Sylvia moved as though locked in a dream from which there was no escape.

They sat in the headmaster's hot, fusty, study in front of his large desk, like two naughty children caught fighting in the dorms. The headmaster cleared his throat.

'This is rather unfortunate,' Richard said.

The headmaster nodded. 'It rather clouds the original causes of complaint we held against Charles. I'm sure you'll understand that it is an irreversible decision upon our part.'

'What about his examinations?' Sylvia asked, her thoughts emerging from their thick fog.

The steely man sighed and looked grim-faced. 'Mrs McLeod, expelling Charles is letting him off rather lightly.' He turned to Richard. 'The long tradition of the McLeod family here at Ectonford has resulted in us, shall we say, containing this matter.' He spoke as a conspirator with Richard the accomplice. He looked very sad for

115

Richard, his obvious humiliation, first a feckless wife and now a drug addicted son to cope with. Generations of McLeods rolled over in their respective graves, quite obviously Charley was not the chip off the old McLeod block they had hoped for.

The headmaster turned his attention back to Sylvia, fiddling with a pen as he spoke. 'We are keeping the details of this sorry episode quiet, at great risk to our reputation I might add, but we feel quite sure that it will go no further.' He gave her a warning smile.

Sylvia started to say something but refrained from commenting. This man obviously had visions of her writing an article entitled 'My Junkie Son' naming his glorious school.

'We quite understand, we both appreciate your discretion, Headmaster,' Richard replied, sounding just like the Head Boy he once had been.

'Did Charley's housemaster not see any of this happening?' Sylvia asked.

The headmaster watched her, putting his pen carefully down. 'I don't quite understand, Mrs McLeod. If you're asking do we take our responsibilities for our boys seriously, then, I have to insist that, indeed, we most certainly do.'

'Not so seriously that our son ends up involved in a drugs scandal. Charley is a boarder here, we cannot expect to account for his movements during term time. This is what we *pay* you to do.'

Richard looked aghast but said nothing.

'I am quite satisfied,' the headmaster began, 'that we have done everything expected of us in the circumstances. Charles, after all, quite obviously became involved with these . . . these substances when he was away from Ectonford.' He smiled, a patronizing, sad little smile. 'We obviously cannot be expected to take responsibility for our boys when they are supposed to be under the care and jurisdiction of their own parents.'

Sylvia knew that he had her, that it was her fault, of course, how stupid of her not to see that from the beginning.

Sylvia brought Charley to London where they met Richard at his office which she considered rather ludicrous in the circumstances, after all, they were supposed to be offering Charley a warm and loving home atmosphere in which to recuperate. Sylvia sat herself on the large red leather Chesterfield. Charley sat on the matching armchair and Richard walked in, pacing around a bit, ill at ease, unused to having them inside his working environment, the inner sanctum. A secretary came in with a tray of coffee and biscuits; Richard waited until she had left the office before speaking. When the secretary had been there he had smiled and even appeared happy, now he was very serious again, launching into a diatribe about how much money he had spent on Charley and how he was wasting his life, wrecking his future, causing everyone pain and upset. Sylvia had never seen Richard like this before and wondered if it was Miranda's influence.

'. . . And there's a school close to my house you can attend,' Richard finished suddenly.

'I'm not going to that school,' Charley replied immediately. 'Why should I?'

Sylvia listened to the easy polish of his expensive voice, acting as a counterpoint to his ragged frame, the unkempt appearance of this long-haired, sallow-skinned, untidy-looking child.

'Because,' Richard fumed, gathering steam like a

117

locomotive, 'you have your examinations to complete and I'll be damned if you'll waste any more time.'

'Why do I have to do what you say?' Charley rounded upon his father, standing up now, shouting.

'Because you are sixteen years old . . .'

'Seventeen . . .' Charley interrupted.

'Because you are seventeen years old and you are not going to waste all of that time and effort . . .'

'And money, don't forget the most important thing,' Charley said with disgust.

'I've certainly ploughed enough of it into your education, to try and give you a good start in life.'

That was it then, Sylvia thought, not the drugs, not even the ignominy of expulsion from the old Alma Mater, the 'crime' in Richard's eyes was not getting a sound return on his investment.

'Why can't I live with you?' Charley was directing a question at her now.

She looked at him blankly, her mind whirring in search of a satisfactory answer, but Richard saved her from replying.

'Never mind about living with your mother, you'll live with me and you'll learn that in order to achieve things in this life one has to work and keep some discipline.'

'You may force me into school but you can't force me to work. And I won't live with you and that woman.' Charley was shouting once more.

Richard's face went deathly white. Sylvia could never remember seeing him so angry, she was afraid that blows may be exchanged. 'You will do as you are told.' Richard sounded horribly calm. He turned to Sylvia. 'I trust that I have your backing on this?' It was a question but still a command.

Sylvia nodded.

'I won't stay,' Charley shouted. 'You'll have to keep guards at the house or I'll run away.'

'Don't think that can't be arranged,' Richard said. 'You don't have any choices, son.' He spoke wearily now, sitting back in his plush desk chair. 'When you've completed your education then, perhaps, we can talk again about just what it is *you* want. Until then you do as I say.' He pointed at Charley, stabbing the air. 'All right?'

Charley stared sullenly at his father. Sylvia felt completely numbed; she didn't especially want him living with Richard and Miranda but neither was it practical for him to be with her, that would be impossible. Perhaps Richard was right to command and insist, child care and upbringing by diktat. She felt incredibly tired and stood up to leave. 'I'll call you in the morning, Charley.' She attempted to smile. 'I'll call you both.'

'I won't stay,' Charley told her as she left.

'Just do as your father suggests, just for a little while and you'll see that it'll all turn out for the best.' She cringed at her platitudes. They were already watching him slither down a messy, slippery slope and no one seemed capable of stopping him or even helping him back.

Chapter 6

When she had been married her life, Sylvia understood, was confined within a set of very restricted, not to say constricting, parameters. Whilst it was never actually stated, she was very much Richard's appendage. The landed wife who was eminently suited to entertain or be on show when his career required it. Educated, able and bright she may have been, brighter than many who sat down to dine with them, but still Richard's appendage and her pretending to go along with it, his clever darling, his beautiful, dressed-up, all-talking, all-academic Barbie-wife. Sylvia knew it from the start, of course she did, but she had been genuine in her desire to love Richard and her 'career', whatever it might have been, was put aside and then almost forgotten about after the boys were born.

Life carried on. They had moved to a mansion in Hampstead where Sylvia didn't actually have to do anything, they had people to 'do' for them, to pick up after them, to cook and to clean, to garden and to maintain. She would often spend entire days leafing through the heaviest of glossy magazines which showed replica homes to her own and suggested colour schemes for the bathroom or new designs for the arbour, new plants to trail, new drinks to fix. She spent hours in the bath, minutes in real thought about the future or what she had become, or had been reduced to. She had little to do with the day-to-day care of the boys, they were presented to her at meal times and if she wanted to take them anywhere, otherwise their large, robust nanny kept them occupied and fed and clean. On average she saw them after breakfast, over lunch and in the afternoon for an hour or so. The first seven years of her married life all seemed to blend together in her memory so that it became almost impossible to untangle one year from the next. When Charley went off to boarding school in 1966 she really hardly noticed the difference.

Molly would chide her at their regular monthly lunches.

'Why don't you *do* something if you're so bloody bored?' she asked one day after sitting in Sylvia's immaculate sitting-room listening patiently to Sylvia's usual catalogue of woe.

'Richard would be difficult about it,' Sylvia replied. It was the only answer she ever gave.

Molly found it hard to restrain herself. 'Listen, Carroux, you need a job, something to interest you. Quite frankly, Sylvia, I don't understand what you can possibly find to do here all day. You can hardly spend your time in housework or child care.'

Sylvia blushed. 'I have lots of things to do, things to arrange,' she finished rather desperately.

'What things?' Molly asked with irritation.

'We're always entertaining here . . . and going out to meet people.'

'Richard is the one who's always entertaining, you're wheeled in as wifey.' She took Sylvia firmly by the hands, as though to prevent her from disappearing completely. 'You're beginning to ossify, stuck out here in this ridiculous house, just what are you doing with your life?'

'It's easy for you to say, you have your career.' Sylvia sounded accusing.

'Yes, my career and my kids and Jack,' she paused, 'and he's as bad as a child at times.'

'Jack encourages your career, Richard sees my job as being here.'

Molly laughed. 'Your job?' she sounded disgusted. 'Your job isn't to sit in Hampstead, it's to bloody well get out there and do something!'

Sylvia had not replied, Molly's words echoed inside her head. How had she come to this? Richard engrossed himself in work, it had taken over his life and she, neglected in a luxurious limbo, put her own life into neutral gear. By the time Peter had been born she felt as if they had been married for fifty years, she could not remember how she had felt before. 'Was there life after marriage?' Molly had joked with her in 1958 as they sat up drinking two days before she was churched. Sylvia shook her head and wandered down through their beautiful garden to the wood where she sat in the wild grass and looked up to watch the sunlight splintering through the canopy of leaves above. It was here, her skin damp against the earth, her nostrils filled with the fragrance of bark and earthy musk and pine that she felt free and alive and real.

She met Peter from school one day and took him into the large park with the grey squirrels and the fat ducks on the lake. It was a warm afternoon and they walked to the lake first where Peter threw the breadcrumbs she had brought for the over-fed ducks. The drakes had beautiful dark green head feathers which shone as they made the water boil in their flapping efforts to reach the soggy bread.

'Teacher Brenda asked us what our mothers did today,' Peter said, throwing the empty bread bag into a waste-paper basket. He followed Sylvia to a bench where they could sit and watch the ducks, 'Alistair Ellwood's mother is a doctor,' he announced.

'Why did she want to know?' Sylvia enquired.

Peter shrugged. 'I said that you didn't do anything.'

'And what did Teacher Brenda say to that?' She spoke more than a little defensively.

Peter smiled and then laughed a little. 'I don't know,' he said slowly, playing with the buckle of a sandal.

Sylvia took Peter's hand and they went to search for their favourite over-fed grey squirrel which they discovered at the base of a cedar tree. She gave Peter some nuts which he held out in his open palm, walking very slowly towards the fat animal and, crouching down on his haunches, waited for it to take the food. After a few nervous seconds the squirrel darted down from the trunk and scampered across to Peter, snatching the nuts and running back to safety once more. Peter turned around delighted. 'He took it, Mummy,' he laughed, running back to her.

They walked on through the park to the small aviary where they watched a rather disenchanted-looking peacock which sat staring back at them in a rather superior way despite his threadbare appearance.

'"Please Don't Feed The Birds",' Peter read out, taking Sylvia's hand as they walked on. 'Who feeds the birds, Mummy?' he asked in a concerned voice.

'A man comes every day, a Park Keeper, he looks after them.'

He thought about that for a while. 'Mummy, would you like that job?'

Sylvia grinned to herself, imagining Richard's horror as she left for the park each morning in her uniform, she had already devised herself a cap with a badge reading 'Head Bird Feeder'. 'No, darling, I don't think it would be entirely suitable for me.'

'Why?' Peter wanted to know. 'I could tell Teacher Brenda then.'

'Because, if I worked in the park I wouldn't be able to meet you from school and take walks like this . . .'

'No, but you would be here all of the time then.'

Sylvia headed towards the ice-cream van in the car-park and let Peter choose, even though it would ruin his tea and annoy the nanny. It served to move his attention away from her choice of career. She drove home, Peter in the back of her car dropping ice-cream all over the book she had given him to read but contented and preoccupied, at least for a while, with something other than *her* future.

They were going out to dinner that evening with some potential business partners and their wives. Sylvia wasn't looking forward to it, expense account dinners in large London hotels were not her idea of fun. Having handed Peter over to nanny she had spent the remainder of the afternoon getting herself ready. She scraped her hair back from her face and made her eyes up very carefully to emphasize their greenness. She painted her perfect nails a brilliant red, holding them up when she had finished, moving her hands in order to allow the light to catch the glossy colour, satisfied with her work, as though admiring completed art. She wore a black silk sheath with décolletage and, looking at herself afterwards, thought the general effect dramatic, even a little severe.

'Christ, Sylvia,' Richard said, ripping off his work suit and attempting to shower and dress in ten minutes, 'is that the best you can do?'

She stared at him, watching as he climbed out of a crumpled heap of clothes and moved, naked, towards the bathroom. 'This dress is an original, I've never worn it!'

'They'll think you're in mourning,' he said from under the steamy shower spray.

'It's classic,' she replied, standing just inside the door, watching him soap himself through the glass stall. 'In any case, what do you know about fashion, what do you know about *haute couture*?'

'Enough to know that you should never wear black.' He was drying himself now, rubbing vigorously at his crotch.

'If you'd rather I didn't come . . .' she began.

'Don't be ridiculous,' he replied, throwing her a clean bath sheet. 'Dry my back, will you?'

She stooped to pick up the towel, tottering across the slippery tiled floor to Richard's back which she rubbed as hard as she could, flicking his bottom with the corner of the wet towel when she had finished, causing a red welt to rise up against his baby-white skin.

'Why aren't you wearing the diamonds I gave you?' he asked as she did up his bow-tie.

'They make me look like a dowager, besides, the bank has them, I'm frightened to leave them in my jewellery box.' She stepped back to admire her expertise, handing his dress-suit trousers over to him. 'Men look absolutely ridiculous without their trousers on,' she laughed.

'What's wrong with my legs?' he asked, annoyed.

'Nothing, it's just the sight of shirt tails hanging down and those long black socks!'

'For God's sake,' he complained, zipping up his fly and slipping into his jacket. 'There, how do I look?' he turned to her.

'All right.'

'I look bloody elegant,' he said, picking at something on his lapel, 'did you have this cleaned?'

'Yes.' She looked closely but could see no mark.

He took one last look at himself in the mirror. 'Come on, then, for God's sake, we're going to be late.' He picked up her fur coat and slung it across her shoulders as he might throw a blanket over a horse, and they rushed out of the house, Richard driving all the way like a maniac.

Sylvia drank too much. There were three North American businessmen representing a large electronics corporation, and their wives, two blondes and a stunning redhead, all three much younger than their husbands. One of the blondes was talking about her impending hysterectomy in a voice too loud for Sylvia's comfort.

'And they will be leaving my ovaries,' the woman said, as if Sylvia were her closest friend rather than a mere dinner-table acquaintance.

'That's nice,' Sylvia smiled encouragingly.

'Have you had it done?' the woman enquired.

Sylvia shook her head. 'I've never had an operation, the only time I've been in hospital was to have my sons.'

The woman looked very surprised, as did her two companions. 'God, but isn't that incredible. I would have imagined that, with your state health care, you would have had everything checked out by now.'

Sylvia smiled rather painfully. 'It doesn't quite work like that.'

'Oh.' The woman sounded disappointed. 'I've had just about everything out it's possible to remove and still function!'

Sylvia looked at her. 'Really?' She prayed that a blow-by-blow account was not about to follow but she was to be disappointed. Around the appendix Sylvia switched off, how anyone could discuss such gory details whilst eating was quite beyond her wit. She closed her mind off, nodding and smiling and watching blood ooze from one of their rare fillet steaks.

Richard had changed the subject of conversation when

he told everyone that Sylvia was the daughter of a real Lord, after which they were anxious for every last detail.

'Does that mean *you* are a real Lady?' the red-head asked excitedly.

'Yes,' Sylvia nodded, 'but I don't use my title.'

'Does it mean you have to meet the Queen?' another wanted to know.

Sylvia shook her head. 'No, never.'

'Do you have a Stately Home?'

'No.'

'Sylvia's father, Lord Wessley-Carroux, has an estate in Norfolk,' Richard said. 'How many thousand acres, darling?' he asked, smarmy and sickening.

'Thousands of acres?' one of them asked. 'My God, it's so romantic. Do you know any of the Royals?'

Sylvia shook her head. 'We're very minor in the league of landed and titled families.'

'Sylvia's father can trace his antecedents to before 1520,' Richard said.

'You seem less interested than your husband, Mrs McLeod, in your own history,' the more elderly of the three businessmen remarked. A thick-set man with silver hair and very bronzed skin.

Sylvia smiled at him enigmatically. 'I've tended to reject my past.' She watched Richard as she said this. 'In fact,' she told them in a confidential tone, leaning forward to make it seem even more conspiratorial, 'I'm a Communist now.'

The woman gasped. 'A *Communist*?' the red-headed one asked.

Richard's sudden burst of nervous laughter broke the silence that had descended upon the table. 'My wife is fond of her little joke, aren't you, darling?'

Sylvia grinned at him. 'Of course, I'm a Socialist not a Communist.'

'Then you support the Labour Party?' old silver-hair asked, more suspicious than ever now.

Sylvia turned to him smiling. 'It's family tradition,' she explained.

'Tradition?' he asked, confused.

'Yes, probably more to do with a dislike of the bourgeoisie,' she continued, stealing a glance at Richard, 'after all, the English aristocracy are renowned for their eccentricity.'

The man was about to ask another question when he seemed to understand that she wasn't really answering him at all.

Richard was furious, he smouldered all the way home, brooding over the steering wheel, eyes fixed firmly on the road ahead. When they reached Hampstead he immediately poured himself a large whisky whilst Sylvia, slowly and carefully, picked her way up the staircase. She was in their bathroom when Richard came up.

'Well, that was pretty bloody of you,' he began, walking into the bathroom, standing there as she scrubbed her teeth. 'You know how terribly conservative these American corporation people are.'

Sylvia rinsed her mouth and dabbed a towel at her lips before answering. 'I'm sorry, Richard,' her words were slightly slurred as she attempted to be contrite, 'but those people were so dire . . .'

'They could be a major source of my income, all that rubbish about communism. I've *told* you time and time again that you cannot handle drink. This kind of behaviour is not very attractive in a mature woman, Sylvia.'

'For God's sake!' She brushed past him and went to her dressing-table where she sat and combed out her long hair. 'There was a time when you would have found it amusing, you used to have a sense of humour or, perhaps, I never noticed before that you haven't one.'

'I don't ask much of you . . .'

'You always bring up my family, my breeding, the glorious blood line, it's demeaning, Richard, you make me feel like an Aberdeen Angus!'

'Don't be ridiculous, I can't understand why you should want to deny your background, it's there, after all, why not use it?'

'You *are* such a snob, Richard. What has any of that got to do with me now?'

'I should have thought that one would have been proud of one's background . . . I know I am.'

'Even my mother and father don't use their titles, they never insist upon that, I think they'd prefer to forget about it. It seems to me that you're the only one bothered about it and it doesn't even concern you.'

'Your mother doesn't even use her married name and your father's rather cranky to say the least. It's quite obvious who you take after.'

Sylvia refused to be drawn into another ridiculous argument. 'Well, I won't apologize. It was an excruciating evening, I don't even believe those women were their wives, and don't expect me to sit through anymore of these dinners. I have a good brain and I'm going to use it.'

'And just what's that supposed to mean?' he asked with rancour, 'and don't think I don't know where you're getting these ideas from. I know that *comrade* Molly is filling your head with nonsense.'

Sylvia climbed into bed, switching her lamp off. She closed her eyes and feigned sleep, listening to Richard urinating loudly, sure that no one needed to make such a noise. She turned over and buried her face into the soft pillow.

In 1969, when the boys were home from school for the summer, she had taken them to the coast. Molly came with her children for a week and, after midnight feasts, pillow fights, beach bonfires and general mayhem, the two women relaxed away from the chaos of children with the odd joint to ease away the tensions of the years.

'When you married Richard is this what you expected?'

Sylvia passed the funny cigarette across to her friend. 'What do you mean? Children?' She laughed. 'I certainly expected one . . .'

'No, I meant didn't you think about a career, too.'

Sylvia shook her head. 'I seem to recall that I was going to do something in journalism, wasn't I?'

'Sylvia Carroux, ace reporter,' Molly smiled, 'are you still interested?' She sat up. 'I know that *Artist's Choice* are looking out for someone . . .'

'I don't know anything about art,' Sylvia replied cautiously.

'I've brought some back copies down with me, you can read them, see the sort of stuff they do.'

'How do you know about this?'

'A friend,' Molly replied. 'Give me a few pieces, write some articles about something current.'

'I don't know about anything current.'

'Don't be pathetic, get a grip, Sylvia, just engage your brain . . . try it and see.'

Sylvia flopped back and looked up at the clear night sky, watching the stars and thinking hard. 'I don't even know if I can write anymore.' She closed her eyes, listening to the dull thud of breakers as they hit the beach. After a while her heart seemed to be beating in rhythm with the ebb and flow of the tide and she woke up face down on the lounge sofa very early the next morning. Molly was crumpled up on the hearth rug covered with an ancient blanket dragged from the chest in the hallway. Sylvia stumbled through into the cold kitchen and made herself some coffee. She took it out and sat in the blue morning light watching over the still grey sea thinking about what might be.

That was how she got her job. It started as an article and she gradually progressed until she became a staff writer for *Artist's Choice*. She began to do some radio and television and everything gathered pace so gradually, almost imperceptibly, that Sylvia didn't really notice the changes in her life. Edmund was on the look-out for a presenter to front his new show when he had first seen Sylvia doing a series of reports from the Edinburgh Festival for an evening news programme. He had found them witty and incisive, attractive and informative. Sylvia was obviously a force to be reckoned with, she was never lost for a question, confident in front of a camera and obviously in control of the situation. He found her professional and able to charm her way through the most defensive or difficult interview whilst squeezing the relevant answers out. She was also photogenic, Sylvia looked good on the screen. When he first met her Edmund found Sylvia to be the same as her on-screen persona complete with an infectious laugh and a wry turn of phrase. It was Edmund's opinion that she was an astute and clever woman who was going to succeed, a woman who knew exactly what she wanted out of her career and who was going to get it, if not on his show, then on another. Edmund was attracted to that whilst being slightly in awe of her pedigree and education and it would always be Sylvia's fate to present this ultra-confident, even daunting, image to the world whilst, inside, she was a mass of doubt and uncertainty. She often considered that the control she exerted in her professional life compensated for the loss of direction which she experienced privately.

'There's been a lot of positive feedback from your Festival reports,' Edmund told her, 'it was a *very* professional job.'

Sylvia smiled. 'Thank you . . . I was with a good crew.'

Edmund shook his head. 'No, it was more than that, you have a good style . . . You come across in a sympathetic yet positive way . . . That's very, very nice.'

Sylvia thanked him again.

'You've done quite a bit of radio work as well,' he nodded his head as he spoke, 'I've been listening, that stuff you did on the British film industry . . .' he sat back and looked at her, examining her face, '. . . excellent work . . . and the series about the old Hollywood actresses . . . really, really fine, was that your idea?'

Sylvia nodded. 'All my own work!'

Edmund had nodded and smiled and, within the month, Sylvia had signed for a series of Edmund's show, 'The Arts Programme'.

When she first left Richard in 1972, Sylvia felt much more adrift than she had ever supposed was possible. She had imagined it as an escape to freedom but it proved nothing of the sort because she was now responsible for everything, felt very isolated and was always having thoughts about Richard – especially at night. She hated to sleep alone. It came as an awful shock to her, the understanding that the quality of her life had not immediately improved, had not been liberated out of all recognition. Molly gave her as much support as was possible for a woman with several young children to bring up and a full-time univer-

132

sity post to sustain. She had brought Sylvia a bunch of flowers from her cottage garden, planting them in a large grey pottery jug which she had found hiding in a cupboard in the flat's hi-tech kitchen. They sat in the lounge on low-slung chairs drinking wine, admiring the flowers which were placed on the huge square table in the middle of the floor upon which rested a portable television set and numerous expensive coffee-table books.

'I never imagined you amongst new things,' Molly began, looking about her, 'it must have cost an absolute fortune.'

Sylvia liked the look of the room. It was painted white and had a wonderful wood-block floor which shone in the morning sunlight. She would buy some rugs though, she decided, to break up its mass a little. 'Do you like it?' she asked her friend. 'I wanted to get away from olde-worlde bits and pieces . . . I'm not sure if it really works or not.'

'Has Richard seen it yet?' Molly asked.

Sylvia nodded. 'A while ago.'

'And what did he have to say?'

'Oh . . . too small, too expensive, too brash . . . too everything, we didn't really discuss it, we tend to argue about everything.'

'Perhaps, in a few months, he'll get himself sorted out.'

'I think he does it just to make me feel guilty.'

'So, tell him to fuck off!'

'That would be terribly mean.'

'You're not having second thoughts, are you?'

'No,' Sylvia looked absently at the flowers, 'of course not . . . I miss him though, sometimes.'

'Of course you do, you've been with him since the late fifties!'

Sylvia laughed out loud. 'Molly, you make me sound so *ancient*! . . . But it's true, isn't it.'

'Anyway, love, it isn't irrevocable, you can always go back to him.'

'Never,' Sylvia replied without hesitation, 'it's final.' She bent forward to pick up her wine glass from the table, taking a sip from it. 'When I was with him I was taking sleeping tablets and tranquillizers and yet I was leading the most tranquil life imaginable.' She examined the glass carefully. 'I suppose love is simply born out of desperation sometimes.'

'Does Richard understand why you left?'

'He thinks it's just a phase, that I'll return, that I want my career and independence but only for a while . . . He thinks that I'll see the error of my ways, give up my job and move back to the happy home . . .' She looked at Molly and grinned. 'Fat chance!'

'And carry on as before?' Molly concluded.

'I expect so.'

'What about the boys, have they been to see you?'

Sylvia shook her head. 'Next week-end.'

'Are you going to divorce him, then?'

Sylvia thought about that, it made her feel strange and even sad, the word seemed so alien to her, increasing her sense of failure. 'I don't really see the point, neither of us wants to marry again . . . I don't want anything from him.'

'He may want to marry again, has he told you that he won't?' Molly spoke with a note of surprise in her voice.

'Well, it's only been a few weeks,' Sylvia replied, shrugging the idea away, 'a month or so.'

'Twelve weeks,' Molly stated firmly.

'Do you think I should divorce him?' She sounded a little unnerved at the idea.

'I think you should see your lawyer.' She looked at her friend's rather doubtful expression. 'You should certainly

134

consider it, Sylvia, rather than simply allow things to blunder along. After all, *you* may want another husband one day.'

'Never,' Sylvia laughed at the suggestion, 'no way.'

'See your lawyer and just talk about it with him, or is it her?'

'Richard is my lawyer,' Sylvia replied, feeling rather foolish.

'Oh, he can't be, Sylvia, you must have one of your own.'

'I'll find out about one then . . .'

'Or why not talk it over with Richard?'

'He won't even think about such a move.'

'You really ought to get yourselves sorted out.'

'It seems so final,' Sylvia said, pouring herself some more wine. 'Do you think I've made an awful mistake?'

'No,' Molly stated firmly, 'do you?'

'No,' Sylvia said, sitting back with a sigh of relief and shaking her head, 'no, I don't.'

In 1976 she didn't know what to do, having counted away the seconds as they ticked by on the ancient grandfather clock, her mind spinning away with thoughts and memories and recriminations. The claustrophobic heat which had dissipated her energy and forced her off the burning sands now seemed to be creeping inside the cool beach house. Sylvia was sitting in her mother's old practice room, she could still see the dents in the carpet where the legs of the grand piano had dug holes. She got up and walked to the open windows looking at the shading bands of water, muddy-yellow over the sandbanks and a darker, greeny blue where the sea floor suddenly shelved away into deep water. Between the banks and the shore line the sea was a perfect, dazzling blue. Her eldest son was a social problem, a statistic she supposed, a drug-dependent child, seventeen years old. A boy who ducked school and treatment and everything she could think up to aid him back to normalcy.

Richard, railing against Charley's behaviour of late, had started talking of an institution, a clinic where proper care and control might be exerted upon his son. Since his expulsion from school Charley had, undoubtedly, made Richard and Miranda's life absolute hell. She wondered about Peter and Charley out there, on the white sands. Sylvia considered how casually she dealt with Peter but with Charley there seemed to be no approach. For all of her fame and 'brilliance' and wealth she felt there was nothing she could do for him. All she did was watch the pain and deal with the unspeakable consequences of his addiction. Richard had completely given up, it was a job for professionals now as far as he was concerned. However, for the moment Charley was 'clean'. She had picked up a whole vocabulary of menacing little words that only spelt death to her but Sylvia liked to be accurate if nothing else, liked to attempt an understanding and yet she found she was hugging herself whenever she thought about Charley or talked about Charley, holding everything in to prevent herself from screaming.

The boys arrived back from their day on the beach and Sylvia watched them from behind her old typewriter, leaning her brown arms over it and resting her chin on her hands. Peter looked bronzed and bursting with health, he had filled out and was more muscular and, at fifteen, already taller than his brother. A fine-looking boy, even though she did say so, like Richard when he was a lad (she hated to admit), his hair almost bleached from the sun and salt water from the usual blond to white. Charley

136

was dark-haired and under-weight for his usual stockier build. She had noticed bruising on his left arm, dark circles under his eyes, the general ragged appearance, the bad skin, the dreadful tell-tale signs and consequences.

An hour or so later, they had all sat out in the warm evening by the swimming pool which shimmered under the lights from the terrace. Peter was practising a dive from the high board, jumping, up and down, up and down, achieving the desired height before cutting through the sultry night air and into the water, bubbling to the surface, calling out for them to watch. Sylvia examined Charley carefully, sitting at her side, rolling his weedy cigarettes and smoking them, one after the other, all through the evening.

'Why don't you swim?' she asked. 'You could show Peter that dive.'

'I can't be bothered.' He glanced across at her as his brother hauled himself out of the water. 'Don't keep on, Mother, I'm okay . . .'

'Are you?' She hadn't been able to resist it. 'You look far from okay to me.'

'Yes, well, living with Dad and Miranda is no party, she treats me as though I have an infectious disease,' he watched Peter tracking wet footprints across the warm concrete towards them, 'it's bloody foul.'

Peter grabbed up his towel from a chair, flopping down on to it and rubbing his wet hair. 'Why aren't you two swimming?' he asked bluntly.

'I'll come in for a while,' Sylvia said, turning to look at him. 'God, but you're brown, people will think you've been to the Caribbean!'

Peter looked down at himself, stretching out his legs in front of him. 'Perhaps one of our ancestors was Italian or Spanish . . .'

'With blond hair?' Charley asked disparagingly.

Peter shrugged. 'You don't tan because you take after the Russian side of this family, you just burn up . . .'

'That's right,' Sylvia said. 'Charley takes after me, dark hair, white skin, Natalia Fiodor's Russians, there's no doubt about it.'

Peter stood up and headed off towards the pool again, turning at the edge just before jumping back into the water. 'Come on, Comrades!'

'He's like Dad, isn't he,' Charley said, as though trying hard not to hold this fact against his brother, 'all muscles and athleticism . . . and brains, no doubt . . .'

'You used to enjoy sports, Charley.'

'Peter has the easy success of this family in him, good looks, good mind, kind, considerate, trusting, trustworthy . . .' He stopped to light another cigarette.

Sylvia stood up and unzipped her skirt, allowing it to drop to the ground. 'Don't use his talents and his beauty as a weapon against him, you have all those things and more, wasting time in regret and jealousy is futile, it'll cause untold harm and unhappiness.' She stepped out of the crumpled heap of her skirt and, smoothing down the material of her bathing costume, walked to the pool, pushing her hair up into a ridiculous flowery cap as she went.

When they emerged from the pool Charley had gone. They sat drying themselves, Sylvia watching the sun's final descent, the sea red at the horizon just before darkness fell. In the twilight she looked at Peter with a kind of wonderment that this muscular youth had emerged from her, defenceless and dependent. He smiled at her, in the half-light it could have been Richard, she told him so.

'Is that good or bad?' he asked, draping the large colourful towel around his shoulders.

'What an odd question, Peter. It was merely a statement of fact, an observation not a value judgement.'

He shrugged.

'Has Charley said anything to you?' she asked as they walked back to the house.

Peter shook his head. 'He was expelled from school, Mum. I hardly think he wants to discuss that with me, especially as I'm still there!'

'Haven't the other boys said anything about him leaving?'

'No one knows why he left,' he replied.

'Don't those sort of things get around?' she asked. 'How have they kept it quiet?'

'It only involved four or five others . . .'

'Why haven't they said anything?'

'Because they've all gone on an exchange for two terms, to Quebec.' He looked at her, nodding against her look of disbelief. 'La Belle Province, there's an exchange deal with a school there.'

Sylvia smiled, the irony of the situation getting to her, the tidy end to the whole mess, Charley out of the way for good and the others removed until the dust settled. She had to admire such strategy, however distasteful it was to her.

Later, Sylvia came down after showering off the swimming pool chlorine, wrapped up in her robe. The boys were sprawled out in front of the television watching a noisy American detective film. She made them all a cup of cocoa, taking it through on a tray and curling herself up into a chair.

'What's David working on now?' Peter asked.

'A science fiction epic,' Sylvia replied. 'I don't know too much about it.'

139

'Is he living there permanently?' Charley enquired.

'As long as there's work,' she said.

'You don't think much of his films, do you?' Charley seemed determined to pursue this topic.

'He's only completed three.' Sylvia watched as a policeman was shot during a high-speed car chase. 'They're very lucrative,' she said, 'and he seems to enjoy making them.'

'But not very serious,' Charley continued.

'No,' Sylvia agreed, 'he has a lot of time to make serious films.'

'Do you mind?'

'Mind?' She looked at Charley over her steaming cup. 'Why should I mind?'

'You have a reputation to uphold.'

'Reputation?' She laughed at the idea. 'I don't know what you mean.'

'Your TV show, don't you deal with rather esoteric issues?'

'No,' she shook her head, 'I look at a wide variety of things, they're not all serious.'

'I see.' He turned his attention back to the film. 'Well, I don't always watch your programme,' he concluded.

Sylvia felt herself bristling. Charley's dismissive attitude to her work annoyed her but she would not be goaded into an argument over it. She settled back into her chair, half listening to the raucous film but mostly remembering that when they first arrived for this holiday on a sweltering afternoon she had surreptitiously examined Charley's room for signs of his drugs habit. The boys had gone down to the beach and the house was very still and silent. The windows in his room were open, the curtains drawn together against the hot sun. Charley had put his suitcase on top of the bed and had opened it but not unpacked. She carefully examined it, lifting out his sponge-bag,

140

unzipping it and searching inside. She lifted the freshly laundered clothes and searched the case for any hidden drugs. She looked all around the room, in the drawers, under the bed, in the bed, behind the curtains, in the bathroom, anywhere that he could have secreted his illicit hoard. Her searching proved futile, he was too clever for her though she was sure he had drugs with him.

She wandered along the cool corridor into her own room where she opened the curtains and looked out at the boys who were at the water's edge with their sailing boat. Her head ached from the long drive and the bright sunlight. She was constantly worried and in a state of tension about Charley but she could not follow him and be with him twenty-four hours a day. She had closed the curtains again and lay down on her bed listening to the distant surf and had fallen asleep. It was late afternoon when she awoke, showering and changing into shorts and T-shirt and going off to find the boys sitting by the pool listening to pop music.

'Everybody all right?' she asked brightly.

'Fine,' Charley had replied, 'it's good to be back.'

Sylvia had attempted to convince herself that all was well, that her search had proved fruitless because he was 'clean'. However, one look at his eyes told a different story, that odd, haunted appearance. There may have been some words that she could have spoken to Charley then, to make him stop, to pull him away from danger, but none were apparent to her. Instead she felt like shaking him, making him tell her where he had hidden his supply and destroying it but, impotent and afraid, she sat and waited and watched.

Chapter 7

David came over for a few days at the end of that summer. She met him at Heathrow and they spent a few days at the coast just before the good weather finally broke and the autumn tides began to turn in on the beaches. The garden looked brown and tired from the hot summer days, the house looked in need of a fresh coat of paint. Sylvia made a mental note to arrange for someone to come and take a look at it. He looked tired and she was concerned that he was on a production line, moving from film to film without a long enough break.

'So,' he said, looking around the large house, 'this is where you hide away.'

'Some hide-away,' she said, 'the boys have been down over the summer.'

'How are things?'

They walked into her bedroom. Sylvia stood at the window looking hard over the sea from her vantage point. 'Things are problematical,' she admitted, turning to him. 'Charley isn't really getting on very well, he's still living with Richard and Miranda, he's still taking drugs . . .'

'Are you sure about that? I thought he was going to some day clinic.'

'He's not doing anything, he's wasting his time,' she caught her breath, 'and his life . . .'

David came across to her, putting his arms around her. 'Poor you,' he said, their foreheads touching.

Sylvia smiled, turning her head up to kiss his lips. 'It's not your problem, David, I shouldn't go on about it.'

'I'm glad you do.' He held her close to him. 'If I'm to be a *real* part of your life, I want to know . . . I want to help if I can . . .'

'Well,' she said, breaking away from him at last, 'it shouldn't be your problem, I don't want it to be . . . we have to sort this out between ourselves.'

'It sounds as though it's getting out of hand.'

Sylvia was forced to laugh, but out of desperation rather than humour. 'It was getting out of hand months ago. Richard has a clinic lined up . . .' her eyes stung with tears. 'My God, I say that quite naturally, as though it were quite a natural thing, a fact of life . . .'

'Charley must know it's for the best,' David said, attempting to comfort her.

Sylvia wondered just how many times she had heard that phrase, everything will be for the best. 'Charley wouldn't know what was *best* for him if it stood up and bashed him in the face!'

'Oh,' David replied, pushing his hands into the pockets of his jeans and shrugging.

Sylvia looked at him. She considered him to be an alien in a foreign land, his own land. He dressed the same, spoke almost the same language but he was no longer even really English. He looked different, burnished to perfection, Hollywood's high-gloss wunderkind, the living actuality, the personification of his screen image, star incarnate, present as though he had just stepped down out of a moving picture to be with her. Larger than life, each tousled hair expensively cut, each feature, somehow, enhanced, all of it hers, everything she wanted from him or of him she could have, complete possession. She followed the generous curves of his mouth, the terribly white teeth, perfectly straight now.

They swam and walked the beach and made love and

the few days of his visit seemed to blend together from bed to beach to sea to bed again. She kept the conversation away from her domestic troubles. She wondered just what he must think of her, of her children, of her life, but she felt a need to keep everything separated out. There was David and there were her children and for the sake of her own existence she did not want them to blend. It was probably wrong, a mistake, she knew that but she was afraid. Sylvia considered Charley to be *her* failure and, therefore, she wanted David to keep away, she did not want him dragged into all of that mess.

She watched him in the light of a drift-wood fire they had built in the dunes beneath the house. The late sky of summer was still light blue but fading fast as the fire became brighter. She lay back and listened to the crackling wood and the distant waves. She smelt the beach and the wood smoke and him next to her. He had just come out of the water and the sand had stuck to his body where he sat. His hair was slicked back and flat, it made him look older and striking.

'I shall miss this place,' he said, turning to look at her, 'it's been great, hasn't it.' He took her hand, the firelight dancing in her eyes. 'I love you very much, Sylvia.'

She felt a lump in her throat, his words had such an earnest, innocent, almost child-like quality. She could not talk but looked down at her hand in his and felt herself a child, divested of all the trappings of maturity and independence. 'You don't know me,' she said at last.

'What else do I have to know?' he smiled.

'There's the guile and the cunning.' She looked up. 'You don't know any of those things. I get to where I want no matter what, no matter who's trampled in the process . . .'

'For God's sake, Sylvia,' he looked into her eyes, 'what are you talking like this for? None of it's true . . .'

'Isn't it?' she only wanted to make love, she had no desire to talk.

'No,' he insisted, 'don't shut me out like this.'

It was the very last thing she wanted to do. 'No,' she agreed, shaking her head, 'I won't shut you out. For God's sake, it's *you* I want most of all.'

David seemed confused. 'So?'

'So, we'd better do something about it fast as it's your last night with me for a while.' She grinned into the sparky flames.

Sylvia took David to Heathrow before returning to Camden Square where Vanny was frantic, rushing up to her almost before she had one foot inside the door.

'Charley's missing,' he announced, with all the weight and gravity of a bad Shakespearian actor.

'Missing?' She put her bags down on the shiny hall floor. 'What do you mean, missing?' She felt panic beginning to rise.

'Missing, your ex-husband has been ringing every hour . . .'

Sylvia went to the telephone, and called Richard's office. He was unobtainable, in a meeting. 'Bloody typical,' Sylvia said, slamming the receiver down. Vanny stood, white-faced, at the door. The telephone rang making them both jump. It was Miranda, she had received a confused message, something about Charley and an address in Camberwell which she had written down. Sylvia reached for a pen and scribbled the information on to the back of an envelope. 'Camberwell,' she said to Vanny, rushing out of the house.

'Camberwell?' he asked, confused, following her down the front steps to the car.

'Camberwell,' she repeated, tyres screeching as she accelerated away at full speed.

She traced Charley to a squalid room, so disgusting she could not imagine it having anything to do with her son. She would always remember his eyes on that day, how they stared at her from the dirty shroud of blanket wrapped around his nude body. It was a warm day and the room was small and square at the top of a crumbling terrace. It felt stuffy and the smell of rotting food, pungent urine and stale bodies turned her stomach. She could hear a voice repeating inside her head, over and over again, 'Oh God, oh God, oh God . . .' There was fresh blood in the scummy wash basin, dirty hypodermic syringes all over the place, scorched silver paper and a carpet of cigarette ends.

She was an age in that awful room, all of her life, inspecting every broken detail from the ripped and peeling wallpaper to her collapsed, destroyed child. She sat tentatively on the edge of the damp, stained mattress looking intently at his arm, examining it as though it were a laboratory specimen. Under the soiled rag of blanket his skin was very white, his exposed arm etched with septic sores. It all revolted her, the corruption, the violent evidence she had often refused to admit now confronting her. She looked and could not stop looking, attempting an understanding of this room and this boy now so totally full of pain and searching for his own destruction.

When she finally broke the appalling spell which rooted her there, she raced along the hot pavement to a telephone box at the end of the dirty street from where she dialled Richard's number.

* * *

It was a warm autumn afternoon, stiff breezes blowing smoke from bonfires piled high with leaves, swirling it around, turning it in many directions, making it impossible to escape.

The Freeman-Lapp Clinic was housed in a Georgian mansion standing amidst several acres of parkland. It was in a pretty area of the Churnet Valley in the north Midlands, the house hidden from the road by a high stone wall. One approached the estate through huge gates which opened automatically once it had been established, via an intercom, who you were. From the main house the trees were set in rigid parallel lines, following the neat gravel driveway down to the high entrance gates. It was another Saturday, smoky and warm, a clear blue afternoon.

Sylvia watched the trees flash by as Richard drove quickly towards the imposing house, she listened to the gravel spattering against the car and was the first to get out when they had stopped. She smelt the sweet country air and the acrid smoke from the bonfires. It was a beautiful scene. Charley was the last to emerge, Richard already climbing the entrance steps. Sylvia stood between them, no one spoke. They entered a dark hall where a nurse in crisp blue uniform smiled, checking off their names on a list before inviting them to sit, pointing to some armchairs which were grouped together at the bottom of the grand staircase. There was a smell of polished wood and new carpets; Sylvia had anticipated white walls and a hygienic, sterilized hospital atmosphere, instead it reminded her of home when she was a child. They all sat silently, Richard fidgeting with his car keys, Charley staring at his feet. Sylvia sat back, her hands firmly gripping the arms of her chair. She suddenly realized that she was wearing a black suit, her hair tied tightly back, a white blouse caught at the neck with a gold pin, dark tights, black patent shoes. She considered how austere she must look. Richard hated her in black; it gave her a little comfort.

The same nurse came back after a short while preceded by her echoing footsteps along the passageway. She took them all to meet Dr Freeman, the male half of Freeman-Lapp. He was young and smiled at them, introducing himself as 'Mike Freeman' with the easy charm and studied informality of a West-Coast American, his accent soft and attractive. He cleared the easy chairs of books and papers and sat them all around in a circle. He was slim with a delicately formed face, high cheek-bones and straight, sandy hair cut quite short. He wore round spectacles with fine gold frames which he removed frequently to wipe or simply to relieve the pressure where they dug little grooves into the sides of his nose.

'Martha Lapp usually likes to meet newcomers to the clinic but, unfortunately, she has to be away in Paris for a seminar right now,' he smiled. 'Now then, we have a very nice room for you, Charley, and we can all go take a look at that in a short while. Firstly, I guess that you'll all want to know a little about this clinic and just how it's going to help you.'

Richard spoke for the first time. 'Our own doctor has explained the philosophy behind the treatment you provide here, Doctor . . .'

'Please, call me Mike.'

Richard cleared his throat. '. . . he was very impressed with the results you've achieved.'

The doctor smiled his easy smile. 'You understand that we run a strict regime here. Stricter than your boarding school, Charley, stricter than being at home with your Dad. You'll have a programme to follow and your day will be filled up from early in the morning until late in the

148

evening. You earn any concessions like TV, cigarettes, magazines, even visits from your family as you progress – '

Charley interrupted him. 'I . . . I think you should know from the start . . . I don't want to come here. My parents have found this place . . . It's a last resort,' he finished abruptly.

'Well, now, that's a pretty normal reaction. Come on,' the doctor smiled encouragingly, 'let's have a look around.'

They left Charley unpacking the things Sylvia had bought for him in the few days prior to his departure for the clinic. Dr Freeman smiled and told them not to worry, that Charley's hostility towards them was quite natural. What he saw as rejection now would be forgotten as the course of treatment got underway.

'We've done everything anyone could possibly expect of us,' Richard insisted as they drove away, 'and this is the very best treatment there is.'

'Don't you dare talk about how much this is costing,' Sylvia demanded. She still had an image of Charley staring at her with a mixture of distress and recrimination, his eyes red-rimmed and cold. It made her shudder. Sylvia felt as though she was beginning to break up, little pieces of her were chipping away, very gradually, hardly noticeable but, little by little, she knew she was becoming, somehow, smaller and that her life was unbearable to her at times. She could not understand why, after seventeen years, she had still failed to reconcile herself to Charley, that he was paying the price for her own stupidity and arrogance. Why, when she loved Peter so much, did she feel such emptiness for Charley? It was a recurring and fatal theme, playing as a continuous accompaniment to her life, plaguing her and making her distrust those who would only love her.

Soon after Christmas and early in the new year Sylvia was filming at the National Theatre. She and Peter had spent the holidays together, Charley was at the clinic, no visitors allowed due to a bad, unco-operative patch, and Richard and Miranda had gone to the Seychelles.

David called her on New Year's Eve.

'Happy 1977,' he yelled over the bad connection.

'Why aren't you here celebrating it with me?' she asked.

He laughed. 'I'll be with you soon.'

The line broke up but she thought she heard him telling her that he loved her, 'I *love* you,' she said rather desperately, clinging on to the receiver until she was sure his voice had finally gone. It was a miserable start to the new year and she was glad to be working.

They were devoting a programme to new actors of the English stage. Sylvia was struck by the youthful enthusiasm these people showed, their incredible dedication to their craft, it made her wonder what David might have achieved had he not been seduced by Hollywood. Peter came along with her and watched with interest as the interviews took place throughout the morning. Sylvia finished her last interview for the piece and spoke to the girl afterwards, a vivacious blonde with dark roots called Greer, someone to look out for.

'That was very good,' Sylvia said, 'thank you.' She handed her clipboard of notes to Peter.

'Is that your son?' Greer asked, smiling at Peter, 'he's terribly attractive.' She laughed in a friendly way. 'I was at Central with David Christensen,' she said to Sylvia.

'Oh, really?' Sylvia looked interested. 'I'll mention that to him.'

150

'He's done terribly well,' Greer said.

'Yes,' Sylvia replied, wishing to know just how well they had known one another, 'but, so have you, of course. I'm told you're destined for great things.'

Greer laughed. 'How does David like California?' she asked as they began to leave the auditorium.

'Fine,' Sylvia nodded, 'he enjoys the life Stateside.'

'He has international success now, a couple of years and he's a movie star, incredible!'

'Yes,' Sylvia agreed, noticing Peter waiting for her at the exit.

'I expect David's told you all about his time at Central,' the young woman continued.

'Yes.'

'Oh, then I expect he's mentioned me, we were quite close.' She smiled stunningly. 'And this is your son,' she said again as they approached Peter. 'How old are you?'

'Sixteen,' he replied with a grin towards his mother.

'Sixteen!' Greer feigned amazement. She turned to Sylvia. 'You know, when I saw you on the box I'd never have *dreamed* you were old enough to have a son this age.'

Sylvia smiled back sickly, knowing exactly what this girl meant.

'Well,' Greer said, flashing her wonderful smile again, 'it has been *so* nice to have met you . . . When will it be on?'

'Next month, I think.'

'Fabulous,' Greer replied, waving and turning to walk away, her legs showing to great advantage in her short skirt and very high heels.

Sylvia placed her arm around Peter's waist. 'Help your old mother across the lobby, dear,' she said.

Peter laughed. 'Who was that?'

'My dear, don't you know that Greer Browne, with an e, is a star of tomorrow, one of England's finest?'

'I hate actors,' he said, 'they're all so bloody phoney . . . except David,' he corrected himself quickly.

'It's their insecurity, dearest heart.'

'Oh.'

'She knew David at drama school, she says.'

'Don't worry, Mother, she's not his type.'

'And what's that supposed to mean?'

Peter smiled at her. 'Too unsophisticated.'

'Thank you, darling, but I'm not sure if that's quite true.'

'Well, he's asked you to marry him, so don't worry.'

'I'll try not to,' she said as they walked out into the cold winter sunshine, looking over the river.

'Are you going to marry him?' Peter asked directly.

'Do I have to answer that?' She looked into his serious eyes.

'I thought you might, he seems an awfully nice man and he makes you laugh. Why aren't you?'

'I haven't said that I won't, I think it's rather unlikely . . .'

'Why? Because of the age difference?'

She smiled. 'Not only that.'

'What then?' It was almost a demand to know.

'Peter,' she began with an embarrassed laugh, 'I'm not altogether sure if a mother should be holding this conversation with her son.'

'Come on, Mum, don't be a stiff, I'm not a child.'

'No, you're most certainly not,' she replied ruefully.

'I know you're in love with him.' They began to walk back to her car.

'How do you know?'

'I can tell by the way you look at one another when you don't think anyone else is watching.'

'Sneaky.'

'And besides, Grandmother told me!'

'So, you've been conspiring with Natalia Fiodor,' she jokingly accused him. 'Haven't I warned you about that Russian?'

He grinned. 'You've been seeing one another for a long time, it's about time you did something!'

'Is that Natalia Fiodor or you speaking?'

'After all,' he continued, ignoring her last remark, 'none of us is getting any younger!'

'Now that's straight out of mother's repertoire of guilt-inducing observations!'

'Is marriage so awful, then?'

'It's perfectly fine. It just isn't what I want, I've been through it once.'

'But David wants to be married,' he stated flatly.

'Perhaps he'll change his mind,' Sylvia said. 'Why are you so keen to have me married off, does my wicked life-style shock you?'

Peter shook his head. 'You're not thinking of dumping David, are you?'

'What a horrible expression, Peter, is that what you think I do? Do you think I "dumped" your father?'

'No.'

'This is 1977, I thought all young people rejected the ideas of monogamous life-styles.'

'That was in the sixties, anyway, you're my mother and I just happen to think that you should be married to David.'

'So, I do embarrass you, then.' She stopped walking to look at him. 'When I first married, almost twenty years ago now,' she thought about that for a moment, 'it was really the only thing to do, now it seems the only thing *not* to do.' She laughed. 'I hope Mother isn't confusing you, darling.'

Peter smiled but made no reply, and they walked on until they came to her car. 'So, you're not going to marry him?' he asked as she pulled out into the traffic.

'Everyone thinks I'm mad not to. I don't know what will happen . . .' She paused to look over her shoulder as she changed into the right-hand lane. '. . . I think it's unlikely, he wants children, you know.' She glanced quickly over at him.

'He wants you to have a child?'

'Ah, I thought that would alter your mind.'

'I think that's great, what a super idea . . .'

'Oh, you're just saying that,' Sylvia replied, irritated that her trump card had failed to have the desired effect. 'Can you imagine me with a baby?' She turned to him as they pulled up for a red light. 'At my age?' She sounded appalled.

'Grandmother was telling me that one of her relatives had a child when she was over fifty!'

'For God's sake,' Sylvia said, exasperated with her mother's family sagas.

'It would be fun,' Peter insisted brightly.

'You should ask your dear grandmother why she only had *one* child if it's such jolly fun.' Sylvia pulled away from the green light with a distinct jerk.

'Do you think that actress really knew David?' he asked after a long silence.

Sylvia turned left into Camden Park Road. 'I expect so but whether in the Biblical sense or not I have no idea!'

'I didn't mean that,' Peter said, 'I just wondered if she was saying it for effect.'

'No,' Sylvia said, calming down, 'she was about the right age, you know, young.'

Peter chuckled. 'You're annoyed now, aren't you.'

'No, darling, I'm not annoyed.'

'I can tell by the way you're gripping the steering wheel, your knuckles are white.'

Sylvia pulled the car up in front of the house. 'Come on, quickly,' she said, getting out. 'Lunch and then I have to be at the studio to tape a show.'

Peter was leaning across the roof of the car laughing. 'You never stop, do you? You just *never* pause for a minute.'

'Nonsense,' she said firmly, 'I suppose you think I ought to give up my job as well as marry David.'

He smiled. 'I thought you weren't going to marry him.'

Sylvia turned away and went into the house, into the kitchen where the shopping was piled up in a large wicker basket with a note on the top from Vanny: 'No cooked chicken, no mixed salad, no skimmed milk, got salt and vinegar crisps by mistake! Sorry.'

'My God,' she turned to Peter, 'Vanny has had his usual brain storm in the Co-op. It'll have to be something and cheese.' She began to open the fridge door where she discovered a note on the cheese dish: 'Forgot the cheese.' 'Pub lunch, then,' she said, already picking up her bag from the kitchen table. 'Come on!'

Peter stood, bemused for a moment, before following her back out of the house and across the square to their local.

Sylvia sat in front of her dressing-room mirror surveying the damage. She was wiping off the make-up and feeling shattered. 'Another one in the can', she had heard Edmund say in her ear as the camera lights dimmed. She looked at herself in the brightly lit mirror, neat, she looked ever so neat, pin-stripe fitted skirt and jacket, hair scraped back, everything in control. All she needed now to complete the picture was a bowler hat! She walked to the pub with Edmund where they had their usual argument about content and control. She took the drinks over to his favourite booth, a pint of bitter for him, a glass of white wine for herself.

'The problem is,' Edmund said, continuing their discussion, 'that you want to write it, produce it *and* bloody well direct it.'

'Why not?' Sylvia asked. 'You do two of those things, no one thinks it odd that you produce and direct the show.'

'Because I've been at this business for a long time and, besides, the autonomy you crave is illusory.'

'Yes, I know, you answer to executives and they answer to their bosses and the advertisers are the ones with the real power . . .' She paused for breath, Edmund was smiling at her. 'You have the immediate control over what I do, that's what concerns me, you're stopping me from putting what *I* want on to the screen.'

'I have to make the final decisions,' he nodded, 'but you have lots of freedom, Sylvia, why complain so much?' He frowned across at her, as though she were a naughty little girl. 'Listen to me, you're fronting a very prestigious programme, very well I might add . . .'

'Oh, don't patronize me,' she interrupted him.

'It's true, nevertheless and, when you front a live show the power is all yours, you're in control then.'

'Not the *real* power, Edmund. You allow me my bits and pieces to keep me quiet but we never tackle any real issues.'

'That's untrue, why only tonight you had that avant-garde lesbian painter, an American television actor, now there was a handsome man and he was flirting with you outrageously, and that loopy woman who publishes Red Indian poetry. There now,' he sat back, satisfied that he had made his case, 'how can you possibly go on about us not looking at interesting and unusual issues?'

'We're miles apart, Edmund, you know exactly what I mean but, before you start, let me say it for you, we are not current affairs.'

'Precisely. You know, darling, you're being terribly well rewarded for your efforts and we have a top-ten rated programme.' He looked at her hard. 'Do you seriously suppose this would have been the case if we'd filled the programme with all of these co-operatives and teepee people?'

'I want more control, I'm fed up having to fight for everything I want to include. You know, you're the kind of man who asks someone a question, gives them the answer and then tells them that they've got it wrong, you never *listen* to me.'

Edmund finished off his pint in one go. 'I really have to be off, Sylvia. Don't take it all so seriously, this is show-business, we're here to entertain.' He slid out of the booth and left her to her wine.

She watched him leave, noticing that one of her inter-viewees had walked in and was drinking at the bar alone. It was the American television actor who was here to do Shakespeare in the park. Edmund stopped to pat him on the back as he left, they exchanged a few words. The actor turned and their eyes caught; Sylvia smiled. She watched as he picked up his beer and came over to her. He was handsome, probably couldn't have been mistaken for anything other than the all-American hunk, late thirties, she thought, strong-looking, the type who always kept in shape.

'Hi, mind if I join you?' he asked, throwing his tweedy jacket on to the curved bench seat before sliding in after it. He smiled and noticed her empty glass. 'Let me get you a drink,' and he was sliding out again before she could protest that she was about to leave. 'What's it to be?' he asked. 'Another white wine?'

Sylvia sat back, picking up a beer mat and examining it, standing it on a corner and turning it around under her finger. He returned with her wine, a bag of crisps, a bag of nuts and a fresh pint for himself. The pub was beginning to fill with people now, it was just after eight o' clock.

'I thought it was a good interview,' he began. 'You asked some unusual questions, not many about the TV show, that's good.' He smiled and Sylvia found it very attractive.

'Your programme is very popular over here, American police series often are. I thought Shakespeare more appealing from "The Arts Programme's" point of view.' She was appalled at her own pomposity.

He nodded. 'You were having a pretty heavy conversation with your man just now.'

'Edmund.' She sighed. 'We don't seem to be seeing eye to eye about much recently.'

'Your show seems . . .' he paused, '. . . I guess the word is radical, I saw it last week, also.'

'Radical?' She was surprised. 'Do you think so?'

'The women's group theatre was very powerful.'

Sylvia nodded. 'I would like to develop those kind of ideas and anyway Edmund wants to broaden our approach.'

'Won't that please you?'

Sylvia looked at him. She drank her wine, not wishing to discuss it very much.

He took the hint and changed the subject. 'There's quite a bit about you and David Christensen in our press at home. Does it bother you?'

'What, David and his older woman?' She smiled. 'It's inevitable, isn't it?'

He nodded. 'He's *very* big right now, very successful . . . Do you spend much time in the States?'

'It's terribly difficult at the moment, there seems to be no set pattern to when we meet. I go whenever I can.' She smiled. 'Are you married?'

'No.'

'Divorced?'

'No.'

'Attached in any way?'

'No,' he laughed.

'I'm sorry, prying, aren't I.'

'I once lived with someone for about ten years, we split up a while ago,' he explained.

Sylvia looked at her watch. 'I really have to be going.'

'Maybe you'd like to come to the play sometime,' he suggested, standing up with her.

'I'm not sure,' she looked into his eyes, 'I may be in America by then.'

He seemed disappointed. 'I hope we have another chance to meet whilst we're both still in England.' They were standing outside now in the cool evening.

Sylvia nodded and smiled but did not reply.

'Well,' he said, not knowing what to say.

'It was super to meet you,' she said, extending her hand.

'I sure hope that we meet up again.'

Sylvia had taken his hand. 'That would be nice,' she said.

'Perhaps I could call you?' he asked.

She nodded.

'I have Sunday free, you could show me some of the English countryside.' He was still holding her hand.

'All right.' She made up her mind quickly. 'I have a place at the coast, in Norfolk, what about that?'

'Sounds marvellous.'

'We're going there for the week-end and you could join us there,' she suggested.

'We?'

'My son is going with me, do join us for the day.' She broke away from him, retrieving her hand.

'I'd have to hire a car,' he sounded unsure.

'Well, let me know,' Sylvia replied, turning to walk away, 'I'll give you details then.' She waved and left him outside the pub.

Peter was sitting on the stairs as she came in. 'Hello,' she smiled, putting her bag on the hall table, 'win your tennis match?'

'You're late,' Peter said, 'I cooked supper.'

'Did you, darling?' She ruffled his hair as she went by him. 'Is there any left?'

Peter followed her into the kitchen where he proceeded to stir up a large saucepan of Bolognese sauce. 'Have you eaten?'

Sylvia peered into the pan. 'No, I went to the pub with Edmund. Did you see the show?'

Peter nodded.

'Geoff Meredith joined me for a drink.' She took the wooden spoon from his hand and tasted the sauce.

'Delicious, darling, do you want me to do anything to help?'

He shook his head and, replacing the lid on the saucepan, he began to put the strings of spaghetti into boiling water. 'David rang,' he told her.

'Oh yes, did you speak to him?'

He nodded, his back to her as she sat at the table. 'Said he'd ring back.'

'Is he all right? Did he say anything?' she asked, nibbling at the French stick.

'Not much, asked me if you were okay.'

'How's the film going?'

'To schedule,' he said. 'What's Geoff Meredith like?' he asked. 'All these TV stars look the same.'

'He seems okay, he might join us at the week-end.'

Peter nodded but made no comment. He pulled out a length of spaghetti and threw it against the kitchen wall where it stuck above the cooker. 'That's almost ready, then,' he said.

'Don't leave spaghetti on the walls, darling, Vanny has a fit when he sees it.' Sylvia broke off another piece from the French stick.

Peter dished out the food and carried the two piled and steaming plates over to the kitchen table, sitting opposite Sylvia, watching until she'd started to eat.

'It's fabulous, Peter, I'm starved, thank God one man in the family can master domestic tasks. I bet your father never cooked anything in his entire life.'

Peter grinned. 'Dad called round after you'd left this afternoon,' he told her through a mouthful of food.

'Oh yes, what did he want?'

'Said he was passing and called in on the off chance.'

'What did he have to say for himself?'

161

'Asked me to play golf with him this week-end, they're driving up to St Andrew's.'

'Do you want to go?' Sylvia asked without looking up from her fork-twirling.

'I said I'd already arranged to go to Norfolk with you.'

'Why not change your plans if you want to,' she smiled, dabbing at her saucy lips. 'Is Miranda going?'

Peter shook his head. 'He's meeting up with some business associates, someone from work's going.'

'Go then, you'll enjoy that, you know you enjoy golf, it would be nice for you both.' She took a sip of water. 'Ring him after supper.'

'Are you sure you don't mind?'

'Don't be silly, Peter, I can go by myself, have a lazy week-end and not have to bother about anything.'

'What about Geoff Meredith?' he asked.

Sylvia shrugged. 'I bet he won't call, it was a very provisional arrangement.'

Peter looked doubtful.

'I don't need a chaperon.' She laughed at him. 'Don't be such a fuddy-duddy.'

'So you don't mind, then.'

'No, I *want* you to go.'

'Sure?'

'Yes, what do you want, my signature in blood?'

Peter reached up to the wall-phone and dialled Richard's number.

It rained for most of the week-end and when it wasn't raining the wind across the North Sea was enough to keep Sylvia indoors with her work and her thoughts. She got up early on Sunday morning to find a patchwork of blue sky behind the heavy grey clouds and decided to walk the empty beach. She pulled on an old pair of faded jeans

162

and a thick crew-neck pullover on top of her thermal vest. She dragged on a yellow waterproof coat and slipped into matching boots before setting off, down through the garden and on to the sand dunes. She found a hedgehog, drowned in the swimming pool and decided to deal with it on the return journey. Large white gulls screeched at her, swooping low and flashing white against the dull sky. The tide was out and she walked beyond the groynes, looking up at the tall mast-like structures at their ends, coated with dark-green seaweed which flailed in the strong wind. It seemed strange for her to be walking where the sea would be, to look at the rusting groynes zigzagging away from her, soon to be covered with the rolling grey water. Sylvia trudged the wet sand, the tide running up to her boots and falling back again, drawing away and heaving back, gaining more ground as it began to turn. She walked on, pacing the distance between each sea defence as though a soldier patrolling her land against the enemy.

At last she turned away, moving further down the beach until she reached the dunes. The wind was behind her now and the roaring hiss of the sea distant in her ears. She kicked at a rusty drink can and looked at the litter amongst the marram grass.

After a while she decided to go home and returned to the house along the back lane, which wound around the fields amidst high hedgerows and stunted bent-over trees, like ancient men stooping away from the sea, gnarled into grotesque forms by the gales of winter. She climbed a five-bar gate and looked over the flat lands, at the church, solid and square, a crisp flint outline in the distance. A part of the landscape with little turrets on the square steeple end, a fortress in which to hide from the wrath of wind and rain and sea, thick walls in which to keep one's prayers safe. She climbed down and walked on until she could see her house in the distance. She felt hungry and could almost smell the coffee in the pot.

The small red saloon car was parked by her own in front of the house. There was no sign of the driver and Sylvia walked around into the garden where she saw a man standing looking into the pool. She called out to him, he turned and waved. It was Geoff Meredith.

'So, you came, then,' she stated rather obviously, joining him by the pool.

'You have a visitor.' He pointed at the hedgehog.

'Poor thing,' Sylvia said, 'I'll fish it out in a while.' She turned to him. 'How long have you been here . . . How did you know where it was?'

He laughed. 'I arrived about half an hour ago, and your houseboy, or whatever he is, told me how to find you.'

'Vanny,' she explained, 'was cleaning today because he's off to a hairdressing competition with his boyfriend on Monday and Tuesday.'

He raised his eyebrows. 'Such decadence!'

'Not at all,' Sylvia replied, walking him back towards the house and breakfast. 'They're the least decent people you could wish to meet.'

'Where's your son? I rang the bell and knocked the knocker but no one answered.'

'Peter didn't come, he went away with his father instead.' She unlocked the kitchen door and they went inside. 'You can make the coffee,' she decided, 'I'll cook the breakfast.'

'Lead on, just show me where everything's kept.'

She sat down on a chair and stuck her legs out in front of her. 'Please,' she pointed to her yellow boots.

He obliged and, bending to the task, eased them off her feet. 'Cute outfit,' he said.

'I've been beach walking, no one sees me there.' Sylvia got up and began to prepare the food.

'You seem to enjoy a very pleasant style of life here in Norfolk,' he said, pouring the last of the coffee. 'I bet you wouldn't like to give it up.'

'Why should I have to?' Sylvia asked.

'What about David Christensen?'

'What about David Christensen?'

'Don't you find it difficult, one of you in California, one of you in England?'

'Difficult?' Sylvia pondered that.

'Yes, he being an attractive young man and you being a *very* attractive woman.' He grinned, somewhat salaciously Sylvia thought.

'Oh, I see,' she replied, clattering the plates together as she started to clear the table. 'We *do* see one another from time to time, you know.'

'Are you in love with him?' he asked directly.

She turned, plates in hand. 'Why should you want to know that?'

He smiled. 'I'm just interested, a woman in love with someone else is . . . interesting.'

'In what way?' she asked, turning on the hot tap, steam rising, billowing up at her from the sink.

'In every way.'

'I'm not sure what you mean.' She began to wash up.

'What's he like?' he asked, picking up a tea-towel and beginning to dry one of the large breakfast plates.

'Are you interviewing me now?' Sylvia asked, turning to look at him.

'Sure, why not?'

'Well, he's like you see on the screen.'

'No, I mean as a person, how would you describe him?'

Sylvia thought for a moment. 'Like anyone else really,

165

like any other man, very kind, humorous, I think, makes jokes against himself and doesn't take his work too seriously.' She picked up a cup from the basin and concentrated on cleaning around inside it. 'Oh, I don't know,' she continued, 'he's just . . . very dependable and I feel more at ease and more secure when I'm with him than I have with anyone before . . .'

'In my experience men as handsome as him are a real pain in the arse, you know, vain, arrogant, cocky, absolute bastards . . .'

'He's not that . . .' Sylvia shook her head. 'I mean, I'm sure he's aware of his looks, what a great asset they are to him but he's never struck me as a vain man.'

'It's early days yet,' he replied.

'No, I don't think so.' She tipped the soapy water out of the washing-up basin. 'Why do you say that? You're in the same boat as him, pretty-boy actor resorting to Shakespearian tragedy to gain credibility as a serious player.'

'One doesn't resort to Shakespeare . . .'

'You know what I mean. For God's sake don't start getting precious, you began this conversation!'

He clattered some knives and forks he had been drying into their drawer. 'So, this fabulous young film star comes along and really sweeps you off your feet . . .'

'Hardly,' Sylvia corrected. 'He wasn't even famous when we first met.'

He waved her response away with a flick of the wet tea-towel. 'Whatever. What I don't understand, what I find hard to figure out is this living apart business.'

'There's nothing to figure out, we both have our careers to follow.'

'But aren't you crazy not being with him?'

'No, not crazy.'

'You miss him, though.'

'Of course.'

'You miss sex with him?'

'For God's sake,' Sylvia had to smile, 'what are you?' She snatched the tea-towel from his hand and dried her wet hands on it. 'Are you the *Kinsey Report*?'

He laughed. 'Come on, we're both grown-up people.'

'I know I am,' Sylvia retorted.

'You haven't answered my question.'

'Why should I?'

'Does it embarrass you? I'm sorry.'

'No, it doesn't embarrass me and you're not sorry.' She sat down and smiled across the kitchen at him. 'If you wanted to go to bed with me you didn't have to go through all this pantomime.' She threw her head back and laughed seeing just how ridiculous this all was, knowing exactly what the outcome was to be. 'You didn't have to hire a car and drive all the way to Norfolk.'

He smiled, bemused now, uncomfortable. 'I'm sorry.'

She stopped laughing and leant back in her chair, examining the split ends in her long black hair. 'We're both grown up, you just said it, come on then, let's go upstairs and be grown up!'

'Just like that?'

'What do you want?' She stood up, facing him. 'An engraved invitation?'

She didn't really know all the reasons why she'd done it; out of a sense of grievance perhaps at David's long absence or, perhaps, he had simply been around when it seemed appropriate. Whatever the reasons, timing, luck, chance, recklessness she never had any second thoughts. He was smooth-skinned, it seemed that every other man she had ever slept with had been hairy, very black hair and smooth, marble white, creamy skin, almost feminine, over rounded, firm muscle. He had been proficient, workman-like, a little bit of this, a hand here, mouth there, stroking, bringing her to an aroused state so that when he entered her, rather more quickly than she would have really desired, it was not uncomfortable but then neither was it particularly gratifying. At times it was as though she were not really part of this act as he pushed and shoved himself into her, coming in great grunts of gasping satisfaction, leaving her on some plateau in between foreplay and orgasm. He eased out and rolled away just when she would have wanted him to start, leaving her, like so many before, aching and tantalizingly close. She felt cold and wrapped herself around his back, he turned and smiled into her eyes, kissing her gently on the lips.

'Was it all right for you?' he asked gruffly.

She couldn't believe it, was it something to do with the house? Why did men have to ask such questions. She recalled Richard and shivered. It was a competition, then; had he won? Had he achieved the desired results? She smiled at him and he lay back for a while looking contented. Sylvia began to feel guilty that she hadn't protested her desire and longing for him enough, they were suddenly like old married partners, going through the motions of the old routine. She looked across at him and felt an odd sensation, a feeling of fondness. He had survived on his own terms, had been a *man*. She had lain back and thought of all sorts of unrelated things, as soon as she realized that she wasn't really going to be required, just a loan of her body, she was able to contemplate the practicalities of life, not quite shopping lists but close enough.

After a time he went into the bathroom and emerged,

leaning against the bedroom wall, arms folded across his chest, a square shock of black pubic hair standing out in wild contrast to the rest of his napless body, his penis, still seemingly semi-erect, jutting out at her. He looked serious, dramatic, slightly pouting lips, terribly black eyes which a real heroine, if she had been one in romantic fiction, would have drowned in ('. . . drowning in his deep dark eye pools,'), she thought to herself, unable to contain the smile this brought to her lips. He seemed to take this as a sign that all was well, that duty had been done whilst all the time Sylvia was thinking that she wanted to be fucked by him and involved – not treated as though she was no longer there. She got off the bed and kissed him on the lips as she went past into the bathroom, where she closed the door behind her and took a long, hot shower. He was sitting in the armchair by the window, bare torso and tight jeans, white socks and no shoes, reading a Sunday paper. He didn't look up as she came into the room and began to dress.

She had waved Geoff Meredith out of the driveway, not sure if she was relieved to see him go or not. It had begun to rain again and she went down to the poolside where she took the shrimping net on the long pole and fished out the dead hedgehog, laying it on the wet paving stones for a while whilst she decided what to do with it. In the end she dug a respectable little grave in the corner of the garden close to a climbing rose and shoved the soggy, prickly creature down into the wet hole. She walked back into the house and quickly packed her things. She pushed the crumpled sheets into a pillow case and carried everything downstairs.

They had eaten a sandwich lunch along the coast in a small pub where other week-enders clutched their drinks and mixed with the local characters imbibing the atmosphere whilst discussing their yachts. She looked around her; middle-aged businessmen and their wives in matching wet-weather wear laughing in that haw-haw way that really irritated Sylvia. Steaming wet dogs lay around the floor at their owners' feet waiting for another wet Sunday lunch-time at the pub to come to its boozy end.

'This is cute,' he had remarked, looking up at the oak beams and the horse-brass.

She had known he would say that, so bloody predictable. She smiled, forcing it across her face. 'I'm glad you like it, when I was married, my husband used to keep a yacht down here, so, this was really our local.'

'You sail?' he asked.

'Infrequently, although it has been known. I still have a small boat down here.'

He nodded. 'A woman of many parts, eh?'

'Most of them wearing out!'

He had laughed at that and looked at his watch, 'I really shall have to be making tracks.'

Sylvia had breathed a silent sigh of relief, and finished her lunch quickly in order that they might leave before he suggested more drinks to hold up their progress any further.

Now she stood, the house locked, the car packed, taking one last look at the sea before driving back to London. The tide was in, the dark water rolling up under the leaden skies. She watched the sea birds skimming the surface of the waves and then turned, glancing at the mound of hedgehog tomb, before leaving the garden and walking over the wet grass at the front of the house to where her car was parked. As she drove away she thought about herself, considering, wondering, trying to decide just why she did certain things, what her motives were, what her reasons must be. She accelerated the powerful car away along the narrow country lane leaving a plume of exhaust smoke trailing in the air. She could come to no conclusions about herself but knew that Geoff Meredith, for all his considerable charm, was no answer. She thought of David, he had merely enhanced her longing to be with him. She thought of him in California. She looked out at the pouring rain, the sea to her left, flatlands to her right, the world closed in around her, the strange pull of Norfolk that, somehow, infuriated her but which she also loved. David in a blue swimming pool, Sylvia under a downpour, David on golden sands, Sylvia burying dead animals in sodden earth. There was no justice to all of this but, whatever there was, Sylvia had brought it all on herself. She pulled up at a road junction and turned right on to the main Norwich road, finding a cassette tape and pushing it into the machine, the car filling with the sounds of Joni Mitchell. Sylvia looked ahead and gunned the engine, faster and faster, the wide tyres hissing through the rain. Time was running out, she thought, her decisions had to be made, perhaps her answers could be found with David. It was time for another trip to Tinsel City to find out.

Chapter 8

'Hollywood is like a vile smog,' Sylvia said to David as he drove them back to his low-slung Canyon home in his brand new low-slung Italian sports car. 'How can you believe anything anymore? How can you believe anything anyone says to you?'

'It's not like home,' David replied, 'it's all cut and thrust . . . None of your gentleman's agreement stuff.'

'And your agent is *so* crude,' Sylvia complained. 'Does that woman have to swear all the time?'

David laughed. 'Marsha has her own style, that's why she's top of the ladder. People respect her in this town.'

'She's terrifying,' Sylvia said from the heart.

'She's pushy,' he countered, slightly defensively, 'knows what she wants and gets stuck in there. I'm grateful to have her on my side.'

'I need a drink,' Sylvia said as soon as they entered the dark house. She found it odd that he didn't live behind high walls rather than in this secluded but accessible house.

David flicked on the lights. It was a house Sylvia knew well, straight out of a film, interior designer spartan to fit an image, lots of wood – floors, ceilings, walls – leather chairs, Mexican throw-rugs, very austere in an expensive way. Hi-tech electronics, a clinical-white kitchen which, she was convinced, would easily adapt for major heart surgery, spotless, white, shining, freshly cleaned and unused. The only room with any character was the bedroom. It had muddled surfaces, crumpled clothes dropped carelessly around, some partially uncrated pictures which they had picked out together a few months previously. There were cigarette burns on his bedside table, a half-empty bottle of J and B, a dog-eared selection of books scattered around, a picture of her (smiling), a picture of him (serious), a picture of them (laughing) on a beach, taken a year ago . . . bills and scraps of paper and scripts and letters piled up on the floor at his side of the vast American bed with English newspapers muddled in amongst them. David never allowed his Mexican cleaner to touch this room, it was like the inside of a giant, untidy drawer and only David knew where everything was kept, where each script or important document lay at any given time. The curtains were rarely drawn open, the room smelt of him and of tobacco and paper and drink and expensive perfume.

'You're too famous,' she said at last, standing over by the picture window.

He laughed at her. 'You're too drunk.'

'Never too drunk for this place.'

'You love it, really,' he said.

'I *hate* it, really,' she snarled, like Marsha. 'You came here for one film *two* years ago . . . I would like to know how much longer you intend to stay.'

'Are you serious?' he looked at her. 'We're not getting into my rotten films versus my serious stage career argument again, are we?'

'Do you want to get into that argument?' Sylvia asked.

'No, I'm going to bed now, I have to be up early.' He smiled at her before turning away.

'You look tired,' she said, feeling sorry for him now, 'wrecked.'

David smiled. 'It was one of those Hollywood days,' he was joking, 'know what I mean?'

173

'No, I don't, not really.' She watched him beginning to undress.

'Well, I don't see this bloody picture ever being completed with that *bloody* man directing it.'

Sylvia nodded, David had been complaining about his director since she had arrived. 'Mother's in New York, David, and I thought I'd leave a day early and stay over with her.' Sylvia blurted this out as though she had been preparing it all day.

David lay down on top of the bed in his underpants. 'You're leaving early to see your mother?' He stared at her for a long moment, incredulity in his voice. 'Why are you always running away from here . . . from me?'

'Don't be ridiculous . . .'

'You can see your mother any time you want!'

'I can't, she's always on tour. She's always travelling about.' Sylvia was adamant.

'Sylvia,' David sighed, closing his eyes tightly as though attempting to gather his thoughts together, 'I know I haven't spent a lot of time with you this trip. I know I haven't been very attentive.' He opened his eyes. 'I'm exhausted, Sylvia.' It was almost a complaint directed at her, as if she had been making too many demands upon him. 'I want you to like it out here, to feel comfortable.'

Sylvia thought about that, her hands in tight fists now, the nails digging into the palms. 'You want me to make it very easy for you. The problem is I don't like it . . .'

'So, you're going off to see your mother.' He sat up. 'When will I see you again?' he asked, resigned to the fact.

'When will you be free?'

'God knows, three weeks, a month.'

'What about your next epic? When does that go into production?'

174

'I'm having a rest before that, Goddamn it!'

'What will Marsha have to say about that?'

'Marsha will have to sort it all out,' he replied angrily.

'Lucky Marsha.'

'Come on, Sylvia, what can I do to make everything right for you?'

'Do?' she watched him lighting a cigarette, 'for me? You don't do anything, just don't expect me to sustain this trans-Atlantic-Little-Miss-Showbusiness routine for the remainder of your career, that's all.'

'I have obligations and a stack of commitments here, I don't know what you expect me to do.' He looked at her, 'You know I love you.'

'Well, I'm not demanding choices, David, I just think, that in terms of our relationship, things are pretty bloody silly. I'm usually jet-lagged and shattered, you're always exhausted and have to be in bed by nine o'clock, up at some hour of the morning no sane person sees. At least no one could accuse us of being obsessed with sex.'

'I love you,' he told her again, sounding sad and looking lost.

This look of his always got to her, she had even seen it employed by him on the screen, but it stopped her from saying something bitter. 'I hope your love will be enough, David, because I've drifted beyond the point of careful deceptions and I have to be selfish and abide by my own set of rules.' She swallowed back her tears which came so easily now, 'I love you very much and I recognize all these conflicting feelings within myself . . . I cannot fall out of control because of you. I *have* to keep hold of the things that I've worked to achieve.'

'Your career,' he slumped back onto the bed, 'your career above all else.'

'No, not above all else, why should it have to be seen in those terms?'

'I want to marry you, that should mean something, shouldn't it? Why aren't we married by now? Jesus, we've been together for two years and I've been asking you since 1975. Why are we *always* having this same Goddamn argument?'

Sylvia bit her lip, looking into his eyes full of hurt. She took a deep breath. 'I know you want us to marry but I don't want to be a wife again. I can't cope with the responsibility of that role again. I don't want to marry and I don't want to have your children because I'm too old and too damn selfish.'

'You're obsessed with age,' he said bitterly.

'One day you'll fall out of love with me. When I'm an old woman you'll still be a young man and I will not be dependent upon someone who no longer wants me . . . I have no desire to become your mother!'

He smiled at that, despite himself. 'I'm in love with you, you foolish woman, what else matters? What else is there. You know, Sylvia, people spend their whole lives searching for that. Don't throw it away for us, for my sake.' He watched her for a long moment. 'Do you love me?'

'I love you,' she replied simply.

'This is absolutely hopeless,' he began to laugh, 'for Christ's sake, give a sucker an even break.'

For once she left the house at the same time as David. It was a strange, wet dawn. She wandered on to the back terrace and noticed the cat dish still full of food from the previous day. Perhaps the cat had realized that she might be leaving and wandered, padding on those sticky legs, off to another foolish woman who would pity it and then rue the day. David could not drive her to the airport, a sleek black limousine had already arrived to take him to the studio but he waited with her until a cab arrived. He kissed her with an urgency that began to panic her, he kept repeating that he loved her, insisting that she should marry him. Sylvia had wept all the way to the plane. She could not give him up.

Her mother took her to a restaurant full of dark panelling and signed photographs of famous patrons discreetly hung. A young Katharine Hepburn in pensive mood studied them at their dim table. Sylvia wondered if any of the dark shadows in the spaces around them were the elderly images of these youthful faces caught forty or fifty or more years before when, in their prime, they set out to conquer. She felt consumed by age and history and doom. Sylvia watched her mother, old but still working hard, in her middle sixties but still in demand, giving concerts and master classes, fresh as ever, astute and brilliant.

'Why do you always bring me to this place?' Sylvia asked, sulking like a child.

'Because it's convenient for my apartment and the concert hall. I can't think why you have to fly back to London before the week-end.' Her mother had a wonderfully crisp accent which became almost unbearable when chastising her daughter. 'I hardly ever get a chance to see you these days.'

'I can't stay, Mother, I have to get back to record an interview.'

Natalia Fiodor sighed. 'You haven't said anything about David, how is the film star?'

Sylvia flinched. 'He wants to marry me.'

'Excellent,' she beamed at her daughter, 'that's very good.' She paused. 'Isn't it?'

'Mother, be serious.'

'What's wrong with that?'

'Everything,' Sylvia complained.

'Isn't he a very nice man, as well as being so terribly attractive? Why don't you want to marry him?' She sounded amazed at such stupidity.

'He's too young, Mother,' Sylvia warned.

'Too young?' she sounded incredulous.

'Too young, yes.'

'Your great-grandmother, Natalia Alexandrov, married a boy, a princeling, when she was eighty-three years of age.'

'Oh, Mother, really,' Sylvia laughed, 'that's just one of your family stories.'

'You have Russian blood in you, Sylvia, it's hot!'

'For God's sake.' Sylvia blushed.

'You're still a young woman, of course you are, don't be ridiculous.'

'Well,' Sylvia said, raising her water glass, 'here's to Mother Russia.'

Her mother continued, ignoring Sylvia's disrespect. 'David is a very attractive person, nice. You don't have to let him go for the sake of one of your wretched principles. Don't let him go or you'll live to regret it, Sylvia,' she said, wagging a finger.

'Don't you think I *have* thought, Mother. He wants children.'

'You could have children.'

'Mother,' Sylvia said patiently, as though explaining to a child, 'I'm forty.'

'You could have children.' Natalia Fiodor sighed and waved a hand dismissively. 'Darling, most women would be pleased that David even looked their way.' She smiled at her foolish daughter. 'Why do you always make life so

178

awfully difficult, don't you love him? What more do you want?'

'Yes, I love him, yes, I know it looks ridiculous, but why should I have to compromise my life to fit into David's scheme of things?'

Natalia Fiodor looked away in disgust. 'Marry him and be done, you need him.'

'I have my job, I won't let him destroy that. What he fails to understand is that without it I cease to be the same person.'

'I fail to understand why things should change.'

'Yes, you do, you're just being deliberately obtuse.'

'Couldn't you do the same things in America?'

'But I don't want to live in America,' she was adamant, 'and I certainly don't want to live in Los Angeles,' she said contemptuously.

'You make everything sound so final, Sylvia.'

'He could work in Europe,' Sylvia said, showing her anger. 'It was supposed to be a two-film contract. That was three films and two years ago.'

'Well, one can hardly deny him his fame, you want yours, don't you?' It was an accusation.

'My fame is limited, you can hardly call it that.'

'Whatever, you're still loath to give it up.'

'Because I worked damned hard for it and because it's mine.'

'And David didn't work for his?'

'He's twenty-five years old,' Sylvia said, infuriated.

'Well, now, here's the crux of the matter. Don't you think it's rather patronizing of you to take such a view?'

'I meant that he'd rather fallen into success.'

'You worked hard, Sylvia, there's no denying that, but you've never had to struggle exactly.'

'Oh, yes, I struggled, Mother, a debilitating marriage

to Richard, two children before I could even get started.'
The emotions that this raised inside her surprised even
Sylvia.

'You regret your children, now?' her mother asked,
disgusted.

'In certain instances, yes,' she replied, defiantly, staring
her mother out.

Natalia Fiodor shrugged. 'It was always your decision.
You didn't have to marry Richard, I certainly never had
any intention of making you. He may be a little dull but
he always struck me as being rather dependable . . .'

'It was 1958 and I was pregnant,' Sylvia interrupted
sourly.

'How can you write off fourteen years of your life, it's
perverse.'

'So, I'm perverse,' Sylvia said, sounding tired. 'I have
to catch up with myself, time is running away with me and
I don't want to be trapped, why should I? You never
were, you always had your fabulous career,' she accused.

'I play the piano, Sylvia, I can do that anywhere, I've
never been very particular about where I work. You seem
to be hell bent upon doing what *you* want irrespective of
what damage it does to you or anyone else.'

Sylvia picked at her meal, moving the food around the
plate, just as she had done when a child. 'You think I'm a
fool not to grab him whilst I have this chance,' she said.

'I think you'll be unhappy, ultimately, but, only you
know what has to be done.'

'That's not very helpful, Mother.'

Natalia Fiodor raised her eyes to the ceiling. 'You only
want to argue today, Sylvia, there's no sense to you.
You've lived with him, I don't understand how marriage
will be any different. You can have David, your career,
your freedom.'

'I only want him. I don't want all the rest that seems to accompany him.'

'Marry him, take your chances and stop being a fool.'

'He insists upon marriage now.'

'Do it, Sylvia, just do it.'

'But you say that because you're an incurable romantic, you think it'll solve everything.'

'I'm rather an incurable realist. What if you don't marry him and, in five or ten years' time you find out what a dreadful mistake you've made, what then?'

Sylvia felt panicky and she wouldn't answer her mother.

They took a short walk after lunch, looking strangely at odds with one another. Sylvia in jeans and polo-neck underneath her red plastic coat. Natalia Fiodor immaculate in black fur, coat and hat, and black leather boots under a mid-length black skirt. Sylvia's hair flew wildly in the Park Avenue down draught, Natalia Fiodor's careful blonde locks were coiffeured to lacquered perfection, the strands of hair glistening, pristine, under the black fur. Sylvia slouched along, hands in pockets holding the plastic coat together. Natalia Fiodor walked straight, head erect, purposeful, majestic. Sylvia envied her mother's control.

'Do you want me to come to JFK with you?' her mother asked.

Sylvia was sitting on the window seat in her mother's bedroom, knees pulled up tightly against her chest, her hair veiling one side of her face as she looked down on to the city. 'Of course not.' She turned to her mother and smiled.

Natalia Fiodor walked over and stroked Sylvia's long hair. 'Why can't you simply be happy for once in your life?'

Sylvia took her mother's hand and squeezed it, shaking

her head. 'Until I know what's going to happen to Charley I just feel that I can't make any decisions that may affect his life.'

The older woman sat down next to Sylvia. 'Charley's eighteen now, how long are you going to wait? Have you considered he may never change?'

'Well, Dr Freeman feels he's made good progress . . .'

'He's been in that clinic for six months now, how much longer will it take?'

'It doesn't matter how much time it takes, he's able to come home every month or so, he's able to function . . .'

'Sylvia, you cannot afford to wait. Charley's receiving the very best treatment, what have you to feel guilty about?'

'Letting them go when they were so small?' She searched her mother's face for an answer.

Natalia Fiodor looked away. 'That has nothing to do with it, I was always away from you . . . and what about Peter?'

'I don't know,' Sylvia replied hopelessly, 'I don't know.'

The flight back was interminable. Sylvia had never really considered things in terms of motives although she was convinced that they were there all the same. Rather, she attempted to see things with a kind of logical self-assurance, even detachment, which enabled her to battle through when all else fell to pieces around her. David was insisting upon marriage but she didn't want that because it made absolutely no sense to her. She could have his child without marriage, she had once even considered it as a possibility. David was someone she really wanted, she enjoyed him, she liked him, she liked sex with him, craving him when they were apart. If it was love, though, why couldn't she marry him just for the sake of some peace and quiet? Why not just do it for him? There was no one else after all for either of them and, therefore, the truth must be, she concluded, that she didn't want to give up any part of herself to anyone after so long, so many years of controlling things for herself. After all, hadn't she *had* marriage?

The steward handed her a vodka in a plastic glass and tonic in a little canister. She pulled the tab and added some to the alcohol. Sylvia tried to imagine herself at sixty-five with porky feet and puffy ankles that spilt over the edges of her Minnie Mouse shoes. David could keep that picture away from her, at least for a while. She shuddered, he would still be relatively young when she was a pensioner. Sylvia found herself staring at the middle-aged woman in the aisle seat opposite, the woman caught her eye and smiled, Sylvia turned back to her drink and her magazines and her scattered thoughts.

Within a few days of her arrival in London, Molly rang to hear how the trip had been and suggested they had lunch together. Sylvia arrived at their usual rendezvous, a dark restaurant down a steep flight of steps, a converted wine cellar which did a nice line in whole, vegetarian foods with a good house wine on which they invariably became loose-tongued and, occasionally, even raucous. She was listening to a crackling Gershwin record whilst reading a book by Lillian Hellman, *Maybe*, which was only one-hundred-and-two pages long but which seemed to go on for ever, when Molly arrived clutching at a package of books and a huge bunch of roses which she had cut herself and brought up from the country. She dumped everything on to the blue check table-cloth and, leaning across, gave Sylvia a big kiss.

'Hello, love, sorry I'm so late. Damned bookshop, I

ordered this lot months ago, they swore blind that I'd never done any such thing.' She sat down and grinned. 'And so, how are you? You look a bit peaky. How was America?'

Sylvia bit into her lip. 'David has asked me again to marry him.'

'And?' Molly asked expectantly.

Sylvia shrugged. 'I don't want to marry again.'

'Is it his age that puts you off?'

A waiter came and took their orders, Molly asked for a bottle of wine. 'It's a big consideration, yes, of course,' Sylvia replied, watching the waiter walking away, absently admiring his behind encased in tight denim jeans.

'What else is there to hold you back?' Molly asked.

'He wants a child, I can't start all of that again.'

'I had Benjamin last year,' Molly replied, 'it's possible, you know.'

'Yes, but you're different, you've always had children and career and husband.' She looked at Molly dressed in her peasant-style smock made up like a patchwork quilt, bare feet inside red, hand-made sandals, her hair henna red and cropped short, her face scrubbed clean, a slight flush to her cheeks from the alcohol or high blood pressure. Molly had grown large, plump in the mould of a real earthmother, all welcoming, luxuriant and fecund, open and warm and full of life giving promise. Sylvia could feel safe with her but also resent Molly's fortune at the same time, sanctified within a marriage and surrounded by five healthy children. 'You've always enjoyed the role you play, I was never fitted for that, for motherhood, happy families . . . all of that.'

'You've had two children, what are you talking about?' Molly stared at her, pouring them some wine. 'Stop being so damned self-pitying. You have to make your choices

184

as events dictate them, and, once you have, then it becomes history and nothing can alter that.'

The waiter returned with their salad and quiche, smiling at Sylvia but ignoring Molly.

'I know what you're going to say,' Sylvia began in an accusatory way, 'that I should marry David and be damned, never mind about the consequences.'

'Yes, marry him, why not? What's to stop you? It's easy.'

'You just want everybody to be like you,' Sylvia replied bitterly, 'married and nursing babies and having their work in between times.'

'My work isn't in between times,' Molly protested. 'You have, *one* has, a family *and* a career, if you're lucky, and it all just fits together somehow . . .'

'Well, let's just hope one of your children doesn't end up like Charley, let's pray it never happens to you and Jack, but, if it should, *then* talk to me about how easy everything is and the historical inevitability of life . . .'

'Oh, Sylvia,' Molly sounded appalled, 'you're consumed with guilt, for Richard, for Charley, even for David and you've got to stop it!'

'How?' Sylvia demanded. 'You tell me.'

'By going forwards.'

'However the past may affect everything, whatever it may bring?'

'Sylvia,' Molly spoke calmly, 'you either love David or you don't, if you do, then nothing else should matter.'

'Not even Charley?'

'Charley isn't a child any longer, you cannot be held responsible for ever!'

Sylvia thought about that. 'I couldn't face everything going wrong at this stage of my life. There is Charley to consider, whatever you may say.' She concentrated upon lunch, cutting her quiche into small squares.

'You cannot simply continue embellishing your present life with all the crap from what is now a redundant past, you go forward and grab at whatever chances come your way.'

'You're just talking about David again, you and my mother, you're both obsessed with the subject.'

'Because we want you to be *happy*.' Molly poured more wine for them. 'You've always been such a mixture, Sylvia, everything about you is a contradiction, everything is always opposite . . . you're the child of an aristocrat but insist upon being socialist, there's no consistency in your life at all.' She chuckled to herself.

'Well, now, you're just laughing at me,' Sylvia replied, feeling rather annoyed.

'I'm not, love, I'm attempting to understand your rationale.'

'There's nothing to understand.' She gave her friend a withering look. 'Anyway, my parents are hardly traditional aristos, my father doesn't ever use his title, my mother has *never* even used her married name!'

'Why aren't you following her advice?' Molly asked. 'You know she's a very practical woman.'

'Because she's taken in by David just like everyone else.'

'What's that suposed to mean exactly?' Molly asked, unconvinced.

'David has this incredible bourgeois morality, he feels guilty because we're having a relationship outside unholy matrimony.'

'Are you serious?' Molly asked, laughing and pouring more wine. 'You're not serious.'

Sylvia didn't answer her, she drank more instead.

'You think too much about everything,' Molly concluded.

'I don't think enough, if I'd thought about things I would never have married Richard, or rather, ended up having to marry him.'

'No, you would have married someone else and divorced them instead.'

After lunch Molly walked Sylvia to her car. 'What happened to the Porsche?' she asked as Sylvia opened up the tail-gate of a bulky Volvo estate.

'Not very practical,' Sylvia replied laying the roses carefully down and slamming the door. 'I'm having Doug's farmhouse renovated and this is useful for carting stuff up and down.'

'I don't know why you bother hanging on to that place,' Molly said, shifting her parcel of books from one arm to the other.

'Doug liked it,' Sylvia said. 'I suppose I ought to sell it really, I have three houses and I'm barely in any of them, I never use them.'

Molly put her books on top of the car and then took Sylvia into her arms, hugging her warmly. 'Call me in a few days?' she asked, looking at her closely. 'Are you all right?'

Sylvia nodded. 'Don't worry . . . I know you think I'm being stupid.'

'Not at all,' Molly protested, 'a little misguided perhaps, but never stupid.'

It began to rain. Sylvia sat waiting for a red light to change, looking out at the smudged images behind the steamy windows of a run-down greasy café. It reminded her of a painting Douglas had done whilst in New York. She smiled and bared her teeth at herself in the driving-mirror. 'You poor old bastard,' she said, 'you stupid old thing.' In California the sun would be shining brightly, catching his hair, golden against the perfect movie blue sky and framing him in his glory days of youth and power and fame. Sylvia understood that this was the stuff mistakes were made of but longed for him just the same. The sound of car horns and the green light through the pouring rain made her return to reality.

She met Edmund in his office. He was sitting behind his desk in his large fake leather chair with the executive swivel, the back reclined, looking through a sheaf of neat typescript. Sylvia sat down on a sofa against the wall on the opposite side of the room. She adjusted her long summer skirt, looking at her bare legs and wondering if they required shaving. Her espadrilles looked tatty, the plaited-fibre soles beginning to wear rather badly. She tucked a finger under the inside of her embroidered cheese-cloth shirt which scratched at her collar bone.

'So, Sylvia,' Edmund began after their initial greeting, 'and how are you?'

'Hot,' Sylvia replied, easing off her right shoe and massaging her heel, looking at the dark rain spots on her light skirt. She had a vague headache from all the lunch-time wine.

'There are some rumblings from on high concerning your choice of material for the coming series.' He looked back at his notes and then came forward to face her across the wide desk, his hands clasped together in front of him. 'I thought we should have a chat, unofficially, Sylvia.'

'Unofficial, eh?' The office was hot; even with the windows open and the downpour outside it was still very close. There were dark wet circles under his armpits. 'Sounds serious, Edmund,' she said with mock gravity.

'The word is out that the programme has become, and

I'm quoting here, "a receptacle for trendy, lefty, feminist pleadings", that we've moved too far away from our original, wider, broader based, brief.'

'A receptacle?' she asked innocently. 'You mean like a toilet or a spittoon?'

Edmund looked very serious. 'If we step over the mark, Sylvia, they can pull the plug.'

'Well, let's see, now,' Sylvia replied, pondering the situation, 'for this season we have a women's theatre group from Lambeth, an artists' collective from Manchester, a writers' co-operative from Norwich and a radical film-making workshop from Bristol.' She paused, Edmund was already looking pained. 'Then we have The Royal Ballet, a programme about Marc Chagall, a profile of Dustin Hoffman,' she raised her eyes, 'a piece about advertisements as art, a programme about British film stars, Mason, Lockwood et al., my piece about graffiti in New York, a film about David Hockney, a report . . .'

'Okay,' Edmund said, stopping her, 'there's no need to go through the entire schedule, I do know what's in there.'

'Then why aren't you putting the record straight on our behalf?'

'Sylvia . . . Sylvia,' he sighed, 'last season the show was full of some very contentious items which I let through because of my belief in you and in your judgement . . .'

'Oh, God, Edmund, don't flatter me, it's so bloody demeaning, just say what you have to say and save me the crap.'

'Now don't start, Sylvia, there's no need . . .'

'There's every need, Edmund, for Christ's sake. I thought we were supposed to be working together with the same ideals and aspirations for the programme. Just because some creep in admin gets the wind up you're trying to use the old scare tactics routine on me . . . I agreed to do this programme on the firm understanding that we were broadening the scope of arts TV, I was under the impression that you went along with that aim.'

'Yes, yes, yes, Sylvia, that's all very well but we're in the real world now, and we're still an arts programme . . .'

'And not a current affairs show,' Sylvia interrupted, finishing the well-worn phrase for him.

'The last series ended with a film full of radical lesbians talking about group sex.' He tapped the desk-top to emphasize his words.

'Women's politics, Edmund, *politics*.'

Edmund ignored the interruption. 'That was supposed to be a group of serious painters from Wales. You promise one thing, I let you loose with a camera crew and you come back with something completely different!' He sounded very upset. 'It places me in a very insidious position.' He sat back into the refuge of his chair, rocking it slightly from side to side, pointing at her now. 'You have editorial say on all your filmed pieces . . . I sometimes wonder why I'm here at all,' he finished accusingly.

'Well, now, there's a thing, perhaps that's the real problem here, Edmund.'

'I don't see this as a personal issue,' Edmund insisted, 'let's not get carried away.'

'I can't work with these kinds of threats and constraints hanging over me . . .' She paused and thought for a moment. 'Perhaps two years is enough.'

'I don't want to hear that kind of talk, Sylvia, we can work this out to everyone's satisfaction. *I* have to answer for my actions as well, you know,' Edmund finished, opening his hands in an expression of innocence.

Sylvia, considering him to be ostensibly culpable, was

not convinced by this honest-broker routine. 'I have to film the New York piece, I assume that I still have your support on that.' She looked at him questioningly.

'Of course,' Edmund said, 'absolutely, right down the line.'

Sylvia nodded. 'Perhaps you'd like to be more specific then,' she suggested.

'I've been working on some possible rescheduling ideas,' he replied, pushing papers across the desk-top towards her.

Sylvia limped over to the desk and, sitting on the comfortable chair in front of it, picked up the papers and examined them quickly. 'You seem to have cut the women's theatre group,' she said with barely contained rancour.

'They've received some awfully bad press just recently . . . I want us to shelve them for the time being.'

'Cut them, you mean,' she replied, irritated with his semantics. 'After all, we're talking censorship here, aren't we,' she stated.

'Not at all,' Edmund said firmly, defending his decision. '*Shelve*,' he insisted, 'for the time being.'

Sylvia paused, laying the papers back on the desk. 'And what have you in mind to replace them with?' she asked disgustedly.

'I thought we might do something on the London theatre scene . . .'

'Oh, great,' she responded sarcastically, 'a sort of "In Town Tonight", something we can really get our teeth into!'

'Every programme doesn't have to be controversial, Sylvia, contrast is a useful device. Why can't it just be a straightforward look at something, we don't have to delve into politics and feminism *every* time we point a camera.'

'No, but I don't see art as something abstract, something divorced from everyday life, it should be an integral part of it. The London theatre is hardly going to appeal to the sort of audience we're attracting.'

'No, well, that may not be an altogether bad thing.' He looked at her searchingly. 'That thing you did on "The Clash", for example, we're supposed to be reaching for a wide audience.'

'Look, Edmund, listen to me, you're taking work out of context. The week after the punk programme we did a profile about Rubenstein, and, besides, "The Punk Rock Show" got our highest ever ratings and *very* good reviews. Christ, if we were to follow your tastes it would be Dame June Skipworth and the *Desert Song*!'

There was silence for a while, just the sound of rain and the fresh smell of it against the hot buildings and pavements. 'Do you really feel Joe Strummer and the like have artistic integrity, Sylvia?'

'Oh, Edmund, shame on you. For God's sake, I'm not about to start an ideological argument with you about punk rock, it's absolutely pointless.'

'Well, just answer my question,' he said with an edge of irritation now present in his voice, 'please.'

'Yes, I do, of course I do, they're reflecting something important and the whole movement is interesting sociologically. It's . . .'

'I think it's terribly sordid,' Edmund interrupted.

'Yes,' she said, giving him a withering look, 'well, I can't answer for your closed-off mind.'

'I'm trying to have a serious discussion, Sylvia, *please*,' he insisted.

'Edmund, you're the director, *you* have the power to make the cuts or not . . . I'm sick of these perpetual arguments . . .'

192

'Are you unhappy with the show?' Edmund enquired.

'In 1975 I felt we had a common goal. We've moved from an original and exciting idea to a run of the mill wallpaper show, it's becoming far too careful, Edmund.'

'A sign of the times perhaps,' he suggested rather sinisterly.

'A sign that I'm getting too old for this type of thing.'

'Rubbish,' he said.

'Is it?'

'We must bend with the wind or break, Sylvia.'

Sylvia thought about that. 'You make it sound as though some dark malevolence is out to get us.'

He didn't respond to that. 'Can I leave you to consider the changes?'

Sylvia picked up the papers again, limping back to the sofa where she put her shoe back on. 'I'll call you in a few days,' she said, leaving him to his reclining comfort, his pages of typescript clenched tightly in her fist.

She was sitting on her bed listening to the remaining messages on her answering machine. Richard was the final caller, would she drive up to Freeman-Lapp at the week-end to fetch Charley? Sometimes she felt more hopeful about Charley but she saw things generally in a negative way; recently she had come to view the situation as having no absolute resolution. Charley had not completed his schooling or been in a position to make any long-term decisions. He had no ideas about what it was he wanted to do (even if he had been fit to make such a choice) and he was eighteen years old with absolutely nowhere to go. Sometimes she felt desperate about such an uncertain future.

She took Charley from the clinic to the coast where Peter joined them. Storms were breaking up the hot spell and they arrived late on Friday afternoon when the clouds were low over the sea and there was rain in the cold wind which whipped the slashing dune grass around their legs. The tide was out and the beach empty, stretching away, seemingly for miles. Sunlight streaked down from between the louring dark clouds illuminating the sand which looked a garish yellow against the churning roll of dark ocean and tossing white caps. Sylvia could see no ships, black sky touched the horizon and she shivered at the thought of being out there on such a day. She watched Charley and Peter from her vantage point on the dunes. They were walking out to meet the tide, parallel to the rusty groynes. They walked on against the strong wind, their bright wind-cheater jackets ballooning up, orange and red, like two fat old men. At the tide line was the jutting débris of the old sea-wall or, perhaps, part of a house that had been swept away years ago, the sea having taken away the sand exposing old brick and sea defence. They began to clamber over these ruins and Sylvia turned back to the house, her face glowing from the stinging wind.

Peter bent down to pick up a conical shell and discovered a hermit-crab shut up inside. Charley came back along the top of the ruined sea-wall to look.

'Shall we try to prise him out?' Peter asked.

'No, better to leave him in his home,' Charley replied.

Peter replaced the little shell and watched the flowing tide washing up on to the old red bricks, scoured smooth by the elements. He walked on to catch up with his brother. 'So, how are things?' he asked as they strode along wet sands at the water's edge.

'Things?' He looked at Peter. 'Things are okay.' He nodded as though to reinforce his own conviction of this fact. He stooped to pick up a flat pebble, attempting to skim it through the oncoming surf. 'I've become institutionalized, a Freeman-Lapp junkie, habitual clinic user, that's me,' he said and smiled about it. 'Nearly a year . . . What did the parents say? Ah, yes, that it was all for the very best . . .' He moved on and climbed over the next rusty groyne, jumping down on to the other side leaving deep footprints where he landed.

'They never say much about it now,' Peter said, joining him, 'but I would say they're pretty relieved about everything . . .'

'My cure,' Charley said, stepping up on to the top of a pillbox, submerged in the sand. Ripples of water were starting slowly to creep around it; Peter climbed on too and they both stood facing the turning tide. 'Well, they know there's no cure . . . there's no point in beating around the bush over that.' His words were distant, carried away on the wind, he turned to Peter. 'I'm still drug addicted if that's what you wanted to know.'

'But you'll be leaving the clinic soon,' Peter said, stepping down on to the sands again, 'and you should get off there now, the tide's coming in fast,' he walked on, 'if you don't want to drown.'

'I can't go back to live with the old man or with Mother,' Charley said, catching up. 'Christ knows what I'll do.'

'You could stay at Camden Square, she's hardly ever there . . .'

'Ah, yes, the film actor. We saw one of his films a few weeks ago, a special treat for my group therapy class,' he said with derision. 'It was an all-action film, he's terribly pretty, isn't he, and so *terribly* young.'

'There's a big age gap, fifteen years. Does it bother you to think about that?'

'Jesus,' Charley whistled.

'He's a really nice chap, and very serious about her. I thought you said you liked him.'

'He seems okay, I hardly know him. Do you think they'll do it?' He turned to his brother. 'Marry?'

Peter shrugged. 'As long as she's happy what does it matter . . .'

Charley laughed nastily. 'God, you always look on the bright side, I bet the old man is furious . . .'

'I can't see what it has to do with him, why should it concern Dad?'

'Imagine the publicity,' Charley said.

They began to walk up from the beach and on to the dunes. Charley pulled at the blades of marram, slicing a sharp wound in his right hand. It was deliberate. Peter watched him inflicting this upon himself. They crossed the dunes and found the back lane which took them to the house. 'Why did you do that?' Peter asked him.

'What?' Charley asked innocently, winding a rough bandage, a grimy-looking handkerchief, around the wound. He smiled at his brother. 'Sometimes having a family like ours is a bit of a liability.'

'What do you mean?'

'Oh, you know, everybody so successful, world famous this, world famous that. You're following along in all their footsteps, it's really no wonder one of us turned out to be such a crashing failure.'

'You're rambling, Charley,' Peter said, disenchanted and worried by his brother's sour comments.

'It's true, I don't exactly fit the good old family tradition. Charles McLeod, conceived by mistake, responsible for our parent's marriage, wayward, hapless, no talent, no brains, no future.'

'You can always console yourself with the fact that you

stand to inherit all their fortunes.' Peter saw the house and ran ahead, along the driveway and into the hallway.

Sylvia looked at Charley, resting her book against her bosom and surveying him standing there. It seemed to be growing darker by the second, rain tumbled down and the strong wind whistled and gusted around the house, she could hear the old timbers creak and groan. The bright fire cast long black shadows on the sitting-room walls, which danced and moved in strange, eerie ways. She reached and switched on the lamp at her side.

'Tide's coming in now,' Charley said, 'the old sea-wall is quite exposed. Must be odd for the people who were here thirty years ago to see bits of their old homes poking up through the sand.' He came into the room and squatted down in front of the fire, holding out his hands to the flames which licked over the crackling logs.

He had begun to fill out again, somehow returned to her in a form she recognized, a physical resemblance but no longer the same person. There was a hardness to him that she could not remember and a remoteness, as though he could never be reached. Sylvia noticed the bloody handkerchief. 'What have you done?'

'I scraped it on the old wall, it's nothing.'

'Do you want a plaster?'

'Don't fuss, Mother.' He didn't look up from the fire.

'How's your examination work going?' she asked after a long pause. 'Can you manage it?'

Charley shrugged. 'It's okay . . . I find the history a fag.'

'What does your tutor have to say about that?' she sounded stern, never able to really relax with him.

'He thinks I'll do well if I work hard, you know, the usual stuff.'

'And are you?' she asked plainly.

'Sometimes . . . It's hard, though.' There was an element of defeat in his voice, it sounded like a whine or an apology for impending failure.

Sylvia found this very annoying, she wanted him to be positive and sure, she felt it unnatural that he should be in a position of non-achievement, a failure. She disliked herself for feeling like this. 'When I was young and felt like that, your grandmother would quote something to me about ploughing the proper furrow in order to grow the most productive wheat . . .'

'You were a natural, bright, eager to learn,' he said.

'Well, so are you.' She felt surprised that he should almost accuse her of this.

'Pete's bright, I've always plodded . . . I find everything terribly hard . . . that's why I landed up in this mess, I suppose.'

'And now you're getting out of the mess,' she insisted, looking at him as though that was enough to justify it all. 'You're better, I can see that with my own eyes.'

'Come on, Mother,' he said, turning to look at her at last, his large black eyes reflecting the fire, 'you know that there are no cures, there are just second chances and some relief.'

'So, you must take your second chance and go forward now.' Sylvia felt angry with herself for failing to notice the more obvious signs that something had been wrong in the very beginning. She supposed that she had known, she had simply allowed herself the luxury of not thinking the worst. After all, it was ridiculous to imagine that a child of hers could be involved with dangerous drugs, weren't her children safe amidst their slice of wealth and privilege? Charley had proved her terribly wrong and had added insult to injury, her hurt pride, by stealing from her to support his habit, taking whatever he could find to

198

be sold for drugs. It was this underhand action, the deception and the lies, that she found herself unable to forgive. Sylvia understood that it was really not a blameworthy act, such blame as there was, she knew, lay more with Richard and herself.

'I don't know what it is I want to do, even if I manage to pass these wretched examinations.'

'You can decide later, perhaps you'll go to university . . .'

'What would be the point of that?' he asked, moving from fire to window. 'When pressure isn't good for me university would be the worst place in the world.' He turned to her. 'All anyone in this family ever talks about is *doing* well . . . Maybe I'll never amount to anything in your eyes. Have there never been any like me in the family, any roués, any cads, rakes . . . habitual drug users?'

'I'm not asking you for anything, I want you to get over this horrible experience and discover something good about the world. I don't care how you do this as long as it's something more positive.' She began to sound just like her mother. 'I'd like you to be happy for once . . .'

'Ah, yes, happy,' he sneered. 'I wonder, perhaps you might care to define that for me one day . . .'

'Don't be so ridiculous, there's no point in wallowing about in self-pity. Charley, you are alive and complete and on the brink of a brand new start, don't fall back again, resolve now that you'll never do that.'

He was silent for a while. 'Perhaps, when I leave Freeman-Lapp for good, I could spend some time down here, away from institutions.'

'Whatever you want,' Sylvia replied, feeling very unenthusiastic about the idea. 'Perhaps a holiday would be beneficial.' She looked across at him. He was standing, arms folded, grim-faced, miserable.

He followed her into the kitchen later as she prepared supper. 'What's the matter with Peter this evening?' she asked.

Charley shrugged, picking at a lettuce leaf and nibbling a corner of it. 'Pete's all right, takes after you.'

She ignored that. 'He seemed upset, was he?'

Charley shook his head. 'Not that I know of, we had a walk and a talk, I think he finds me hard to cope with.'

'I'm sure that isn't true, you were probably being objectionable,' Sylvia replied, dumping the lettuce into a shaker.

'Probably,' he readily agreed.

She could hear the waves crashing on to the shore through the darkness. 'Would you go and tell him that it's almost supper time?'

Charley laughed. 'This is real Cain and Abel stuff, isn't it?'

'I sometimes think you'd like it to be. Sibling rivalry is to be expected but at your age it's a bit daft, don't you think?' She brushed past him to the oven where she looked in at the baked potatoes, touching them, making sure they were ready.

'I'll tell him, then,' Charley said, walking out of the kitchen.

The kettle began to whistle, piercing through her thoughts. She picked up a spoon and found her hand trembling.

They drove over to Wells next the Sea the following morning where they strolled along the quayside, looking down at the boats stranded there on the mudflats, their anchor ropes trailing behind, a shiny ribbon of water

200

remaining in between the banking flats glistening and reflecting the watery sun. Seabirds stepped across the mud, feeding. Sylvia watched a grey-brown curlew stalking slowly, probing the ground with its long bill. Gulls floated on the still brine whilst others soared above, crying out noisily. They walked out away from the small town and along the top of the sea defences, dropping down after a while to cross on to the salt-marsh where they criss-crossed the spongy vegetation, jumping the deep salt-water pools left by the outgoing tide. Charley had gone on ahead of them, striding purposefully, as if intent upon reaching the open sea. Sylvia and Peter had come to a broken bridge which once had spanned a tidal inlet. Peter stood out on the remaining timbers looking down.

'It's pretty rotten,' Sylvia warned, 'don't fall in.'

He came back on to the marsh. 'Just where does Charley think he's going?' Peter said, pointing across to his brother, still walking out.

'Do you think he's all right?' Sylvia asked.

'What do you mean?' Peter was still following his brother's progress.

'Oh, it's nothing. Did you two have words last night, when you were out?' They began to trudge on. 'We'll have to attract his attention soon, I don't want to go all that way.'

Peter didn't answer her question. 'Has he told you what he's going to do when he leaves the clinic?'

Sylvia shook her head, adjusting her headscarf. 'I have to talk with Dr Freeman about that. Charley can't just leave. I would imagine they have some ideas cooked up between them. They're terribly secretive up there. Charley probably knows exactly what he's going to do.'

Peter began waving his arms above his head to attract

Charley. 'He isn't looking,' he said after a while of frantic effort.

'Damn,' Sylvia looked at Charley's distant figure, 'what does he think he's up to?'

Peter turned back to her. 'I'll go ahead and get him, we can meet you back at the car if you want.'

Sylvia watched the threatening sky. 'You go on, I'll plod along at my own pace, maybe he'll remember one of us is here and turn back.' She watched Peter moving away from her, always the same story, Peter responsible for Charley. She paused to catch her breath after another few minutes, Peter far ahead by now. She seemed to be surrounded by deep inlets barring her further progress. She searched around until she found one which looked reasonable and, taking a few steps back, ran forward to jump across. Her right foot found the opposite side, lost its hold and she tumbled down into the filthy mess of viscid mud which caked her jeans and oozed inside her shoes. Somehow she managed to haul herself off the bottom and scramble back up to the marsh, her front covered with muck, feeling stupid, wet and uncomfortable. Sylvia looked down at herself and suddenly started to laugh, finding it all too ridiculous, stuck out in the middle of a salt-marsh covered in mud from head to toe. Peter and Charley came up to her, looking amazed.

'Are you all right, Mother?' Peter asked.

'What happened?' Charley sounded concerned.

'It's all right, really. Mother took a dip, that's all.' She bit into her caked lip, attempting to stop another paroxysm of laughter from escaping; she didn't want them to think she had cracked up completely! 'Come on, let's get back,' she said, finally gaining some control over the situation.

Peter took the lead, Charley the rear, as though escorting a prisoner, guiding her homeward.

After that the rest of the week-end seemed to go better, whatever tensions had existed before had dissipated and they all seemed to carry on as normal. The boys took out their boat whilst Sylvia got down to some work, passing the afternoon engrossed in some ideas she had for a documentary film, forgetting the children or, at least, if not forgetting, putting them to one side. They arrived back close to dusk wet and ruddy in their yellow oilskins talking excitedly about their afternoon messing about on the water.

'You wouldn't mind if I spent some time here, would you?' Charley asked her over dinner that night.

Sylvia shook her head. 'You'll get bored, but if you want to use the house it's up to you.' He seemed set on the idea, she remembered later, full of the weeks he would spend there and what he would do. Peter had been taken with the idea, too, and was already planning to take part of his vacation there.

Late on that last night Charley came down into Sylvia's work-room where she was still typing long after the boys had gone to bed.

'What's the matter, can't you sleep, either?' she asked, watching him pad over to the dying embers of the fire.

'I always find sleep hard. I was tired out when I went to bed but I'm wide awake again now. Thought I'd try some hot milk, it always used to do the trick, do you remember?'

Sylvia smiled. 'Yes, when you were both tiny.'

'So,' he poked at the fire, attempting to encourage a flame, 'how are you, Mother?'

'Me? Oh, I'm fine.' She sat back, watching.

203

'I sometimes get to see you on the box. I've enjoyed the stuff you've done.'

'Thank you.' She wasn't sure what this was leading up to.

'How's David?' He looked across at her.

'David's fine, busy as ever in California.'

'Peter said you were probably going to marry David.'

Sylvia didn't feel much like discussing this topic. 'David has asked me, yes, I . . . I haven't come to any decision as yet.' She tried to read his thoughts. 'Does it bother you?'

Charley shrugged. 'No, it's up to you, isn't it.'

'I suppose it is.'

'Night,' he said, moving away into the darkness.

They packed up and left early the next morning. Peter was staying at Camden Square for a few days on study leave before returning to school. Sylvia made them all a quick lunch before leaving with Charley en route for the north Midlands. She disliked motorway driving and tended to become hypnotized by the boredom of it. To counter this she generally played tape cassettes of her favourite Benny Goodman music. It was raining hard by the time they were out of London and the M1 was crowded with returning week-enders. After an hour Charley was fast asleep despite the Benny Goodman concert blaring at full volume. He was playing 'Life Goes To A Party' to a jammed concert hall as Sylvia indicated to pull out in order to overtake the articulated lorry which loomed up out of the gathering dusk, smearing her windscreen with an oily water spray. She moved the big estate car out into the overtaking lane and heard a loud bang just before they began to move erratically across the carriageway and she lost control. Charley was shouting something to her and the last thing she could remember was the feel of wet grass underneath her hands.

Chapter 9

Sylvia was holding a picture of Charley, he had been fifteen, laughing out at her, an image of everything a fifteen-year-old boy should be, before everything started to go wrong. She recalled taking it, she remembered the day, the warmth of the sun and the sound of the surf. She remembered his laughter. But Richard was talking to her, he had made all the arrangements, the funeral was in two days' time, in Norfolk, held in the church on her father's estate.

'I've contacted everyone now, I think.' Richard spoke in a monotone, his voice reduced by emotion and fatigue.

'How are you? she asked. He looked old, suddenly grey.

'Not so bad,' he replied. They were standing together in the kitchen at Camden Square. 'I don't think it's quite hit me yet, though.' His eyes filled with tears.

Sylvia took his hand in her own, squeezing it and then he was in her arms sobbing like a child and all the time she was telling him that it would be all right and trying to soothe away the pain.

'I did love him, Sylvia, I *did*,' Richard said.

'I know,' Sylvia replied firmly, hugging him tighter now, her own tears spilling down. Then, looking into his eyes, for a moment in love with him all over again, remembered how it had all begun.

They all stood by the grave on a blustery, cold July day whilst brilliant shafts of sunlight streamed through the ragged grey clouds. She was standing in between Richard and Peter, her parents to the right of them, Richard's father standing apart from the main grouping. Miranda and David waited together, a respectful distance from the graveside. Sylvia watched but was barely aware; everyone was in black, it revolted her. She had worn an emerald green silk scarf which blew in the gusty wind, fluttering against her cheek. The rites continued but, having no beliefs, she didn't feel part of the proceedings; it was for Richard and her parents now. Having seen Charley dead, having seen him released and removed from his pain she had resolved in her own mind, even before the funeral, that the blame was all hers. Looking down at him he had appeared to be just asleep, as if he might have woken at any moment. Sylvia's memories of death were all associated with her grandmother. She always carried this vision of Death with its gaunt face and jutting sharp bones and hollow cheeks, lips pulled back, drawn in a tight, almost fiendish grimace over teeth which were bared slightly, making the old woman look hostile and frightening. With Charley, death had served to remove the haunted look that he had developed and so returned him to the child she had loved. It had made her feel calmer.

David drove Sylvia back to the house along the estate roads. They had been the last to leave, Sylvia remaining at the graveside for a long, long time. He saw the great house for the first time amidst parkland at the top of a long, straight, driveway. He swung the large dark BMW into the gravel curve in front of the imposing entrance steps which formed a graceful horseshoe.

'Oh God,' Sylvia breathed, 'this is going to be bloody awful. I don't think I can face it.' She sat back, making no attempt to get out of the car.

David turned to her. 'Come on,' he spoke gently, 'we're

here now.' He began to open his door. 'You don't have to be with them for long.'

Sylvia smiled at him and reached to brush his hair straight at the front. 'Thank you for coming.'

'Come on,' he insisted, climbing out.

Sylvia went first, up the long entrance steps, across the terrace and into the front hall, turning to the left and following a corridor from which they could look out into a central paved courtyard, a pristine oblong of lawn at its centre. Sylvia turned into the drawing-room, with its carvings by Grinling Gibbons and nineteenth-century plaster ceiling, dark oak panelling hung with precious paintings and drapes. A pair of ormolu and glass chandeliers were lit against the darkness of the day, their light reflecting off the shining wood and gilt of the furniture with its crimson coverings.

Natalia Fiodor crossed the Savonnerie carpet and hugged her daughter. David kissed her hand and then her cheeks. 'Thank you for coming,' she said to him, holding his hand and guiding them across the large room. 'Have a drink.' She motioned to a uniformed maid who came up to them with a tray.

Sylvia sat next to Peter and took his hand, he appeared to be completely lost but, after a short time, she moved him quietly out of the room, David watching them leave through another door.

'How is she?' Natalia Fiodor asked David. 'She's hardly spoken a word to me about it . . . It's scary.'

David shrugged, looking across at the others, standing and drinking close to the large marble fireplace where the flames danced cheerily. 'I've only been here for a short while, we've hardly had a minute to ourselves.'

The old woman nodded. 'God knows, she'll blame herself now for the rest of her life, stupid, *stupid* accident.'

207

She spoke in a low voice, emphasizing her words by tapping a fist of one hand into the other.

'Sylvia hasn't had a chance to tell me what happened.' David caught their reflection in a large looking-glass, he suddenly realized just how 'American', tanned and pristine, he appeared amidst this room full of slightly tatty family history.

'A tyre burst as she was overtaking on the motorway and she was unable to control the car, it spun over the carriageway in the rain, turned round and hit the central crash barrier. Charley's side of the car received the full impact.' She took his hand and squeezed it as she related the story. 'Sylvia was thrown clear and found unconscious a little way from the wreck. Charley was killed instantly.' She stopped talking, her words seeming to hang in the air around them.

'My God,' was all David said.

Sylvia had asked for tea which was brought to them in the library along with some home-made cake. The tray was set down in front of Sylvia and Peter. She poured the hot liquid, the aroma of the freshly baked cake mixing with the smells of lavender polish and musty old books and the wood burning in the hearth. She passed a steaming cup to Peter. His hand shook slightly, spilling tea into the deep saucer. She took a sip from her cup before speaking. 'How are you feeling?' she asked, concerned. He had said very little since the accident, he seemed to be very controlled, too much so for her liking, holding everything in. At the graveside he had looked at her, his head slightly to one side, his eyes hurt and questioning, his jaw set firm, the lower lip slightly pouting. It had reminded Sylvia of when he was a little boy, it was the same expression, even then he would rarely cry.

'I'm all right.' He put his tea down. 'Is your head any better?'

Sylvia touched involuntarily at the patch where the stitches had been sewn, it felt quite strange. 'I always did have a thick head.' She smiled at him. 'Are you staying in Norfolk for a while?'

Peter nodded. 'What about you?'

She hadn't thought. 'I don't know. David may have to get back to America in a hurry . . . I haven't spent any time with him . . .'

'It seems unreal, doesn't it,' Peter said. 'I haven't quite come to terms with the fact that Charley is dead.'

Sylvia nodded. 'You mustn't be afraid to grieve for him, Peter, don't be strong for me,' she looked into his serious eyes, 'I can cope . . . just about.'

'It's okay, really . . .' He looked away. 'I don't want to burden you . . . you have enough . . .'

'Peter, don't be ridiculous . . .'

'I'm all right. Mother, really I am, don't fuss.' He walked over to the high, library windows, looking out across parkland.

Sylvia listened to the loud ticking of the long case clock which seemed to fill the room. 'Your father and Miranda will be leaving soon. Will you join them or shall I tell them to see you in here?'

'No,' his voice sounded strained, 'I'll be out in a minute.'

Sylvia walked to the window and hugged him. 'See you in a moment, then,' she said, breaking away, her footsteps echoing up into the high ceiling as she left the library.

Sylvia stood on the long front terrace with her parents and David whilst Peter was beneath them saying goodbye to his father and Miranda. After a short conversation with

Richard the new Rolls Royce began to pull away, Peter waving until they were out of sight.

'What hateful weather,' Natalia Fiodor said, taking Peter's arm as he reached the terrace and leading the way into the house.

Sylvia hung back, clutching at the heavy coat which she had draped over her shoulders against the chill, watching David waiting for her at the entrance.

'Are you coming in?' he called.

She took a deep breath. 'I don't want to.'

'Come on, it's cold out here, you'll freeze.'

Sylvia nodded but remained where she was.

'Sylvia,' David said more sharply, walking towards her. 'Sylvia, what is it?'

'What is it,' she repeated to herself and then, looking at him as though she had only just realized he was there, 'I was just thinking how I wished I believed in the hereafter. It might be some consolation now to believe that Charley might be floating around up there laughing down at us all . . .'

'Why laughing?' David asked.

Sylvia shrugged. 'Wouldn't you be, freed from all of this?'

David put his arm around her and guided her into the house.

Sylvia's room looked over the ornamental lake at the back of the house. It was a beautiful sunny morning and she awoke to find David standing at the window in his underpants.

'I forgot to thank the vicar yesterday,' Sylvia began, sitting up in bed looking at him.

David turned around. 'You slept well, it's almost nine-thirty.'

She stretched. 'I don't remember anything after my head hit the pillow. Did you sleep?'

'Norfolk air and jet-lag are a potent combination,' he yawned.

'It was all so unreal yesterday, I don't think it's really hit me yet. I sometimes wonder if it ever will, all my crying of the last few days doesn't seem to have released anything . . . I simply feel as though I'm suffocating half the time and numbed for the rest of it.'

'Time,' David replied, 'give it time.'

'Yes,' Sylvia nodded. 'When do you have to go back?'

'Tomorrow afternoon.'

'I'm glad you came.' She climbed off the bed and went over to him, holding him around the waist, her head on his shoulder. 'Thank God you came.'

As they drove away Sylvia turned back to wave at her family, left standing at the bottom of the horseshoe staircase. She continued to wave until it was impossible to see them any longer. Turning around she reached into her bag for a handkerchief and wiped her eyes, blowing her nose hard.

'Peter seemed very subdued,' she said, worry evident in her voice.

'What do you expect, Sylvia?' David replied calmly. 'Peter's all right, he's sixteen, he can handle it.'

She pulled the sun visor down and inspected her face in its mirror. 'My *God*!' She sounded appalled. Her eyes looked puffy and red, her skin blotchy. She snapped the visor back into place. 'It's much worse than I expected . . .'

'Don't worry,' he said, 'it's not important, come on now.'

'Do you think he'll be all right, then?'

David nodded. 'He's better to be here with your folks, there are a million things to distract him on the estate. Look at the way he spent the morning out with your father. They'll keep him fully occupied and he gets on with them, doesn't he?'

'Oh, God, yes, he absolutely adores them. Peter has a musical ear and can listen to Mother's playing for hours . . .' She stopped talking as they approached the main entrance gates where a crowd of people had gathered. David slowed down to allow the police car parked across the roadway to move aside and then accelerated through. Sylvia was blinded for a moment by the camera flashes. 'What absolute ghouls they are sometimes. Do you think they'll be at Camden Square?'

'I expect so, Sylvia,' he replied as though it were an obvious fact of life.

'I can't stand it, it's really too much . . .'

'You don't have to say anything.'

'It's because you're here, of course,' she spoke as though to herself now. 'Doesn't it bother you?' she asked.

'Only when it hurts you.'

'There's a back entrance to the house . . .'

'Sylvia, I'm not about the creep down back alleys. If the press are waiting we'll handle it,' he said firmly.

She nodded. 'I think we were right to keep the funeral strictly private, don't you? I hope Molly understood . . . I know she was very sweet about it but I expect she felt she should be with us . . .'

'Stop worrying about everything, of course Molly understands . . .'

'I'm sorry,' Sylvia said.

'Don't apologize . . .'

'I think I'm going to be sick,' she said quite suddenly.

David began to slow down, pulling the large car over

212

on to the grass verge, Sylvia was already opening her door. He ran around to her, standing hopelessly as she began to vomit.

Vanny came down the steps to meet them, pushing his way through the assembled press, helping David with the bags whilst everyone closed in asking questions or taking photographs.

'Piss off,' Vanny kept repeating, struggling back across the pavement through the throng of people and up the steep steps into the house, slamming the door behind him and leaning back against it breathing hard. 'Do you want anything?' he asked Sylvia. 'I'm not stopping . . . I thought you'd want to be on your own.'

'No, no, thank you, Vanny.' Sylvia was sipping a glass of water in the kitchen.

He looked very concerned. 'Everything all right?'

Sylvia nodded. 'Yes . . . fine.' She smiled to reassure him.

'Well, then, if you're sure . . . See you soon, then.'

'I feel so stupid,' she told David, watching Vanny scurrying down the garden path.

'Why?'

'I don't seem to be coping with this situation very cleverly.'

He took her into his arms. 'Come on, you need rest. You'd better take one of the sleeping tablets the doctor gave you, you're exhausted.'

'I want to talk to you,' she protested.

'Sleep,' he insisted.

Sylvia undressed and slipped under the cold sheets, taking the tablet David offered and lying back, waiting for him to finish in the bathroom, wanting to say something to him. She heard the shower and turned over on to her side, closing her eyes for a moment against the brightness of the bedside lamps. The blackness seemed to roll over her in soft waves and, forgetting to struggle against it, she fell into a deep, dreamless sleep.

It was almost noon when she finally came down to find David reading the paper in the kitchen. She sat down next to him, taking his hand in her own.

'Thank you,' she said, leaning over to kiss him.

David smiled. 'I haven't done anything.'

'I don't know what I would have done if you hadn't turned up.'

'You'd have managed.'

She shook her head. 'I just wish you didn't have to go.'

He frowned. 'Afraid it's impossible for me to stay any longer, they've already filmed around me for two days . . .'

'So much in demand,' she said, letting go of his hand.

'Come back with me,' he suggested.

'I can't.'

'Why not?'

'Peter.'

'Peter's okay for a few days,' he argued.

'It would look bad.'

'To whom?'

She looked into his very blue eyes.' 'What?'

'It wouldn't look bad, Sylvia, it would look natural, perhaps you should have a break for a few days.'

'It's impossible.'

'Why?'

'I have to film a piece for the programme early next week.'

'Film a piece?' He sounded amazed. 'You'd do that but you won't travel with me?'

'It isn't like that, David,' she warned.

214

He sighed. 'Okay . . . I'm sorry.'

'We'll take that holiday as planned, when it's my birthday.'

He nodded. 'Okay.'

'If I work it'll help me, if I come with you I'll brood . . .'

He nodded. 'That's fine.'

'I'm sorry . . .' she began.

'Don't be, you're quite right.' He stood up. 'Listen, I have to pack and get out of here if I'm to make my flight.'

She watched him go and listened to him running up the stairs. Sitting back in her chair she began to cry.

Chapter 10

Edmund was waiting in her office when Sylvia arrived at the studios, he was sitting at her desk which annoyed her, invading her space and blowing filthy cigar smoke over her carefully nurtured yucca plant.

'Can you see me, Sylvia?'

She put her briefcase down on to the cluttered desktop. 'When?' She was exhausted through lack of sleep, every time she closed her eyes Charley seemed to appear.

Edmund looked at his watch. 'My office . . . say, in an hour?' He got up from her chair and left the room.

Sylvia sat back and wearily opened her morning mail. She was preparing to interview a young American film actor. In an attempt to bend towards Edmund's wishes, in an effort to popularize the programme, she had agreed to the piece about this boy who looked at her from the glossy publicity package she had at her side. He was dark with brooding good looks, at least, that was what it said. 'Samuel Marshall . . . twenty-three years old . . . already the star of four major films . . . darkly handsome with brooding good looks.' She felt she was helping to destroy all the initial promise and originality 'The Arts Programme' had once stood for.

She wandered into Edmund's office at ten-thirty carrying a mug of coffee and sat down in front of his desk. He was shouting down the phone, a trans-Atlantic call that was obviously causing some distress, his cheeks had turned deep red. At last he finished and sat back. 'We have a problem,' he began.

'Do we?' she met his eyes.

'Yes.' He flipped a typescript across the desk towards her, it was the usual ritual, confront her with the evidence and then make her squirm out of it.' 'This thing . . . this show you're planning to do about a gay theatre group . . .'

'Oh God, Edmund,' she put her hand to her head in exasperation, 'do I have to fight now *every* inch of the way?'

'We can't go with that,' he insisted pointing to the script, 'we mustn't.'

'We've already advertised it,' Sylvia protested angrily.

'Well, we can call it rescheduling if you like but it's not going out.'

'We'll be a bloody laughing stock . . . *I'll* be a bloody laughing stock!'

'It's much too much, Sylvia, you have your way over most things but not this, not this time.'

'Balls!' Sylvia shouted at him. 'We never do anything. Christ, I'm working on some dross about an American teen idol who no one will remember next year!'

Edmund opened his hands in that familiar expression, what more could he do? 'There's no discussion about this, Sylvia, no argument.' He drew his first finger across his neck. 'It's cut.'

'I see.' Sylvia felt dreadful. 'I cannot possibly be expected to come up with good quality work when the material I'm allowed to work with, the people *you* want, the subjects *you* agree, are so fucking facile.' She was shouting again

'I should have thought, Sylvia, that a Hollywood heart-throb would be something attractive to you.' Edmund spoke quietly, very controlled and still. She recognized this as Edmund at his most furious.

'Really, Edmund,' she said almost wearily, 'shame on you.' Sylvia stood up abruptly to leave and, in doing so, knocked the contents of her mug over Edmund's desktop. They both watched the muddy liquid soaking into the pages of the typescript, running in rivulets towards him.

'For God's sake, be careful,' he said in disgust.

'It was a bloody accident,' she replied, picking up her mug and storming out of his office feeling about ten years old and returning to the sanctuary of her own desk.

Samuel Marshall was young and very Californian in that everything was either cut or polished to perfection but in a laid-back, casual, crafty way. She couldn't help but regard these 'types' as an alien species. This one had probably been snorting coke and sleeping around at twelve. He had obviously been *around* movies for most of his life, and he was huge and darkly tanned with straight jet-black hair, cut very short, the shadow of a beard under his make-up and very black eyes. She met him on the set of 'The Arts Programme' and shook his hand, looking into those dark eyes and finding herself developing ideas other than appropriate questions to ask.

'I'm Samuel Marshall,' he said.

'Sylvia McLeod,' she smiled, 'I'm very pleased to meet you. We've been trying to get you on to the show for some time.' It was completely untrue but she was being nice to him because it wasn't his fault that Edmund had such revolting bad taste (and such cowardice). She motioned him to one of the chromium tubular-steel chairs and a minion came scurrying out of the studio gloom to afix a microphone. He was dressed in black, black silk shirt, black jeans and expensive black leather hand-tooled cowboy boots with silver caps on their pointed ends. Sylvia was also in black, her smart black interview suit, therefore, they became an unintentional matching pair. The interview had begun easily enough. He was obviously a dab hand at giving interviews and could probably have done this one in his sleep, having taken up a sprawled rather slovenly position, slumped down in the seat, his legs splayed out in front of him. He was in the midst of an anecdote concerning his latest film, his leading lady and a tame mouse when, laughing heartily, he toppled backwards right out of his chair, falling out of shot and bouncing off the raised set and on to the dusty studio floor, the chair, somehow, wrapping itself around him. Edmund, who had been watching the scene, was amazed to see the boy suddenly disappearing in a brief but extremely noisy exit whilst, on another monitor, he watched Sylvia dissolving into fits of hysterical laughter almost bent double. Eventually, regaining her composure, but still smiling, Sylvia went to help Samuel Marshall on to his feet. He was slightly dazed and taken away for a drink and a change of clothes. During the fall his tight trousers had split exposing rather more than just his all-over Californian tan!

Sylvia arrived home late. Vanny had left some sandwiches for her and all she had to do was make a drink. She took her tray into the sitting-room where she sat for a long time. Charley kept coming into her thoughts and she tried to trace his life, pin-pointing the cause or the moment which triggered off everything that had been negative and bad for him. She knew she had ignored many of the signs mainly because of her ignorance but, as Richard might say, ignorance is no defence.

Sylvia could look back and see it all so very clearly and she worked hard and attempted to move forward but her grief was such that, at times, it became almost impossible for her to go on, to function. It was as though she were consumed with some terrible disease which slowly ate away at her insides whilst, outwardly, she looked exactly the same.

'He's not a drop-out who turned to drugs,' she remembered insisting to Dr Freeman, 'it's a vile part of life that's infected him.' The doctor had smiled sympathetically, he must have heard the same thing from almost every frantic parent who crossed over his threshold. Charley turned inward, like some odd creature that fed upon itself. When she had found him close to death Sylvia had telephoned Richard and not for an ambulance. When seconds could have been vital in resuscitating him she had squandered them contacting his father. She recognized now that she had hoped they would discover him dead, she supposed she must have been in shock herself. But she could recall quite distinctly saying 'let him go,' in the swaying ambulance as they began to work on him. Hanging on as it raced to hospital, unable to look at Charley who was strapped down with a tube sticking from his blue lips. Richard had been waiting in the emergency ward, dressed in black, straight from court like an angel of death, clenching and unclenching his great fists all the time and smoking endless cigarettes. She had watched them pumping out Charley's stomach, white-coated, plastic-gloved nurses and doctors, fighting to save this wrecked and damaged child, reviving Charley sufficiently for him to be left in a closely monitored side ward. A young doctor, ridiculously young, Sylvia remembered thinking, had spoken to them. Charley would be all right this time but he must receive proper treatment. Sylvia had nodded and walked away. She wanted no more part of it. However, instead of the pain, Sylvia tried hard to remember Charley as a little boy. She was desperate to picture him whole without the distraction of what he had become. Charley on the sands playing with Peter, a thousand holiday snapshots ago, her two boys, one dark and tousle-haired, looking slightly far away, a little mischievous perhaps, grinning madly into her camera, one arm around the shoulder of his blond-haired sibling. She could find no clues in his childhood and could arrive at no answers.

Sylvia returned to New York in time to celebrate her birthday and to be with David who was there to discuss the play he was thinking about doing. Several months had passed since the funeral, it was the middle of November, and very cold. Sylvia walked through her mother's empty apartment, running her finger along the top of the grand piano that dominated the large lounge. The blinds were always kept partially closed and the dark sheen of the piano reflected the cool, blue tones of the room. She went into the small service kitchen to make herself some tea, taking down one of her mother's huge china cups and a saucer. It was late afternoon and she could see the lights of the city beginning to shine brightly in the gathering gloom over Central Park West. She sat in the lounge watching the slatted light through the blinds turning the various shades of blue until the room was almost dark. The telephone rang in the hallway, its loud bell making her jump. She left it to ring for a long time before getting up to answer it, she knew it was David calling from his rented loft space. Sylvia's face was reflected back in the glass of a large, dark, black and white print of a recent Bette Davis photograph. Her black hair was tied up and scraped away from her face, she stared at Bette Davis who stared back, frozen and pensive through a cloud of cigarette smoke.

'When did you get in?' he asked. 'I waited for you to call.'

'The flight was delayed,' she lied, 'I haven't been here for very long.'

'What about supper . . . or should I come over to your place?'

'I'm exhausted, David, I'll be awful company.'

He paused, the wire clicked and buzzed. 'Okay,' he agreed at last, 'what about tomorrow?'

'I have to meet up with my film crew in the afternoon, I could meet you for lunch.'

David agreed, whilst sounding rather put out by her lack of enthusiasm.

She met him outside the Wyndham Hotel on 58th Street where David also had a suite but, instead of taking lunch there, they took a cab back to his loft.

'I've just had a bloody awful meeting with the director of the play.'

'Oh yes,' Sylvia replied, attempting to be interested. She was staring at a squashed cigar butt on the dirty floor. 'I'm filming my first interview this evening.' She turned to him. 'I have to meet everyone at five-thirty.'

David nodded but did not reply, wrapped in a huge sheepskin coat with the high collar turned up so that only his eyes and nose were visible against the cold. They sat on opposite sides of the back seat, the cab dipping and jerking its way through the congested city. They were silent for the remainder of the journey.

Sylvia lay there absently studying the muscles of David's back and shoulders and neck as he sat, knees pulled up, arms resting on them. He turned around towards her. 'It would have been nice if you'd been there, too.' He

222

sounded sour and fed up. 'I can masturbate by myself, you know.'

She closed her eyes and heard him striking a match, smelt the acrid smoke from his cigarette. She looked up at the black ceiling. 'I'm nervous about this interview . . . I'm sorry.' Sylvia got up suddenly and, grabbing his robe, walked into the bathroom. She raised her arms to wash her hair under the needling shower spray, still smelling him on her skin; it was a stale, uncomfortable aroma, one which she had never noticed before. There had been a terrible urgency about him, she had felt his muscles, jutting hard, tensed under his clammy skin. Sylvia had not been ready, she hadn't even really wanted sex and couldn't summon up enough energy to fake it. Sex had always been such a natural and important part of their relationship, she had never felt that she didn't want to before. It was a strange feeling and she spent a long time under the shower but could not rid herself of his odd, stale odour. She towelled vigorously at her skin and hair afterwards. There was a dirty coffee mug on the white tile above the wash basin. The basin was coated with his shaving stubble and soap scum. Sylvia felt annoyed, David really was such a slob. She thought he was asleep when she walked into the bedroom but he opened his eyes and looked at her from his prone position on the giant, rumpled bed.

'You'll wash yourself away into the Hudson River,' he said.

Sylvia began to dress quickly, her clothes felt slightly damp, smelling of the dirty taxi. 'Do you have a fresh shirt I could borrow?'

He pointed towards an expensive antique-looking tall-boy. 'In there,' he spoke softly, 'take whatever you want.'

She found a white cotton shirt with long sleeves which

she put on. She removed her uncomfortable jeans and padded back to the bed wearing just the shirt and her briefs. She sat down in a large armchair watching him. 'I'm sorry, David,' she said. The loft was too hot, it felt oppressive and close.

David propped himself up on one arm and looked at her, a trickle of sweat ran down his breastbone where the hair was already slicked down and lay straight against the skin, he did not speak. Instead he reached for the crumpled cigarette packet and then lay back smoking for a while. The sounds of the street filtered into the echoing spaces of the huge loft seeming to take over from any conversation they might have had. David finished the cigarette and fell into a deep sleep. Sylvia sat, as though in a trance, watching him, incapable of movement. She felt as if her eyelids were weighed down and her brain enclosed within an impenetrable fog. When she awoke it was dark, David was still asleep on the bed and she had missed her filming assignment by over two hours.

Later they sat staring at the check table-cloth and the candle stuck into a wax-coated wine bottle. Sylvia was busy twisting her fork around in the midst of a spaghetti mountain which she had curled up from the dish. It was terribly late and she had gone way beyond hunger.

'Okay, so, as far as you're concerned, what I do isn't esoteric enough.' It was the continuation of the argument they had been having on the ride to the restaurant. 'I make films that make money, I suppose you'd prefer me to make sixteen-millimetre hand jobs which you could review on "The Arts Programme" and talk about with a wanker who claims to understand film.'

Sylvia looked into his eyes. There was that word again, *esoteric*. She remembered how Charley had used it in the same derogatory way. 'You let that woman put you up for any part,' she accused, twisting in her fork a little more violently, 'as long as there's a fat cheque at the start of production . . .'

'Up front,' he interrupted nastily.

'. . . safe and sound in your fat bank account, you couldn't care less what the film's about. I don't expect you even bother to read the scripts anymore before accepting, I expect some drone does that for you.'

'What *is* this problem you have all of a sudden about making money?'

'Not suddenly,' Sylvia snapped back.

'I haven't ever noticed you being short of cash exactly.'

She ignored that. 'I was embarrassed to sit through your last film, it was childish and purile in the extreme.'

'Yes, well, for your information, that childish film was number one at the box-office for a whole summer.'

'Point proved,' she smirked, not feeling very proud of herself.

'I suppose you could do better?' he challenged.

'*You* could do better, that's what I'm saying. This play you've been offered, I bet you haven't even finished reading it yet.'

'There seems little point, they keep making changes, besides, Marsha isn't keen . . . I have years for all of that, my film career could end tomorrow.'

'No such luck,' Sylvia said with feeling, 'you have this chance to create a role, how could you possibly not be interested?'

'What if it fails? Why should I wreck my career, open myself up to all of that criticism? I don't need it.'

'I thought you were supposed to be an actor.'

He laughed at her. 'Oh, but that's very good, Sylvia, *supposed* to be an actor.' He shook his head. 'Maybe you thought wrong, then.' Their eyes met across the small

225

table. 'I'm a film star, a commodity up for sale to the highest bidder.'

'I think you're the goose that lays the golden eggs for that jackal of an agent. I don't care how much you get paid or how famous you are there's always a need to take risks, you must in order to grow and become a great stage actor.'

'You're a cultural snob,' he said in disbelief. 'What if I don't want to become a *great* stage actor?' He stared at her. 'I suppose you'd prefer me to be starving in London right now. The thing is,' he said, leaning forward, 'you never really came to terms with my becoming successful. You feel that I've somehow cheated, that I should've really had to struggle which is a bit of a sham when we consider just where your life chances came from.'

'If insulting me makes you feel any better, then so be it, just don't turn around later and tell me how much you wish you'd done more stage work when your film career is washed up and you're lying bored with your millions.'

'The stage is the answer, then?'

'Go back and find out.'

He took a deep breath. 'Listen, I don't want to argue,' he said more contritely.

'No?' She looked into his tired face. 'What's the matter?'

'I don't want to look a fool, that's all.'

'My God, David, it's just a play, get it into perspective, you won't die if the critics don't like it!'

'I don't know,' he said.

'I have to go home,' she replied, exasperated. 'I'm so tired, I think it's the years of accumulated jet-lag finally catching up with me.'

* * *

Sylvia breakfasted alone the next morning in the hotel coffee shop. She couldn't stand to go back to his loft and he didn't like her mother's apartment, therefore, the hotel was a suitable compromise to their sleeping arrangements. Marsha had suddenly exploded on to the scene that morning and had '. . . to take an urgent meeting with David . . .'. Sylvia sat and waited and watched, air-conditioned and musak cold. She watched everyone coming in and leaving. Fat little men with puffy pink cheeks and puffy pink wives in garish clothes and ill-fitting teeth. An incredibly ugly woman, very ancient and gutted, weighed down with gold, clanking by on the strong supporting arm of a beautiful young man. Sylvia had been both intrigued and horrified, the woman's face, plastered in make-up and without discernible expression except for the eyes which looked frightened as they stared out from behind the cosmetic mask. Seventy-five going on forty, clutching at the young man's hand with sharp red nails, speaking loudly in a voice of grating venality. Sylvia watched them as they passed by and shuddered. She looked at her watch again. David appeared from out of the elevator with Marsha who was '. . . rushing back to LA now . . .' leaving them in a breathless fug of cigar smoke, for she only ever smoked little black cigars, and Chanel. Sylvia grinned and stood up to meet him, their reflections being caught in a large mirror. David looked terribly handsome she thought whilst she looked scared, out of place against his careless beauty, looking her age. He laughed as they stumbled out into the bright November sunshine, laughing about something or other, some stupid story he had just told her. It was suddenly absolutely fine and Sylvia was as much in love with him as she would ever be. He took her hand as they walked down

Fifth Avenue, his dark glasses firmly in place, her doubts tucked away in a corner of her mind for a while.

In the evening they celebrated Sylvia's birthday. She had taken an age to get ready watching herself in her mother's large bathroom mirror, holding her hands at either side of her temples, pulling the skin back tautly. She was forty-one. Sylvia looked closer, listening as an airliner droned overhead, it make her cringe. She had been travelling between London and David like an international yo-yo for the past two and a half years. It concerned her that she could, conceivably, go on like this for another three, or ten or fifteen . . . Sylvia bent forward, she could see clearly how everything, how her whole life, was reflected there, everything building up like layers of Chinese lacquer. She tried to smile and decided that the creases made her look younger but she could not continue smiling for ever, her history proved that. She sat at her dressing-table dabbing on a moisturiser recommended by a Hollywood beautician which, she had been promised, would ease out 'laughter lines and enhance those natural youthful looks'. Sylvia dabbed it on to her arid skin but did not believe. She considered that, perhaps, only cranial surgery would help her now! However, she continued to dab and smooth and thought about David, every detail: David's hair, David's eyes, David's mouth, David's beautifully proportioned muscularity, hard and round and bronzed and smooth and rough and aggressively masculine at times. She had never lost interest in him. She had never stopped finding him attractive and incredibly sexual. She desired him, feeling lustful. Sylvia put down the 'magic' potion and looked carefully at herself again. There was a wicked gleam in her eyes that made her laugh.

David wore some LA designer nightmare involving

228

black, skin-tight, leather trousers, white dress shirt and tailored black evening jacket. Sylvia, for her part, wore a peacock blue evening skirt with a black silk blouse, very low cut, which matched him for audacity if nothing else. She wore her hair long so that it framed her face and fell beyond her shoulders at the back. The maître d'hôtel escorted them to a secluded table and David reacted to being the centre of attention with the stunning cool which Sylvia had always despised in others and secretly admired in him. He was suddenly the sophisticated West-Coast film star out for a night on the town, instead of the insecure youth she had fallen in love with. Their dinner was interrupted on several occasions by autograph hunters but the final straw came when a pretty young woman requested, and received, his scrawled signature on the back of her table napkin. David smiled and reduced her to a nervous, giggling wreck.

'She was wetting herself,' Sylvia remarked acidly, 'how can you subject yourself to that?'

'To what?' he asked, all innocence. 'A young kid wanting my autograph, what's wrong with you, Sylvia?' He laughed at her for being so ridiculous.

'If we can't even go out for dinner without all of this Hollywood nonsense encroaching upon us then . . . The whole point of this evening, after all, is supposed to be *my* birthday . . .'

'Well, we are celebrating, aren't we?' He looked amazed. 'She was just a stupid kid, don't be so paranoid, it happens all the time, you just have to get used to it.'

'It's demeaning . . . all of this crap . . .'

'It's my job,' he replied sharply.

'Don't remind me,' she said, standing up to leave, 'and don't you absolutely revel in it.' She glared at him, throwing her napkin on to the table.

'You're being silly . . .' he said, taking her wrist. 'It doesn't matter.'

She pulled her hand back. 'It matters to me,' she replied, walking quickly away from the table and out of the restaurant.

David followed her back to Natalia Fiodor's apartment where Sylvia was sitting in the darkness by the lounge window looking out over the bright city. They were silent for a long time.

'Sylvia,' he began, 'I know you hate all this, all the travelling and the compromise. I know that . . . The last few years have been difficult for me, too.'

Sylvia didn't reply, she blew her nose because she had been crying for a long time.

'I'm going to do the play, Sylvia,' he spoke softly. 'That's what Marsha was here for.' He looked at her bleakly. 'It was supposed to have been a surprise . . . for your birthday.' He came over to her, taking a small package out of his jacket pocket which he dropped into her lap. 'Along with this. Happy birthday.'

She looked down at the carefully wrapped box but did not make any attempt to open it. She sniffed and wiped her nose again. 'I expect Marsha was pleased,' she said sarcastically.

'Come on, Sylvia,' he said gently, 'I'm doing it for you.'

'Well, don't,' she said adamantly. 'Don't feel you have to make any great sacrifices for me. Do it for yourself or not at all and be gracious about it.' Sylvia picked up the little package, turning it over and over in her hand. 'It's your profession after all.'

He sat down by her side. 'It's not worth anything if you're not there . . . I need you, I need your support.'

Sylvia did not reply. At last she took off the pretty candy-striped wrapping paper and found what she had

230

expected, a little jewel box and, inside, a large diamond ring winking back at her, glinting in the half light.

'Before you say anything,' he began, 'I know that we haven't come to any decisions . . . I just wanted you to have it, something to remember me by if you like.' It was meant to be a joke. 'A small token.'

'A *small* token.' Sylvia sighed, brushing her hair away from her face. 'Oh, God, David!' She laughed but more from nerves than humour. 'It's very beautiful, thank you,' she said finally, contritely

'Are you going to wear it?' he asked.

She remembered Richard giving her a diamond ring, not that they were ever engaged of course, and how she had come to regard it as one might imagine a prisoner did a ball and chain. However, it had become such a part of her that when she, at last, removed it for good she felt, for a long time afterwards, that she was never fully dressed. It was an odd experience. She was wondering now if David had noticed that she no longer wore it. She had never given him much credit for his powers of observation but it was probably the kind of trick he might pull. She held the ring between her thumb and forefinger, hesitating. 'Would it upset you if I didn't wear it just now?' she asked.

'No, not if you don't want to,' he replied, disappointed.

Sylvia nodded, she began to feel threatened, he was applying the pressure, forcing her into making her decisions. 'David, why did you come up and talk to me, that first time at Yolanda's party?'

'You were the most attractive woman there.'

'And then what?' she said in disbelief.

'Nothing else, that's the reason.'

'Why?' she asked, confused. 'The place was full of beautiful young women.'

231

'I wanted you, I wanted to meet you.'

'And now, do you ever consider the future?'

'Yes,' he said firmly.

'That in twenty years' time I shall be a pensioner whilst you will be in your mid-forties . . . in your prime?'

'So?'

'Don't you ever think about that?' she asked.

'Yes.'

'Well?'

'What?'

'Doesn't it concern you?'

He thought for a moment. 'No.'

'I may be all right now, David, but in twenty years' time I will most certainly look my age!'

He brought his face close to hers, examining every detail. 'And?'

'Don't you care?' She was very serious. 'It must bother you.'

'It bothers *you*, obviously.'

'Yes, it does.'

'Why?'

'Don't be so bloody dense.'

'No, really, I don't understand, tell me.'

'I shall be sixty-one, what the hell will you do with me then, pass me off as your mother?'

'Don't be ridiculous, what the hell difference does it make?'

'A lot, that's what difference it makes.'

'I could be dead in twenty years, I can't think twenty years, for God's sake, Sylvia!'

'You should.'

'You're ageless, like Marlene Dietrich, like Cleopatra. "Age cannot wither her, nor custom stale her infinite variety; other women cloy the appetites they feed, but she

232

makes hungry where most she satisfies."' He touched her face with his large hand, bringing her lips to his own and kissing her. 'All right?' He grinned, hugging her close to him. 'Satisfied?'

'You're absolutely impossible.' She was struck by the Shakespearian quote under the cold Manhattan sky. The incongruous nature of the very English Bard amongst the rushing danger of New York City. 'Why can't you ever give me a reasonable response.'

'Listen to me, you're the most attractive woman I've ever met, I'm crazy about you. I'm not interested in any of the beautiful people out in Hollywood, I don't want a Hollywood blonde, I don't want anyone else, I just want you.' He looked at her, his jaw set firm, head cocked slightly, adamant that this would be his final word on the subject. 'Don't talk to me about twenty years from now, let's just concentrate on the immediate future and stop being so negative.'

'Is that it?' she asked. 'Your final word?'

He nodded.

'You know I'll never marry you . . . I certainly don't want any more children.'

'Forget marriage, forget children, whatever the terms, whatever you want I'll accept. You see, there's no chance for me, either . . . I can't face the future without you.'

She looked into his serious eyes and felt panic stricken. So, this was it, they had arrived at the place where she must decide and any decision would be irrevocable. 'I sometimes wonder what would happen if we lived together full-time.'

'Try it and see,' he suggested.

'I'm afraid,' Sylvia admitted. 'I think we sustain our mutual interest by the absences in between, we never have a lot of time in which to tire of one another.'

'I see us as an old married couple, we know one another, it's very comfortable . . .'

'And very boring?' she challenged.

David shook his head. 'Never that.'

'Home tomorrow,' she sighed.

'More arts TV to get on the air,' he reminded her.

'More of Edmund blocking my every idea,' she replied with distaste.

'I don't know why you can't just jack it in and work over here, write and produce your own projects, we can set up our own production company and flog the stuff to the networks.'

'It's a nice idea,' she replied without really considering it as an actual possibility.

'So, why not do it?' he argued reasonably.

'I feel I have to fight my corner in England.'

'I don't see why.'

'I have to try,' she said, feeling doubtful. 'It's all right for you out there in film land.'

'It could be all right for you, too. God knows why you have to keep beating your head against a brick wall.'

'Because I believe in what I'm doing.'

'Ah, a crusader in our midst, you're obsessive about that job . . .'

'If I worked in America everyone would say anything I did was because of you . . .' She laughed. 'Please, don't let's get into this on my last night.'

'Okay, let's get into bed instead.'

Sylvia undressed quickly and was lying on the bed watching him undress. 'You have a great bum,' she said, the outline of his buttocks clear against the tight white cotton of his underpants.

'Don't objectify me,' he said, doing a fake burlesque strip, finally kicking the briefs on to the bed as he flopped down beside her. 'Always love me, Sylvia,' he said before kissing her on the lips.

She put her arms around him, drawing him down on to her, entangling him with her legs, wanting him now, inside her. She could barely wait, moaning as he obliged, thrusting up to meet him. David achieved his own orgasm very quickly but Sylvia reversed their position in order to complete her own, David's erection still being in place and, to her satisfaction (and continual amazement), remaining so until she had finished. Sylvia reached across for a Kleenex before rolling on to her side next to him. 'How do you do that?' she asked. 'No one else ever has.'

He turned his head and smiled at her. 'What about Richard?'

She ignored his question. 'Sex is funny . . . ridiculous really, isn't it?'

David yawned and put his arm around her. 'Hilarious. You're not going to talk, are you?' He snuggled up to her.

'I love you,' she said.

David smiled in his half-sleep. 'Thank God.'

'Are you asleep?' Sylvia asked, *wanting* to talk.

David was silent. She reached out and switched off the lamp.

They breakfasted quietly. Sylvia's bags were packed and in the hallway ready for the car to arrive.

'What are you doing today?' she asked

'More discussions about the play . . . meetings with the producer and the director and a costume designer.'

Sylvia nodded. 'Good.'

'Yes, indeed,' he grinned, 'back on the old boards before you can say "flop"!'

She ignored that. 'It'll be strange for you, I expect.'

'Terrifying.'

'Good for you, then.'

'I wonder if I'll remember how to play a scene in a real live theatre.'

'Of course you will,' she encouraged. 'It's what you were trained to do.'

'I've done more films now than stage work.'

'Haven't you missed the feel of a live audience?' she asked. 'After all, film technicians don't applaud you.'

'Perhaps New Yorkers won't, either!'

'David, don't be so fatalistic . . . I hope Marsha is a little more optimistic, does she encourage you?'

'No,' David laughed, shaking his head, 'she thinks I'm insane.'

'Don't you think it's important to try something different?'

'I might ask you the same question,' he replied.

She said nothing, in half an hour she would be gone and she didn't want to leave in the midst of another argument.

The driver came into the apartment to pick up her cases and they followed him down to the street.

'You didn't have to order this ridiculous car,' Sylvia complained, looking at the sleek, black American monster automobile with its tinted opaque windows, 'people will think we're mobsters.'

David laughed. 'Enjoy the ride,' he said, pushing her into the back and jumping in after her.

'We're terribly early,' Sylvia said.

'That's okay, I'll be able to get you some books and magazines for the flight.'

'My house is bursting at the seams with the books and magazines you've bought me. I never get through them, I *sleep* for most of the journey.'

Once at Kennedy International David bought her a

huge paperback tome, one of the latest blockbusters, and several assorted papers and magazines. 'Read this,' he said, pointing to the door-stopper of a book, 'I may be filming it!'

Sylvia glanced at the lurid front cover. '"Raunchy, ribald and remarkable",' she read the blurb out loud, '"the number one best-seller".' She turned to him. 'You've got to be joking! You can't appear in a film version of this.'

He shrugged. 'I might.'

'You're impossible.'

David nodded in agreement.

Her flight was called and Sylvia kissed him, hating the idea of leaving now. 'Oh, God, here we go again.'

'Wear the ring,' he whispered into her ear before they separated.

'I'll call when I get in,' she told him, still holding on to his hand.

David nodded, smiling and waving, blowing her a kiss as she walked away.

Sylvia settled back into her seat, the flight was half-empty and, therefore, she could spread herself over a complete row. The plane seemed to be full of rabbis who wandered the aisles as though attending some in-flight rabbinical seminar. She amused herself by contemplating the variety of religious flights available and wondered if there was a nine-forty Catholic flight out of New York or a ten o'clock Protestant, a Buddhist flight or one for Hindus. She looked over the clouds and, opening her bag, removed the little package containing the diamond ring. Safe at thousands of feet she took out the beautiful ring and slipped it on to her finger, holding out her hand in order to admire the effect. It was all a dream, she thought, too

237

much for her to contemplate. She put the ring away and, reaching up, pressed the call button. After the steward had brought her some water, she dug further into the reaches of her bag until she found what she was searching for and produced a small plastic drum of sleeping tablets. She took one out and swallowed it, dropping the rest into the bag. She intended to sleep away this flight, she had no desire to think or churn over the events of this trip and, pulling down the window blind, closed her eyes.

Chapter 11

Sylvia turned over and looked at the bedside clock. It was just after nine o'clock and she had slept for almost twelve hours. She stretched and yawned, listening to Vanny clattering about in the kitchen below. As she got up she heard a crash and, grabbing up her robe, went down to discover what he had broken now. Vanny was on his hands and knees when she walked into the kitchen. He was wearing a garish green shirt and his hair had orange streaks, he looked up from his sweeping. 'I'm sorry,' he said and promptly burst into tears.

'Vanny,' Sylvia said, surprised, squatting down beside him, 'whatever is it? Don't get upset over a stupid cup and saucer.'

'It was half a tea set,' he said pathetically, holding half a saucer in his hand.

'It doesn't matter.' She took a crumpled tissue from her robe pocket and handed it to him, guiding him over to the table, sitting him down. 'What's the matter?' she asked firmly.

Vanny blew his nose hard. 'It's Frank,' he said, his eyes flooding with fresh tears.

'Frank?' She was terrified to ask. 'What's happened to him?'

'He's left,' Vanny said hopelessly, 'walked out after six years . . .' He broke down again.

Sylvia made a move to fill the kettle. Tea, she decided, was the order of the day.

'. . . He's going to marry this girl . . . He's only just met her,' Vanny said angrily.

'Marry?' She was confused. 'How can that be?'

'He was married before . . . Oh, not when I met him, he married at sixteen, got a girl in the club. That didn't last for more than a year.'

'What did he say?' Sylvia asked, her curiosity getting the better of her.

'I found them together, in our bed . . .' A further cloud of despair descended upon him as tears welled in his eyes.

'My God, how ghastly.' Sylvia sat down next to him, patting his hand. 'What are you going to do?'

Vanny shrugged pathetically, unable to answer in his emotional state, great tears continuing to fall silently down his cheeks.

Sylvia poured them both some tea, tipping a good measure of whisky into his, sliding the cup and saucer in front of him. 'When did all of this take place?'

Vanny took the cup in his shaking hand and gulped at the spiked tea before attempting an answer. 'A week ago. He told me I was being ridiculous, that we were bound to split up sooner or later.' Vanny turned to her. 'All men are pigs,' he said. 'Six years and it's over, thank you very much, Vanny, and so long!'

'Did he say that?' Sylvia was shocked.

'He didn't say anything, he just packed his things and left. There was a note for me, he said it was nothing personal . . .'

'I'm sorry, Vanny.'

He attempted a little smile which only made him look sadder. 'The thing is, Mrs McLeod, I have to get away . . .'

'Of course, Vanny, a holiday . . .'

'No,' he was shaking his head. 'I mean right away, I can't stay in London.'

'You should think about it carefully, don't give up your flat just because of him, it's your place, you shouldn't have to move, for God's sake.'

'I have a friend who runs a bar in Majorca, I was thinking of going over there.'

'Spain?' Sylvia hadn't imagined Vanny in Spain, she had never imagined him anywhere else other than somewhere in her house in his vivid orange rubber gloves and his constantly changing hair colours.

'If I go now I can help him get ready for the summer season.' Vanny seemed to have made up his mind. 'It'll be a home from home. It's all Brits abroad there, you know, cheap booze and fish and chips . . .'

Sylvia grinned. 'Why don't you take a bit of time off to really think about this, go to the beach house. Don't rush away, Vanny, what am I going to do without you?'

'You'll manage. What about your film actor?'

'He can't help me like you.'

Vanny looked at her. 'I can't give you much notice, I'm afraid.'

'Don't worry about that, when are you going?'

'At the week-end.'

'The week-end?' Sylvia was aghast.

'There's little point in waiting around, Frank won't come back, cut your losses and get out, that's what my old mum would have said.'

So, Vanny had a mother who gave him sage advice, too, Sylvia was fascinated for a moment at the thought of his mum. 'Well,' she said, starting to pour them more tea, 'it looks like your mind's firmly made up, perhaps you're right.'

'I am right,' he replied.

Sylvia nodded. 'That's good, then.' She looked at his rather pretty face, his awful orange streaks. She had never really considered him in terms of sexuality, not really even as a man. He was attractive, why had she never realized it? He was attractive to her. 'I shall miss you very much, Vanny,' she said with feeling. 'Will you write to me?'

'I'm no good at writing, Mrs McLeod,' he said.

'Not even a post-card with a view of Palma Cathedral?'

'You'll be moving on as well, it's obvious.'

'Is it?' She was intrigued.

'You have your film star.'

'Ah yes,' she grinned, 'there is that.'

'I'll finish up today, if it's okay.'

'Don't worry about the house, leave it, you must have a thousand things to do.'

He nodded. 'I'm having my hair bleached, thought I'd go blond. Spaniards are supposed to *really* like blonds.'

Sylvia laughed. 'I meant the packing and the jobs in the flat.'

Vanny sniffed at that idea. 'First things first,' he winked at her, 'that's my philosophy.'

'Do you realize you've worked here for almost four years?' She was shocked at the length of their association.

'A case of all change then, isn't it?'

Later Sylvia watched him walking across the square and felt terribly sad.

She went into her study and sat behind her desk opening letters. She threw all the bills to one side, only looking at the interesting ones. Afterwards she sat back, considering the latest work schedule for 'The Arts Programme'. More of the same, more of Edmund, more headaches, more compromise. She turned to the neat row of videos on the shelf at her side, all neatly titled and dated, she rarely watched them, she didn't really know why she had them, vanity or, perhaps, for posterity, to prove something to her grandchildren when she was old and grey, that the old crone had actually, once, achieved something. She could see herself, a history of Sylvia McLeod captured on video tape, from denim jeans to midi skirts to prissy Laura Ashley print, flowing smocky frocks that seemed to have a life of their own, keeping her body safely tucked away from the viewing millions! The introduction was always the same, music, credits, logo zooming into frame and then her, teeth to the fore, great green eyes sparkling, announcing this, introducing that, extra keen Sylvia, information at the ready, never short of a question or an answer, cool in an emergency, calm and in control. It beamed through the tube at her and this captive woman seemed strange to her, nothing to do with how she felt or what she really was once the camera lights had dimmed and the voice from the gallery had stopped whining into her ear. She could not recognize the Sylvia McLeod of 'Arts Programme' fame because that woman, she felt, had nothing whatever to do with her.

Sylvia worked right up to the last moment that Christmas editing her New York piece and preparing a series of interviews she was to do in the new year. With Vanny gone she was also having to cope with the basic domestic routine, something which she had not been used to doing for a very long time. At first it was fun to prepare her own food but, after a week, the novelty of this wore off and she became irritated as these tasks interfered with her work. In the weeks after returning from New York, she worked from morning to night, every hour seemingly filled with 'The Arts Programme'. She snatched meals where she could but generally she was too tired to bother with food by the time she had arrived back at Camden Square in the evening. She understood just how much she had replied upon Vanny over the years to feed and water her with the minimum of fuss!

Sylvia began to feel unwell a few days before the holiday. She had been sitting in a meeting with Edmund and some production staff when a headache that she had been nursing since getting up that morning began to get steadily worse. Towards the end of the meeting every part of her ached and she was sweating profusely.

'Are you all right?' Edmund asked, giving her a curious look in the corridor as they went back to their respective offices.

'I feel ghastly,' Sylvia admitted, leaning back against the wall, her blouse wet and uncomfortable next to her skin.

'You'd best go home, then, Sylvia,' Edmund said firmly, 'obviously you've got flu.'

'Nonsense, I never even get a cold,' Sylvia insisted, her throat hurting as she spoke.

'*Home,*' Edmund commanded, pointing towards the exit.

She barely remembered the drive back to Camden but by then she was shivering and unable to keep warm. She crawled into bed, switching on the electric blanket and lying under the duvet, her teeth chattering. Vanny was gone, Peter was away abroad on a skiing holiday, her parents were in America and she felt very alone and very sorry for herself. Within an hour or so she began to feel hot again but managed to switch the blanket off before falling into a fractured half-sleep in which she kept hearing Charley's voice calling out for her, sometimes distant and sometimes as though in the next room. The telephone, ringing by her side, finally managed to wake

244

her and, reaching down to pick it up, found Molly at the other end. She croaked her symptoms over the bad line to Molly in Colchester.

'Flu,' Molly said.

'I feel awful.'

'Have you any lemons?'

'Lemons?' Sylvia asked, wondering for a moment if she were hallucinating.

'Lemons. Ask Vanny, put the boy on the line.'

'Vanny's not here,' Sylvia said.

'Then get him to ring me when he gets back.'

Sylvia paused to gather her thoughts, her head thumping again. 'Vanny isn't coming back . . . he's gone.'

'Gone?' Molly sounded shocked. 'What do you mean?'

'He's left.'

'Are you there alone?' Molly asked, light finally dawning.

'Yes,' Sylvia groaned.

'Take some pain killers, keep taking liquid and I'll be up in the morning. Can you last out until then?'

Sylvia was too ill to argue with Molly, even if she had been inclined to and, afterwards, felt a degree of relief that the cavalry was on its way to save her!

Molly took Sylvia back to Colchester where she spent the Christmas holiday being fussed over and cared for. Molly did absolutely everything, bringing her carefully prepared honey and lemon drinks and nourishing home-made soup. She removed any external pressures, no one was allowed to reach Sylvia and even David wasn't allowed to talk with her 'patient' for the first few days.

'You're lucky,' Molly told her, 'it wasn't a very bad dose, you seem to be over the worst.' She was looking at

Sylvia from the end of the bed, her head cocked slightly to one side, arms folded.

'I feel totally wiped out,' Sylvia sighed.

'A few days at the coast would do you the world of good . . . the coast and sea air, what about it?'

'I couldn't drive down,' Sylvia replied.

'I'd go with you, of course.'

'What about Jack and the children?'

'They'll survive, for God's sake, I need a rest, too!'

Sylvia smiled. 'It would be lovely.'

'Good, then that's settled.'

Sylvia lay back on the pillows and smiled at her friend. 'Thank you,' she said.

'It was a pleasure . . . I hope you'll do the same for me some day when I'm in my bed of pain.'

It was a beautiful, clear morning. Sylvia got up early, just as the winter sun rose above the glassy sea, the air sharp and cold. Seagulls skimmed the surface of the water before flying up into the wide arc of blue sky. She took a deep breath of the salty breeze and looked down from her bedroom at the garden, everything muted and dreary, dead. Sylvia dragged a thick pullover on and picked up her warm jacket as she left the house to catch the day, an expression her mother always used, '. . . go catch the day, Sylvia, it's far too good to let go . . .' She walked along the deserted beach following the tide line, following the dirty, frothy spume with its trails of seaweed until she reached the concrete slipway and her boat parked at the top on its rusty trailer. She checked the worn canvas cover for holes and wondered if there was really much point in keeping a boat any longer. She shivered in the breeze at the top of the slipway and remembered her recurring dream, the one about Charley. She had been forced out

246

of bed because of it. He was lying in his coffin whilst she was looking down at him. Charley had opened his eyes and smiled up at her.

'Did I hurt you very much?' he asked.

Sylvia had not replied but had continued to look into his peaceful face.

They were walking on the shore line beneath the beach house, she was able to identify it by the large dark windows which seemed to stare out across the sea. It was a blustery day, high rushing seas and a drifting fog which crossed over the water towards them. Charley was ahead of her but walking backwards, facing her, he was smiling.

'I always admired you a lot,' he said, continuing to grin at her.

'That's a very dangerous thing to do,' she replied.

He began to walk faster and then was running backwards, she attempting to catch up with him as he grew more distant, saying something which she could not understand. Charley was still smiling as the drifting fog suddenly closed in on them, separating and frightening, making her afraid to move any further and then she woke up in a state of panic, his name on her lips.

Sylvia looked over the beach, the winter tides had exposed great chunks of the old sea-wall, the blue sky was becoming ragged with scudding dark clouds whilst a blustery squall was beginning to chop up the quiet water. She zipped her jacket to the neck and then ran down the slipway, following her own tracks back along the sands towards the beach house. The sky was blackening all the time although there was still a silver-bright gap between dark ocean and sky at the horizon. Molly was standing anxiously at the kitchen window watching out for her friend as Sylvia trudged up through the sand dunes and into the garden, drenched from the pouring rain. She

247

stood for a moment at the gate against the force of the gathering storm, watching the breakers rolling in and crashing on to the beach, doubling back, liquid marble within foaming rage. At last she walked on, the thunder and noise of the waves drowning her thoughts, fascinated by the terrifying power that confronted her.

Molly was furious. 'Where the hell have you been?' she demanded. 'You must be insane! You've only just recovered from one bout of flu.'

'I went to check on the boat,' Sylvia replied simply, rain dripping off the end of her nose.

'In this weather?' Molly began to help her to remove the wet clothes. 'You must have a death wish!'

Sylvia shook her wet head. 'It was beautifully clear first thing.'

Molly wrapped her in a towelling robe, making her sit in front of the fire with a glass of brandy and a pot of freshly made coffee. 'You might have told me,' she said, picking up wet clothes and draping them over the log basket at the fireside.

Sylvia peeked over her steaming coffee. 'It was fine when I went out.'

Molly sat back in one of the comfortable old armchairs casting disapproving looks at her friend.

'For God's sake, Molly. Look, I'm safe, don't fuss. I'm perfectly all right.'

Molly looked thoughtful. 'You know, Sylvia, I'm not really sure why you're not in America with that gorgeous man . . . I think you may be in danger of finding enjoyment in your masochism!'

'Don't start,' Sylvia snapped. 'Not another lecture about my awful treatment of everybody's favourite film star.' She rubbed her wet hair with the damp towel. 'What you don't know, what you fail to understand, is that I've done the most ruinous things to the people around me . . .' she looked into the bright flames of the log fire, 'and I'm still doing them.'

'Yes, and you're also responsible for all the wars and the famines and the earthquakes . . .' Molly sounded annoyed and spoke very firmly. 'Come on, Sylvia,' she said, disgustedly.

'What about Charley?' Sylvia asked tearfully. 'He was getting well again, he was so much better, wasn't he?'

'Addicts don't get better,' Molly replied, her words hanging in the still air.

'It was my fault,' Sylvia began to weep, 'it's *all* my fault.'

Molly sighed. 'Perhaps you just want to suffer. Listen to me, thousands of kids go off and do the most appalling things to themselves and to others and you're not seriously trying to tell me their parents are all ogres who hated them and never wanted them.'

'He was better,' Sylvia repeated.

'You must look forward now,' Molly began, 'it was an accident, it was terrible but you have to go on and live your own life.'

Sylvia didn't respond to that, the room felt very warm. She sat silently, exhausted, as though she hadn't slept for many days. She watched the licking flames and listened to the rain against the windows. 'I don't know what to do,' she admitted at last.

'You're in the process of making the biggest mistake of your life . . .'

'There have been so many, which one are you talking about?'

'Refusing to marry David, of course.'

Sylvia sighed. 'Not that again,' she said impatiently.

'Why do you continue to spite yourself and those who

care about you? What about David? He loves you very much . . .'

'I can't be responsible for David,' Sylvia insisted, grim-faced and annoyed.

'But you *are* responsible for him. You can't just leave him out there, abandon him without any hope.'

'He's not my child.' Sylvia poked at a log as she spoke, showering sparks flew up into the darkness. 'He's not my child,' she repeated softly.

'He *needs* you.'

'So, what are you saying, that I should rush out there and propose marriage?'

'Yes, why not? Perhaps that's exactly what you should do . . . Isn't it what you really want?'

Sylvia bit into her bottom lip shaking her head very slowly. 'You're supposed to be giving me the feminist line on this. Instead of that you sound just like my mother . . .'

'Don't you love him? Don't you have this grand passion for him? Who are you trying to fool?'

'You sound just like a Joan Crawford film.'

'You're forty plus, Sylvia, you have to grab your chances now. Don't be a bloody idiot.'

'Why?' She glared at Molly. 'Why can't I live my own life, have my own career, make decisions for myself for a change. I don't have to exist through life with a man always at my side, I'm a person in my own right.'

'Why?' Molly was forced to smile. 'Because, Carroux, you're in love with him and because you're mature and you're intelligent and you're supposed to know your own mind at this late stage in the game . . .'

'Well, I'm not and I don't know. I feel less sure of myself now than when I was eighteen. It just gets harder and harder, all this rubbish talked about the sophisticated older woman. I'm absolutely bloody terrified!'

Molly laughed heartily. 'You know what people will say . . .'

'I'm not interested in what people will say,' Sylvia replied adamantly. 'What will they say?'

'That here you are in love with this ridiculously attractive man who, incidentally, loves you, and you're giving it all up for the sake of some so-called principles.'

'You just refuse to understand.'

'I *do* understand, Sylvia, I just don't want you to throw away the rest of your life, don't do it,' Molly warned.

Sylvia smiled as tears welled in her eyes, she nodded but could not speak.

Sylvia told Molly about the dream as they sat in the lounge after lunch.

'It doesn't mean anything we haven't already spoken of. It would be rather odd if you didn't have such dreams.'

'It was *so* real,' Sylvia said.

'Well, dreams aren't real, are they,' Molly replied sternly.

Sylvia was looking out at the grey sea. It was still raining. 'I know that,' The wind had dropped away and there was a gentle swell. 'I want to go out for a walk,' she announced.

'Are you paying some sort of penance down here or what?' Molly demanded. 'St Sylvia of the Sand Dunes!'

'Don't gripe so much. Come on, we'll have some fun, put your wellies on, it's good for your complexion to walk in the Norfolk rain.'

Molly slouched along at Sylvia's side drowning in a man's waterproof and a sou'wester which kept falling down over her eyes. 'This is ridiculous,' she complained. They trudged along the back lanes meeting two little girls identical in bright blue anoraks with the hoods up, blue jeans tucked into red Wellington boots. As they passed the little girls were chanting:

> 'Nobody loves me, everybody hates me
> I'm going in the garden to eat some worms.
> Long slim slimy ones,
> Short fat fuzzy ones,
> Gooey – ooey – ooey ones.
> The long slim slimy ones slip down easily,
> The short fat fuzzy ones stick to your teeth,
> And make you go yum yum yum . . .'

Sylvia glanced at Molly and suddenly bent double in hysterics, leaning against Molly's slippery shoulder, barely able to stand, gasping for breath. Her words came out, fractured with giggles. 'Nobody loves me, everybody hates me . . . I'm going in the garden to eat some worms . . .'

Molly pushed her away, falling backwards herself on to the wet banking, splitting her sides, holding on to herself, convulsed with laughter. They attempted to complete the silly chant together,

'Long slim slimy ones, Short fat fuzzy ones, Gooey – ooey – ooey ones . . .' but it proved impossible. Sylvia collapsed into a chortling heap, one knee in a puddle, her hands spread out before her, fingers deep in mud and gravel. The sight of Molly crumpled on the bank with the sou'wester fallen over her face, cackling and hooting, made things worse. They were in pain with laughter.

'Oh God,' Sylvia gasped, 'I'm absolutely drenched again.'

Molly stumbled over to her, still tittering, her arms flapping like bright yellow penguin wings in the long sleeves. She tried to help Sylvia up, attempting to brush away some of the mud and stones from Sylvia's clothes. 'You are an idiot, Carroux,' she scolded, starting to laugh again as she noticed that Sylvia's face was streaked with mud.

Sylvia reached over and pulled the sou'wester firmly down over Molly's face. They both dissolved, crying as another paroxysm of hysterical laughter shook them, holding on to one another, unable to move, as the rain poured down over them.

The next morning Sylvia received a letter from Edmund with her new contract. Edmund wished her a quick recovery which annoyed her, she hated to be told to get well soon, why couldn't she just relax? She spread the contract out in front of her, moving the breakfast things to one side, staring at the printed words, looking at the empty spaces were she was supposed to sign.

'Jesus!' Molly said from behind the morning paper.

'What is it?' Sylvia asked, still studying her contract and considering her future.

'Here,' Molly passed the crumpled paper to her, 'you won't have seen this yet.'

Sylvia looked at the folded page, at a picture of David underneath a headline, 'Hollywood Hero Bites Broadway Dust', and in a long article it went on to describe how David's play had closed after only five performances. Sylvia put a hand to her forehead as she continued to read. 'No, my God,' she muttered at each new critical insult to David's ability.

'Didn't you have any ideas?' Molly asked in disbelief.

Sylvia shook her head, staring at Molly. 'What can I do?' she asked feeling sick.

'Do?' Molly asked, amazed at the question. 'I should have thought it was obvious.'

'Yes, yes, yes,' Sylvia stood up, 'it's all my fault, isn't it?' She looked ashen, her eyes wild. 'He'll blame me.' Sylvia shook her head. 'What can I do?'

'You should probably call an airline,' Molly spoke calmly.

'I will,' she agreed, moving quickly to the doorway. 'Molly,' she said, pausing at the door, 'I do love him but . . . but . . .'

'No buts, Carroux, get on that bloody phone and try to find a flight. He needs you, can't you see that, he needs you more than ever now.'

Sylvia's tense features suddenly relaxed, perhaps Molly was right, she was afraid and excited at the same time. Suddenly everything was much clearer and she understood, she knew, that she only wanted to be with David no matter what.

'You're not having any second thoughts, are you?' Molly asked at the airport.

'Yes, lots of them as a matter of fact but, if you're worried about me backing out, don't, I intend to go.'

'Good.'

'Yes, in a way I'll be glad to get away from here, away from Edmund and work . . .'

Molly nodded. 'That's good, then, isn't it?'

'You've always accused me of being a mass of inconsistency, and you're right. I've always traded off my background for what I wanted. It must be easier for me, I mean, the poor-little-rich-girl routine isn't really very attractive, in fact, it's rather nauseating, isn't it? Why be a hypocrite about it?'

'You have got it bad, a touch of the old guilt complexes, is it?'

Sylvia shrugged but did not respond.

'Sylvia, it's a bit late in the day to start worrying about all of this. Life goes on and on and you just have to get on with it.'

'You mean marry him, it's the universal solution, the panacea . . .' she said nastily.

'I mean that you should do whatever it is that'll make you less miserable.'

'I don't think I'm even capable of being happy, it's a condition that seems to have escaped me completely.'

'Nonsense, it really is, *and* you know it.' Molly was annoyed with her. 'You've had the most marvellous things in your life, a wonderful career . . .'

'Ah, yes, well let's not forget about the wonderful career!'

'I would have liked it,' Molly said.

'You?' Sylvia looked surprised.

'Yes, why not me?'

'I never realized.'

'I would have loved it, you get the glamorous career while I get another child, and another year goes by and I'm passed for promotion. You have a great deal to be thankful for, Carroux,' Molly insisted.

'Have I?' Sylvia looked at her coldly. 'One son dead . . .' Her voice trailed away.

Molly was silent for a long time, she listened to the announcements echoing through the departure halls. 'Does this general malaise extend to David?' she asked finally.

'He was depressed when I rang, he sounded awful and I *do* feel responsible, there's no getting away from it . . . David can be so bloody pathetic at times.'

'You always used to complain because Richard hid all of his emotions.'

'Richard was a bastard.'

255

'You loved him once.'

Sylvia nodded. 'But it was never the same as . . .' She stopped speaking and looked away.

'For God's sake, say it,' Molly insisted.

'I never loved anyone as I love David.' Sylvia looked into her friend's eyes. This admission of truth was painful for some reason and she felt battered by the odd emotional response. 'Have I left it too late, Molly?' she asked, a desperate ache for him growing inside her. 'I'm terrified that I might have . . .'

Molly handed Sylvia the large whisky she had bought. 'Drink this and shut up, you're going back, don't talk about defeat, you have to be with him, that's all there is, it's the only thing left . . .'

'And career and independence? What about those things?' Sylvia asked anxiously.

'Oh, you'll have them as well.'

Sylvia looked doubtful.

'You will,' Molly insisted, laughing. 'You'll have everything. Why not, you always have.'

Sylvia grinned uncertainly.

Molly raised her plastic tumbler. 'To us.'

'To you,' Sylvia replied, reaching across to kiss Molly.

'This is it then,' Sylvia said, hugging Molly for a long while as her flight was called for the last time.

Molly was full of comforting smiles. 'Now just go and have a really fantastic time and don't think, just do!'

'That's great advice,' Sylvia said, 'coming from one of the great radical feminists of our time!'

Molly pushed her through the departure gate. 'Go,' she commanded.

Sylvia hesitated for just a moment before turning and walking on. She did not look back.

Chapter 12

Sylvia sat back, watching a jumbo jet lumbering into the sky. She enjoyed the moment of take-off, she still found it exhilarating, rushing concrete and then the separation from earth to air, a spongy kick in the stomach as the beast was airborne. She glanced at the in-flight magazine, flicking through the glossy pages full of expensive watches and perfumery. She watched an airliner coming into land as they were instructed to put their seat belts on and not to smoke. The aircraft was taxiing into position for take-off. Molly had said that she would have liked her kind of success but it wasn't true. Sylvia knew that Molly could only feel safe at home amongst her children and dogs and comfortable husband. That was fine, Molly retired back to the womb of family and nurture and motherhood when the wars of academe became too much for her. Sylvia was afraid to do that, for children grew up and left and no longer needed you. She would not lead a life like that, she was too impatient and living one's life through children was futile, and it was wrong, she felt, to thrive upon the dependence of others. She knew how critical Molly and Natalia Fiodor were of her actions. If they were truthful they were disapproving of her life, her freedom. Molly wanted her married and safe, her mother wanted her to be happy which meant David and, even at this late stage, a child!

Sylvia turned to the thick magazine that Molly had thrust into her hand in the terminal building. There was an article about David: 'David Christensen and His Older

Woman'. There was even a picture of them on the beach, the picture he kept at his bedside. They were laughing at some joke she could not remember and it was a good likeness of her. She was described as 'Lady Sylvia Wessley-Carroux, a youthful forty-one-year-old, famous in her own right and a force to be reckoned with . . .' It was all such a sham. She felt more like an ancient forty-one-year-old and frightened out of her wits, not so much a force to be reckoned with as a crumpled pile of wreckage! In all her life she wanted only peace and yet it was denied her by the associations she made. She would never settle and be contented with her lot, marriage had taught her well. She had to keep moving, afraid to stop now for fear of everything catching up with her, like a train of waggons suddenly shunting up against one another. What did she want ultimately? Sylvia closed the pages feeling angry with herself for her indecision and failure to amend her wayward nature. She wanted David *and* freedom, she wanted him and her own life but she was aware that one would have to be sacrificed, even in part, to the other. In reality she was exhausted and felt she had been in constant motion for almost all of the past three years. Spending time with David, holidays with him, listening, understanding, knowing him. David wasn't a complicated person, she found him intelligent rather than intellectual, he was calm, quite serious, not normally prone to bouts of theatricality, few histrionic outbursts. It was a relief when they were together with no one to perform for, no one pulling the strings. He was certainly driven with a desire for her which she found both flattering and comforting but also worrying. She was always looking forward, beyond the immediate pleasures. It did give her confidence though, she acknowledged. The man over whom girls fantasized, the man they pinned upon their bedroom walls and mooned over, the man women responded to as a sexual object was within her sphere (and in her bed). On news-stands she would see his face looking back, frozen and burnished, selling publications, masturbatory fantasy, clean-cut hero, every mother's favourite son. A man for all markets! By the terms of her own ideology such a man would appear as one more piece of Hollywood junk and her criticism of him was often for the quality of his work, but he was not the image as portrayed. He was an ordinary man, saved, in a way, by extraordinary beauty and using this fact to earn a substantial living. Sylvia took a deep breath as the aeroplane began to ascend, she was busy rationalizing everything out of existence, intent, it would seem, upon destroying what might remain between them. It was a ridiculous exercise and one she no longer wished to pursue.

Sylvia went straight to her mother's creepy old apartment where she slept for a long time and then paced the darkening rooms watching the lights of New York across the park before calling David. He arrived exactly one hour later, looking dangerous with two days of beard, unkempt, wearing a baggy shirt tucked into oversize combat trousers. He looked pale. Sylvia followed him through to the dimly lit lounge standing by his side at the picture window. It was an eyrie above the angry city from which to view and plan, to consider the next move. There was fear in this land and he was aware of that.

'Good flight?' he asked, bending to kiss her quickly on the mouth, his rough beard rubbing against her smooth cheek.

'My ears always pop. You might think I'd be used to it by now.' She touched the sleeve of his shirt before turning away.

'Are you okay?' he asked.

She sat down on the large sofa. 'I'm sorry about the play,' she said.

David smiled wryly. 'I was lousy. There are really no redeeming features . . .'

Sylvia looked at his back, he appeared to be calm. 'Perhaps it's important to have attempted something like that.'

'What's important,' he said, turning to face her, 'is that it was a failure and that I failed most of all.' His words hung in the silence.

She picked at a small stain on the arm of the sofa. 'You learn from every experience.'

'For God's sake, Sylvia, what is there to learn? I learned that I can't act!'

'Nonsense,' she said angrily.

'Well, as you weren't there I fail to see how you can comment. What the hell, it's all water under the old bridge, what's one more kick in the teeth. At least the critics were unanimous.' He reached into a back pocket and produced a wallet from which he extracted some ripped and crumpled squares of newspaper, throwing them down into her lap. 'Here are my critics . . . Read them,' he insisted.

Sylvia looked down at the pile of tattered newspaper cuttings. 'I don't want to.'

'It doesn't matter, I can remember them all, word for word. Jesus, I've read them enough times. "David Christensen moves through this piece as though sleep walking . . .", ". . . David Christensen, for some time the all-action Hollywood star, finds himself unable to hold his own in the company of real, live actors . . .", ". . . Dreary, dreadful and dull, Hollywood's leading man fails to make the transition from screen to stage . . .", ". . .

The celluloid hunk makes a hash of his stage début in New York and falls flat on his muscular face . . .". And the best headline, don't let's forget that, "Throwing Christensen To The Lions," . . .' He sat down at last, breathing heavily.

Sylvia said nothing, shaking her head.

'Well, what about them?' he asked.

'Pretty awful, aren't they,' she replied.

David laughed nastily. 'Sure, my name's mud in this town . . .'

'It was only a stupid play . . .'

'Which I did for you,' he replied sullenly, looking belligerent.

'That's unfair.'

'You virtually insisted I take it.'

'You must have wanted it, you never took my advice in the past.' She watched him sulk. 'You just went on and on making those dreadful films. In any case your fans don't go to the theatre, they don't read what critics write, as long as you're stripped and gleaming by the second reel what do they care?'

'Maybe I don't want to do any more films,' he said airily, walking out into the service kitchen and returning with a can of orange juice. 'You want me to give it up, don't you?' he asked, juice dribbling down his chin.

'You could always come home and work.' Sylvia was attempting to be reasonable.

'This is my home, not England, not London but here, USA. Why should I go back?'

'For me?' Sylvia suggested quietly.

David finished off the contents of the can and crumpled it in his hand. 'Oh, well now, that's very good, Sylvia, *very* clever but, listen, you don't really want me on those kind of terms, do you?'

'I don't know what that's supposed to mean.'

'Will you keep me in the style to which I've become accustomed?'

'You're just being ridiculous, oafish!'

'I've put up with so much crap from you. Everything is wrong; my career, my aspirations, my taste . . . I may not have your advantages, your social cachet, your education, but what I do have is all my own . . .' He was breathing hard now, angry and blowing hot. 'If you cared for me, if you *really* fucking cared, you wouldn't be doing some fucking stupid minority arts programme for a bunch of bloody wankers which, incidentally, you hate.' He challenged her to refute that before continuing. 'No, you'd be here with me – all of the time . . .' His voice broke with despair and he sat down on the nearest chair staring hard at the floor.

Sylvia had rarely seem him so angry or upset. 'My career for your manhood, is that such a prize that I should give up everything *I've* worked so hard to achieve?'

'Then what do you want?' he asked. 'Just what is it, because if you're so secure with your lot, your blessed career,' he said the word with a sneer, 'then what's all this? Why are you here at all?'

'Because,' she began, 'I love you . . . You know that.'

He was silent for a while. 'But your love has all these conditions. I may possess you but I can't actually have you. After all this time you still have to make a decision about us, don't you, Sylvia?' He was accusing her now. 'Maybe if I'd been educated at the right schools, come from the right people, maybe then you'd have found it easier to make a decision about us . . .'

'You're quite wrong. You're almost fifteen years younger than me, fifteen years, my God it's a life-time and it's that . . . that's the difference.' Sylvia swallowed hard and could feel tell-tale tears welling up.

'It doesn't matter, it doesn't matter.' He laughed, a hard, desperate, nervous laughter. 'Don't you think it's time for you to accept your responsibilities where they rest?'

'My responsibilities?' Sylvia asked confused, she had always imagined that she had done so.

'Yes, responsibilities to me and to yourself because, without me, you're sunk,' he pointed a finger at her, 'and you know it, Sylvia.'

'You're an arrogant bastard,' she said, afraid that he was, indeed, close to the truth.

'I haven't the energy to go on like this.' He sounded very weary. 'You stay or you go, it's about as simple as that now. Christ, you talk above love! There should be no choices to be made, I'm not one of your sons, I'm not your ex-husband, I'm not a drunken bastard who beats you up, I'm the man you sleep with and if that isn't enough, not your major priority right now, then you'd better fuck off back to London and suffocate yourself amongst the hacks of "The Arts Programme" fighting your little wars with Edmund.' He stood up and began to pace the room like a caged lion in the Bronx Zoo.

'I'm sorry if you think I've deliberately set out to wreck your life,' Sylvia said at last, as though she were feeble-minded.

'You haven't,' he answered softly, barely audible, 'you've made it worth something.'

Sylvia's thoughts spun around in her mind. 'David,' she said, her voice firm, like a command, 'let's just go to bed now.'

He was silent, the darkness seemed to grow up around

them. 'What will that solve?' he asked bitterly, suspicious of her.

'There's nothing to solve,' she said. 'It might just prove something to both of us.'

He said nothing.

David's skin was pale and he had lost a lot of weight, the Hollywood gloss was tarnished and he seemed very vulnerable to her. She could feel the beat of his heart and his warm breath against her skin. Sylvia wrapped herself around his sweaty muscularity, moving her pelvis against him in jerky, urgent thrusting movements that made her feel him inside her as he remained still. Gradually, very slowly, he began to move and she came quickly and then again, sharp little orgasms; it was impossible, this feeling of such release as she dug further into him, growing agonizingly close once more. He suddenly rode up on her, crying out her name as he came inside her, calling out her name.

'If you weren't so handsome and so nice and sexy I might never have fallen for you like some stupid school-girl,' Sylvia stroked his arm as he held her, 'like a teenager!'

'You were never that, never a teenager, you were a mother and wife before you had that chance, you only became more and more insecure.'

'You think I'm clinging on to make up for lost time,' she said.

He got out of bed. 'No,' he said, walking out of the bedroom to make them coffee. He returned after a while with a plate full of sandwiches and then sat in the armchair munching and smiling at her.

Sylvia sipped her coffee, she wanted him, she could not stop her tumbling desire and she did need him, his strength, the fact that she was so very much in love and he was so very grown up, even from the first really, no clingy insecurities with David, just an expectation of something to follow. It was more than a sexual liaison, he was right, he had become the person she craved, the one she needed above all others, not the father and not the son but the man and it was him who would enable her to go forward.

'I've been looking at a place in Connecticut, an old farmhouse with a piece of land,' he said.

'Are you joking?' She was amazed. 'You're not joking! What about California? What about good old Tinsel Town?'

David shrugged. 'I'll still keep a home there, I'll still make films, I'm just thinking of the future . . . Anyway, it would be an investment.' He smiled. 'I don't want to be making films for ever.'

'What's brought all this on?'

'Nothing. The play folded, I have all these weeks of inactivity before I do anything else. Property is supposed to be an investment for one's old age!'

She sat up. 'That's very responsible of you.'

'What about you?' he asked.

'What about me?'

'What are your plans for the future?'

Sylvia thought about that for a moment. 'My plans?' She smiled. 'Oh, well, now, let's see,' she paused, 'they're not so fixed.'

'Oh no?' He looked interested. 'Since when?'

'Since I realized what a good fuck you are . . . I'd have to be a fool to fix too many plans now, wouldn't I?'

He moved across to the bed, dropping down heavily at her side, propping himself up on one elbow to look at her. 'So, what are you saying?' He eyed her quizzically.

'Nothing.' A Cheshire-cat grin played about her lips.

265

David rolled on top of her, straddling her and pinning her to the bed, their faces almost touching. 'Tell me,' he insisted, his eyes still searching her own for clues.

Sylvia shook her head.

He began to tickle her into submission. 'Tell me.' They rolled over and over across the large bed, dangerously close to the edge, Sylvia gasping for air, shrieking with painful, hysterical laughter.

'Get off me,' she managed to shout, the sheet had slipped away leaving her naked under him.

David paused, raised himself above her on his arms, looking down and then lowering his head to kiss her breasts, taking each nipple in turn into the moist warmth of his mouth, grazing them gently against his teeth as they grew firm. He worked down and down, his tongue brushing against the silky mound of her pubic hair before he was inside her, his hot tongue working, his large hands holding her, guiding Sylvia ever closer to orgasm but never quite allowing it, teasing, cajoling, a forefinger slowly rubbing against her anus, the stubble of his beard rough against the inside of her thighs as she pressed against him, attempting to bring herself to climax by keeping him inside. Suddenly he moved up and his penis entered her, thrusting hard now and coming too quickly leaving her still aroused as he moved away, breathing hard. Sylvia lay across him, playing with the long soft tube of flaccid penis. He looked up; Sylvia's eyes were tightly shut now as she brought herself to a powerful orgasm, moving away from him until, relaxed, she began to breathe more easily. She turned her head and smiled at him, he moved and they embraced one another, holding for a long time, drifting, unspeaking, warm and relaxed almost on the verge of sleep.

'I can never get enough of you,' she said.

'I'm happy to hear that.'

'At this particular moment in my life I would probably accept any condition you cared to make.'

'Except one,' David said.

The hair of his chest curled around her fingers as she lightly brushed them against the dark curling mass. 'I'm open to offers,' she teased.

'What about your job?' he asked. 'What about the old career, then?'

She got up and went into the bathroom. 'I have some thinking to do,' she said, pausing at the door. 'Minority arts programme, indeed!' She laughed, closing the door behind her.

They drove to Boston the following day and walked the Freedom Trail. It was a Sunday and there were a lot of people about, everyone bundled up against the freezing wind and the sleety rain. Bright winter clothing against the dark stones of American history. To Sylvia the day was like the beginning and the end of something. She experienced strong, conflicting emotions towards David. At times she felt angry with him for creating within her such a strong need, this desire for him which could be completely debilitating. No one recognized him, they both looked bedraggled and pale as they walked, untouching, hands deep into coat pockets, collars turned up. They came across a steamy tea-shop where they removed their damp coats and began to thaw out over the hot cups.

'Do you realize this is the first time when we've been together that you haven't had to rush off to begin a new film?'

'What about your show?' he asked, stirring milk into his tea. 'When are you due back for that?'

Sylvia thought for a moment. She recalled the unsigned

contract, it was the potential bridge-burning excuse, she could tell him now, tell him that there was no need for her to return, that her career in television arts was over. 'I'm not sure,' was all she said.

'Not sure?' he asked, surprised. 'That's not like you.'

'No, it isn't, is it.'

'So?' he asked insistently. 'What does it mean?'

'It means I'm not sure . . .'

'Are you going back?'

'At some point, yes, of course.'

'When?'

'When I'm ready,' she replied, finding enjoyment in this particular game.

In the afternoon they drove to the farmhouse in Connecticut where Sylvia's footsteps echoed in the empty rooms against the old oak floor boards.

'Why do you want a house in the country?' she asked. 'You hate the country . . . Are you sure you really want this?'

David was sitting on the window seat in the master bedroom. 'Don't you like it?' He sounded shocked. 'It's a fabulous property and it's a very good investment – my accountant has gone into it.'

Sylvia folded her arms, her coat was still wet from the rainy day, she felt chilled. 'I don't honestly see what use you'll ever get out of it.' She walked across to him, putting her hand on his shoulder, leaning forward to look out at the sleet and down at the green umbrella of the realty woman as it moved, smoke drifting out from underneath it. The woman was waiting outside whilst they discussed his decision, to buy or not to buy, the clouds were low obscuring the surrounding countryside.

'I might make a film in New York.' He looked up at her. 'It's a nice house, we can decorate it . . .'

Sylvia shrugged and walked back across the bare boards. 'Do you have to make that decision now?' she asked. 'That woman will catch her death of cold out there.' She wandered through the rest of the house, in and out of the other five bedrooms, three bathrooms and up and onward into the attic regions where a pale grey light filtered through dusty windows. 'Why do you need all of this room?' she asked as he followed, in and out of the small rooms at the top of the house.

'I'm thinking of this house as being used by both of us.' He sounded distinctly fed up by her negative attitude. 'I would imagine that you have some stuff you could put in it and I've accumulated quite a bit over the years. In any case, New York is just down the road, we can get any furniture we might need from there . . .'

'Well, I suppose we could always start a hotel, or a boarding school for rich New England brats.'

'You don't like it?'

'It's fine.'

'Then say something positive.'

'It's jolly big.'

'Very good, Sylvia, nice try.'

David pulled the front door shut after them and they crunched over the wet gravel to the green umbrella which had moved down to look at the muddy duck pond. The umbrella swung around to greet them and the realty woman smiled in a very professional way.

'We'll be in touch,' David said, 'thank you very much.'

'It's a lovely house,' Sylvia added, feeling pangs of guilt for the cold woman.

'Thank you,' the woman replied.

They watched her trudging back towards the house to lock up and then sat in their borrowed car, a large brown Mercedes, listening to the rain.

'I'm going to have this house,' he began. 'When I was a kid I always wanted a house like this, something with a sense of the past and this has a history all of its own and I want it.' He turned to Sylvia. 'It will be good for you, too. We can set up a studio, what better place to work, you can write and edit your stuff here.'

She felt some surprise that this was amongst his plans. 'You don't have to spend thousands of dollars on this place just for that.'

'Yes, well, you already have your estate and country house to inherit.'

'I don't care if you have nothing,' she quickly countered.

'I want to settle, I want to sit down somewhere solid and stew for a while . . . I would also like an education.'

'Christ, you have another fifty or sixty years ahead of you for all of that. What do you want an education for? You already have your drama training.'

'I'm not like you,' he said. 'I've never had the security of purpose or background to validate me and I don't want to grind on in films for the rest of my life.'

'Yes, you do, it's in your bones now. I can guarantee that you'll be back in Hollywood within the next few months, another blockbuster to complete, another million plus dollars in the bank.'

'I don't have to, it's not inevitable.'

'Yes, it is, in any case you're under contract. A few months here and you'll be suicidal. You belong in California, in Los Angeles, God help you, you like the sun and the smog and the easy way of things out there.'

'And what about you?' he asked.

'What about me?'

'What about you and me?'

Sylvia smiled and looked out at the tumbling rain and

the streaming windscreen. She thought for a long time before answering him. 'I may have something to tell you, something to your advantage, isn't that what they say in those personal adverts when someone distant dies?'

'What news?' he sounded unconvinced.

'Patience is a virtue, find us a cheap motel room before New York and I might tell you afterwards.'

David laughed and started the engine, moving the large car away into the rain, splashing through deep rutted pools of water at the end of the driveway before pulling out on to the highway.

Sylvia was sitting astride him, looking down, his muscles tensed, watching him. She loved that outspread V-shape of his, very broad shoulders which tapered down to a slim waist made firm by his continual work-outs. He had lost so much weight that there wasn't a bit of extra fat. All of his body, both inside and out, which she admired and craved. His head was thrown back, she liked to watch him, neck muscles bulging, wiry cords standing out and afterwards, when he had finished, he looked up at her, smiling like a child. She began to move off him, his penis, still hard, sliding out of her.

'You haven't finished yet.'

'That's all right.'

He shook his head. 'Sylvia . . .' like a warning, his hand on her thigh.

'I sometimes like to do it for myself, it doesn't impune your manhood . . . You don't always have to be part of it for me.' She looked at him. 'It doesn't *mean* anything, for God's sake, don't look like that.' She lay beside him coming very quickly afterwards, rolling on top of David, kissing him repeatedly, stroking his blond hair, peering into his eyes for a long time, neither of them speaking.

She reached across and flicked on the radio, Chet Baker sang 'Do It The Hard Way', she laughed softly and David smiled as he held her and the room grew darker, the slatted light from the motel blinds diminishing into blackness. She rested her head against David's chest.

'Okay,' he asked her.

She eased herself up, a forefinger playing gently across his mouth, following a line over and around his lips. 'You know, I never really made a correct decision in my life. I was always so distant from the truth, from what was actually going on and from what I really wanted to happen. Sometimes it was as though I were looking down at myself, I never seemed to know what it was I really wanted.'

'Can I ask you something?' he sounded thoughtful.

Sylvia nodded, 'Yes, of course.'

'You always seemed to be so much in control, when we first met there you were, your own TV show, liberated female, right there in the centre of things.' He looked up at her, examining her reaction. 'What happened to us in all of your deliberations? Why did you never make any decisions about us?' He reached up to touch her hair. 'You know, Sylvia, I've waited all of this time, there was never anyone else.'

She felt that awful sweet sensation of panic as it rose in her stomach. 'You seem to assume it's been easy for me – you with your hard currency of youth and looks – why did you come to me and then keep on insisting and insisting upon the impossible?'

'Is it impossible, then?'

She held him tightly. 'What do you want from me?' she asked.

'I just want you to stop hiding behind your age and

your career and your kids and your marriage. I want you to stop being so full of martyrdom.'

Sylvia was taken off guard, she wondered if that was the truth or not, hiding behind all the events of her history. She felt defeated and could offer no spirited defence of her cause any longer, battle-fatigue, general exhaustion and a certain guilt pervaded her thoughts. 'It's only because I'm so scared,' she admitted.

'Jesus,' David breathed, 'we're a fine pair.' He wrapped himself around her. 'Why must I prove it's me who has no doubts about us?'

'Because you're so very beautiful and so much younger.'

'Why can't you trust me?'

'It isn't a question of trust, David, it's a question of being realistic.'

'Not that again, not the age difference, *please* not that!'

'It must be faced, you just won't think . . .'

'I've never wanted anyone else, how many more times must I say it.'

'Listen to me,' she said, putting a finger to his lips, stopping him from saying any more. 'I have no conditions to make,' she paused, only their breathing was evident as the music from the radio ended, 'I'm going to stay here with you this time . . . If you want.'

David hugged her tightly, squeezing the breath out of her, laughing as he spoke. 'My God, Mrs McLeod, is that the truth?' He rolled over and over with her until they were completely tangled up with the bed clothes. 'For God's sake, it's about time . . . It's about time. Is that what all the talk was about?'

'Don't you want to know what my future plans are?'

'Sure.'

'I propose to take up your offer and set up an

independent company which will produce films for TV, you know the sort of thing. Are you interested in investing some of your millions?'

'Pushy, aren't you.'

'Ambitious.'

'Did you always plan this move?'

'It's a sound business venture, my brains and your money, it should prove to be both stimulating and profitable.'

'Just one problem,' he said.

'And what's that?'

'What about "The Arts Programme"?'

'My minority arts slot?' she asked, reminding him of his earlier barb. 'I haven't signed for another series yet.'

'Jesus,' he breathed, 'what will Edmund say?'

'Edmund? Oh, he'll have lost a presenter but gained a quiet life in which to nurse his ulcer in peace.'

'I'm not sure where we go from here. It's absolutely incredible.'

'Don't talk now,' she said, 'just get some sleep, tomorrow we have to face the fact that neither one of us is about to depart . . . It may prove too much!'

He laughed at that. 'Not for me.'

'We'll see, then.'

In a short while he was fast asleep and Sylvia drifted off with a thousand thoughts turning over in her mind. Wes Montgomery was wafting over the air taking her back a few hundred years to 1963.

Sylvia joined David at a New York restaurant for lunch a few days later where he was being interviewed by a reporter from *Rolling Stone*. The reporter, a young woman, was just leaving, she smiled at Sylvia, brushing by her as she made her way out.

'How was it?' Sylvia asked.

'Okay,' David nodded. 'She asked some good questions.'

'What did she ask?'

'General stuff, about the play. She saw it, actually had some positive things to say.'

'That's good.'

'She said I've yet to reach my prime, my maturity in film – '

'I was in my prime, now I'm just having primals!'

David laughed. 'I have to present an award at some vast showbusiness extravaganza next week, do you want to come?'

'Will it be painless?' she asked suspiciously.

'You'll have your photograph appear in a paper and a magazine or two . . .'

'Grinning madly . . .'

'Will you come?'

'I suppose so. It won't be too dreadful, will it?'

'I expect so,' he grinned, 'terrible!'

'What the hell.' She raised a glass of water to him. 'Well, here's looking at you, kid, and hooray for Hollywood!'

That evening they were standing on a New York balcony as the day ended. It was freezing and Sylvia looked out over the aggressive skyline. She could see the Empire State building clearly outlined against the crisp sky. David was leaning over the side looking down at the traffic in the street. She didn't know the host, Malc Wraas, but David reminded her that they had been to an exhibition of his at the Guggenheim.

'Sunsets, it was called Sunsets,' he said, irritated that she should forget, or pretend to forget.

'It can't have been very good if I can't even remember going to it,' she replied.

'You said he would be an interesting subject for an interview.'

'Did I?' Sylvia asked, suspicious that he was just making that up to confuse her further. 'I can't remember meeting him.'

'Well, you did.'

'Are you collecting him or what?' Sylvia turned her back on the fading city outlines and moved back to the warmth of the party. 'I don't really know why we're here.' She tugged at his sleeve. 'Do you know why we're here?'

'Malc Wraas invited us.'

Sylvia nodded. 'What do you get for turning up, a free picture? Guest of the evening David Christensen, the rent-a-star to impress your guests!'

'I thought you'd enjoy it, a lot of interesting people will be here, artists, writers, actors . . .'

Sylvia looked unconvinced. She turned to David. 'Come on, then, let's meet these interesting people.'

A crowd of people were brought in to meet David. 'And this is Lady Sylvia Wessley-Carroux.' Malc Wraas beamed in her general direction.

'Please, I never use my title,' Sylvia said, 'my name is Sylvia McLeod.'

'I'm sorry,' their flustered host began, 'I don't quite understand . . .'

'Sylvia works under her married name,' David attempted to explain.

'Oh, really?' a tall woman asked. 'What do you do?'

'Sylvia has her own television show in London,' David began, 'or, rather, she had. We're going to set up our own production company here.'

276

'How interesting,' Malc Wraas said, looking bored, 'I'll look forward to seeing your first production.'

Sylvia felt tired at having to justify her existence and guided David away into the luxurious apartment where they met some of the actors from his play on the verge of leaving. A tide of people entered the room as Sylvia was following David and his actors out of it. They were caught up in between Malc Wraas' 'hi's' and 'goodbyes'.

'He'll never talk to me again,' David hissed as she pushed him into the lift.

'That sounds like a distinct advantage to me,' she replied, producing a bottle of Scotch from underneath her coat, opening it and passing it around in the back of their crowded cab.

'What's got into you?' David asked, laughing as the bottle was thrust into his hand.

She smiled her wicked smile but did not answer his question. 'Your place?' she asked instead. 'Bring your friends if you like.'

David introduced her to everyone as they bumped along to his rented loft. She liked them already and, once at David's place, more recruits were called up and the party began to take shape.

'This will be a first for New York,' Sylvia announced, 'a party where we're not selling you anything!' Her eyes caught an original Malc Wraas, she had not seen it before but was sure it was awful.

Someone had sent out for vast pizzas which they all sat around munching as midnight struck on the grandfather clock at the far end of the long lounge. Sylvia was sitting next to a rather delicious young man who had heard all about her and was interested.

'Were you in the play, too?' she asked, slopping some of her wine on to his jeans.

'No, but I was there,' he smiled. 'I saw it.'

'Was it terrible? As terrible as they said it was?'

'Yes.' He laughed.

Sylvia felt light-headed; she was intoxicated by his laughter. 'Tell me how bad David was.'

'Bad,' the young man replied, 'it wasn't his style.'

'I see.' Sylvia nodded feeling warm and very comfortable. 'And what's your style, would you say?'

He grinned. 'My old lady is somewhere around this cavern . . . I daren't say!'

'God, Americans,' Sylvia said with mock disgust. 'Tell me,' she coaxed but David had arrived and was sitting at her other side.

'Is this woman bothering you?' he asked.

'Not half as much as I'd like,' the young actor replied.

'How gallant,' Sylvia said drunkenly.

'Sylvia McLeod, this is James Teller, James meet Sylvia,' David smiled.

'Pleased to meet you, ma'am.'

'How charming,' Sylvia replied, turning to David and kissing him, open-mouthed, urgent, her arms tight around his neck, her head swimming with desire or lust or alcohol. 'Let's go to bed,' she said.

'We have guests,'

'Tell them to go.'

'You tell them, you were the one who invited them!'

Her hand smoothed back his hair. 'I'm terribly drunk, aren't I?' She took a moment to focus on his face. 'Too drunk . . . How vile,' she said more contritely. 'I'm sorry, you were having such a nice time at Malc Wraas'.'

'They'll go soon,' he said comfortingly, holding her gently.

Sylvia began to cry silently.

'Whatever's the matter?' he asked bemused, laughter in his voice. 'Don't cry, you're soaking my shirt front.'

Sylvia sniffed and hugged him tightly. 'I love you so much, *so* much . . .'

'Is that any reason to cry? It isn't so dreadful, is it?'

She shook her head, taking the handkerchief he offered, blowing her nose with a snorting noise which made them both laugh. 'No, it's very wonderful really . . .' She dabbed at her tear-stained face. 'Jesus, I must be so drunk,' she said, standing up, 'so bloody drunk,' and wandered off in rather unsteady fashion towards their bedroom where David found her, dead to the world, an hour or two later.

'Have they all gone home?' she asked sleepily, rolling over and holding him warm against her.

He brushed a hand over her forehead. 'Shh, go back to sleep.' He lay still and listened for her breathing to become regular and deep, the distant sounds of the city jungle reaching his ears. He felt safe with her there beside him and closed his eyes to the night. Soon there was nothing but dreamless sleep to carry them on.

Sylvia sat up and was wide awake even though it was very early. Wintry sunlight shafted through the tilted slats of the bedroom blinds and the loft felt very warm. David was fast asleep, his head almost underneath his pillows. She stepped on to the cool wooden floor and walked into the lounge where she sat on one of the black leather sofas. The remains of the previous night were scattered about the room, endless wine glasses, spent coffee cups, half-eaten pizza. There were some instant camera snaps on the table in front of her. She reached down to pick them up but she didn't recognize many of the red-eyed faces that looked back. The handsome actor who just looked unspeakably drunk was slopped over his 'old lady', a rather fed-up looking girl who was making no concessions to the camera and had failed to raise even the glimmer of a party smile. A picture of her and David kissing (and she had thought the blinding flash of light had been love!). She flicked through the photographs and then replaced them, easing herself up to make tea. She moved to the long window seat with her tray and stayed there for a long time considering their future.

Sylvia watched the long black tendrils of hair falling around her like hanks of wool. Her head looked ridiculously small and it felt strange not to have the long hair around her shoulders anymore. The young man eased a rubber cap over her shorn head and an assistant busily pulled tufts of the remaining hair through the tiny holes; it smarted as she tugged with her little hook, making Sylvia's eyes water. She smelt the strong chemicals, like bleach, as the colour was applied, a thick purple paste which was painted on to her tufty hair. Afterwards, she was given a cup of coffee and a thick magazine with which to pass away the time between Sylvia old and Sylvia new. Streaked blonde to perfection she had transformed herself into the youthful images she had seen when choosing this particular style in the fashion publications.

She looked at her reflection in the department store windows. At first it shocked her, she hadn't recognized herself, this creature with the rather startling spiked blonde hair. Her hand kept making involuntary journeys up to her head where it touched the firm, moussed remains. Sylvia dumped her packages on to the bed and shook out her new evening dress, hanging it carefully in the closet. She took out the red satin evening shoes, too high really, holding them so that their sheen caught the light. She placed them carefully under the hanging dress, the effect made her grin, the invisible woman look. It all reminded her of when she was a child and had dressing-up days with her mother's old recital gowns. She sat on the bed and picked up Edmund's telegram, 'Where are you?' it asked, 'Contact me immediately.' She supposed that Edmund should be told, it really wasn't right to string him along, to exacerbate the discomfort of his ulcer. Sylvia stared at the crumpled telegram, the end of an era she thought, but the start of something else. She held herself tightly and lay back.

David arrived at five-thirty just as Sylvia's make-up girl, Sheree, was finishing her off with an enormous square box of tricks. He did a perfect double-take. Sylvia had to admit that she was probably unrecognizable by this time. She had experienced make-up hundreds of times for her TV show but never like this; even Sylvia found it hard to comprehend the woman who stared back at her.

'You should practise smiling down,' Sheree suggested, 'like this.' She pulled her top lip down over her teeth and, parting her mouth, had forced her lips into a sort of glossy square. 'Marilyn had to do it,' she explained. 'You have a similar problem – high gum line.' She stood behind Sylvia, peering intently at her reflected image. 'Also, it helps to shorten the length of your nose, try it!' she commanded.

Sylvia attempted this smile but only succeeded in look-ing like a grotesque, a gargoyle.

'Maybe, if you tried sticking out your lower jaw, it might help,' Sheree said, looking very unconvinced at Sylvia's efforts.

Sylvia tried but it made no difference, it did alter the shape of her face but only to the extent of making her look as though a face lift had gone horribly wrong. 'I think I'll use my own smile this evening, thank you, anyway.' She was generally pleased with her new hair and new face, they seemed to be more of a matching pair now.

Sheree clicked her teeth as she prepared to go. 'You look *great*, honey, you'll knock 'em dead. I'll watch out for you.'

'Will you be there?' Sylvia asked.

'God, yes, if you want a re-touch I'll be somewhere back-stage.' She left, brushing by David and smiling broadly, and down, of course, just like Marilyn.

'Well?' Sylvia said, turning to him.

'Well, well,' he replied, 'you look gorgeous. I especially like the housecoat.'

'What about the hair?' She sounded unsure, looking at his own carefully applied make-up.

'Great . . . fantastic.'

'We look like a pair of clowns,' she said.

'We look great. Under camera lights we'll look fabulous.'

He stood behind her; she stared at their mirrored images, attempting to smile down one more time.

They were dressed and ready to go. She looked critically at her designer dress, low cut, too tight, too short, too young, terribly expensive, sheer black stockings and the high-heeled shoes. She felt, to put it mildly, like a woman of the streets.

'Do you remember *Irma La Douce*?' she asked. 'I mean, of course, you won't because you were just a child then. It was a film with Shirley MacLaine and Jack Lemmon,' she began to explain.

David nodded, he couldn't stop looking at her. 'Yes, I've seen it, why?'

'I feel just like her character!'

282

'You look fantastic.'

Sylvia turned to him. 'Don't you dare leave my side, David, they'll throw me out as a hooker!'

'Don't be ridiculous, it's a fabulous dress and you look sensational.'

'I don't appear to look any specific age?'

'Come on,' he laughed. 'The limo awaits.'

In all their time together Sylvia had never once accompanied David to a 'job', as he called them, no premieres, no Oscar ceremonies. He always took a young actress or model, 'the furniture', they were called. Now she was the furniture, a departure for Sylvia if not exactly the one she would have chosen herself. Sylvia took one more look, Richard's diamonds glittered on her wrist and around her exposed neck. 'Okay,' she said, 'Okay, it's now or never, I suppose.'

She had not been prepared for the noise, thousands of people screaming for him, although it might just as well have been for their blood for all the sense it made. 'David, David, David,' they chanted. A battery of photographers let flashes off in their faces, blinding her before she had hardly taken a step away from the ludicrous car, a block and a half of shining black metal with enough room in the back for a small family to live quite comfortably.

'And who is the lovely lady?' the tanned interviewer asked at the canopied entrance as the shrieking continued all around them. David interviewed well, the casual West-Coaster coming to the fore. She heard him mention her name and so she smiled, attempting to remember Sheree's advice, jutting out her chin, catching herself on a small TV monitor nearby, looking like a very bad impression of Benito Mussolini. She felt bilious.

Marsha looked up at her as they reached the huge circular table.

'I didn't recognize you, dear,' Marsha snarled, looking at her in an approving manner, 'you look so . . . so different.'

'Thank you, Marsha, I'll take that as a compliment, anyway.'

Marsha peered through slitty eyes and her cigar smoke. 'This your new image?'

Sylvia took a sip of champagne. 'Do you like it? David thinks there may be a chance for me in soap opera!'

Smoke curled from Marsha's nostrils. 'One actor in the family is enough, dear. Stick to your clever little talk shows.'

'Hello, Sylvia,' a man's voice said.

She turned to find Geoff Meredith sitting down next to her. 'My God!' she exclaimed. 'What are you doing here?'

'I might ask you the same question.'

Sylvia looked at him, feeling slightly embarrassed. 'I'm living here now,' she answered somewhat defiantly.

'I hardly recognized you.'

Sylvia smiled. 'I'm going to work over here, we're setting up a production company to produce my own programmes.'

'No more Edmund, then,' he said, grinning knowingly.

'No more Edmund,' she repeated with relief. 'So, what do you think?'

'Sounds good to me. I'm producing now, over at NBC. So, you're here with your man.' He placed his hand over hers and examined the diamond-encrusted wrist. 'Did our boy buy you those?'

'My ex-husband actually.' Sylvia moved her hand away and changed the subject. 'What do you think my chances are?'

'You'll be all right. When you're ready why not give me a call?' He produced a business card, handing it to her. 'I can introduce you to some people who might be able to help your cause.'

Sylvia took his card and thanked him, watching him stand up to leave. 'It was nice to see you again, Geoff, are you here to present or to receive?'

'Neither,' he shrugged, 'just to watch.' He smiled at her. 'How's Norfolk?'

'Cold,' she replied. 'Very cold.'

'Well, perhaps we'll meet up again soon, give me a call at my office, we could have lunch and, don't worry, with his money and your talent you won't go wrong.'

'And your contacts?' She smiled up at him.

'Sure, why not.'

She watched him disappearing into the crowd, thoughtful for a moment as she remembered. He turned and their eyes held for a second as the lights dimmed and the applause began to greet their host for the evening as he walked out into the spot light. The band struck up and the man began to sing a song about New York and how wonderful it was. Sylvia looked around her at all these Americans and reached for her drink.

Sylvia was drunk, floating along somewhere with David in the back of their rented car, laughing again at a joke she had already forgotten. Halfway between day and night they drove on for hours, it seemed, stopping only as light began to spread at the horizon. The cool air on her face woke her, she watched the tail lights of the large car cruising away into the blue morning light, her red dress looking bright in the dawn.

'Why are we here?' Sylvia asked bemused, looking up at the farmhouse. She felt the wet dew chill and David wrapped her heavy evening cape around her shoulders as they walked to the house. The horizon turned from cold white to warmer pink, the glowing sun began to spill over. Her shoes tripped over the frosted gravel. David opened the large front door and they entered the echoing hallway, walking into the kitchen where a bottle of champagne and two glasses sat on a cloth in the middle of the dusty draining board. He opened the champagne and, as the foamy liquid spewed out, he poured them each a bubbly glass full, handing one to Sylvia. 'I've bought the house, it's ours as from now.'

She stared at him, watching the sun rising through the kitchen windows, sipping at the champagne. 'I don't know what to say . . .' She raised her glass. 'Congratulations, it's what you wanted.'

David smiled. 'What about you? What do you want? We have to stop fooling around, Sylvia, fooling ourselves, that is.' He looked at her as though weighing both her and his next words very carefully. 'This is where we go on from – or not, it's all become real now.'

'Do you love me?' she asked. 'I know you do but . . .'

'Sylvia,' he interrupted her, 'haven't we done enough harm to one another?' and taking her glass away he held her in his arms and kissed her. 'I love you,' he said.

She smelt him, her cheek against the white of his starched evening shirt, his cologne and his distinctive smell, lingering, driving her to him, making her respond.

In the master bedroom, the one that would be theirs she supposed, he stood at the windows watching over the surrounding land, *his* land now.

'Couldn't you be happy here?' he asked, turning to her.

'What makes you think I'm unhappy?' She was standing just inside the doorway.

He shrugged but didn't reply.

Sylvia didn't move from the door, looking, always looking at him, his broad shoulders and tight-waisted trousers which followed the contours of his body closely, too well-cut, custom-made they called such clothes out here, custom-made for him as he might have been for her. She shuddered, feeling someone had walked over her grave. 'What about your desire for marriage?' she asked bluntly.

'What about your career? You haven't even told Edmund yet.'

'That decision has been made, it's history.' She suddenly felt incredibly tired and uncomfortable in her costume. 'How far are we from New York?'

'An hour or so.' His voice echoed slightly, reverberating in the empty spaces. He bent down and picked up a framed photograph he had discovered, a print of a wedding in the 1940s, a war bride in a dark, fitted two-piece suit, a huge flower pinned to her bosom, a reckless smile on her face but such haunted eyes. Her groom in ordinary seaman's uniform, the name of his ship across his hat, a carnation on his white uniform, very young, very good-looking, both so young. 'I like to think that they might have lived here once,' David said.

Sylvia crossed over the bare boards to him and took a closer look at the photograph. 'What about the marriage?' she asked.

He turned to look out of the window again. 'What about it?'

She took the picture and stared hard at the faces, wondering what it must have been like for them, wondering if they ever saw one another again after he returned to sea. She hoped with all her heart that they did.

'I just want you, Sylvia, whatever happens, nothing else matters now.'

They left at last, long shadows greeting them from the rising sun. David had arranged for his car to be parked in the red barn across the yard from the house. Sylvia stamped her feet attempting to keep warm in the frosty morning air.

'David,' she said, running across to him and stopping him for a moment, 'how long do you give us, a year, six months, ten years?'

'Don't be ridiculous, how can you ask me to quantify something like that?' He smiled. 'Are you still drunk, you're rambling.' He put his arm around her shoulders.

She leant against him as they walked to the red barn. 'Drunk and rambling, yes, yes,' she agreed, closing her eyes as they went, 'drunk and old and rambling on . . .' Sylvia waited as he pulled open the large doors and drove his car out, she got in and reclined the seat, sleeping all the way to New York.

She woke up in the late afternoon with David sprawled asleep next to her, everything twisted around him. She surveyed the remains of their gala evening and went off to have a warm soapy bath and, afterwards, sat looking down at the Sunday crowds in Central Park. She sipped strong tea from one of her mother's Russian breakfast cups. She pinched the skin on the back of her hand, watching to see how long it would take to resume its shape, watching to see how much youthful elasticity was left, the longer it took the more aged one was supposed to be. On her reckoning it wouldn't be long before gravity really took hold and gave her a turkey-skin neck and saggy eyes, skin that was creased and liver-spotted on her breastbone and legs and thighs. 'One more chance,' she repeated to herself, 'one more chance.' She sat back, her mother was due in New York soon, she would have to tell her everything and imagined Natalia Fiodor's I-told-you-so smile. Sylvia wondered vaguely how long it would take for the farmhouse to be ready, how quickly before they could move. Her decision now having been made she wanted everything to happen as soon as possible.

He might have been the biggest Broadway success ever from the ovation they gave him. Sylvia felt detached from the scene. David was propped up in bed watching a recording of the show, she was crunched up in the armchair. 'David Christensen,' the compère announced and everyone went insane. They had no idea, she thought. This outpouring of emotion was directed exactly at the qualities he personified on film and which bore no resemblance, even coincidentally, to him. 'And here is David Christensen with his lovely companion, Lady Sylvia Wessley-Carroux, British writer and TV personality . . .' and there she was complete with her Mussolini smile.

'Oh, Christ!' Sylvia said, cringing into her armchair. 'Oh, my God, it's too horrible to watch.'

David laughed. 'It's great. I told you Sheree's make-up would look super.'

'Yes, but I don't really look like that, not in life!'

'You look fabulous, everyone said so.'

Sylvia continued to look at the screen. 'I think that was Lana Turner,' she said, pointing to a group shot of all the celebrities lined up at the end, 'you were next to Lana Turner!' She became excited. 'You might have got her autograph.'

'I didn't think you approved of that sort of thing.'

Sylvia pulled a face. 'An exception for a real star, perhaps, now and again.'

David tossed a pillow at her. 'Thanks a lot.'

She caught the pillow and held it to her face, laughing

into it and then peeking over the top to see herself and the ridiculous red dress sashaying into the theatre. Sylvia groaned. 'Never again,' she said, her voice muffled, 'never again.'

For the second morning in a row Sylvia became nauseous and was, finally, sick in David's bathroom. She sat on the floor and propped her head back on to the bathside. David was out running, pounding the freezing New York streets, risking life and limb getting back into shape again. Sylvia had known it for over a week now, she was absolutely certain that she was pregnant and she was unexpectedly happy about this turn of events. She had always assumed that it would have horrified her, she had certainly not wanted it, there was absolutely no plan involved. However, at forty-one it made her feel, somehow, still part of the community of productive women rather than the *older* woman she so often felt she had become. Being pregnant dispelled the fears she felt about being too old for David, it was a ridiculous admission for her to have to make to herself but it was true. Her whole life seemed turned on to its head. It was odd to contemplate a child and it embarrassed her to remember how she had always refused even to consider the idea when David had suggested it. She now felt full of excitement at the prospect and put this down to a hormonal imbalance as her body prepared her brain for the inevitable. It all seemed quite beyond rationality and common sense. She saw an expensive New York gynaecologist and it was confirmed, as she knew it would be, which meant she could tell David.

'Guess what?' she said, walking in on him as he took a bath.

'What?' he asked, grinning.

'I'm pregnant,' she said it simply, almost matter-of-factly.

'Pregnant?' He didn't seem to comprehend at first.

'Pregnant,' Sylvia nodded.

'My God!' He sounded incredulous. 'Pregnant?' He stood up, stepping out of the water to hug her.

Sylvia threw a large bath sheet over him before he reached her. 'You'll drown us,' she laughed as their lips met.

'Are you serious?' he asked, a smile spreading across his face.

'I'm forty-one years old, David, I'm bloody serious!'

'Are you all right?' he asked.

Sylvia nodded. 'Yes, I'm perfectly fine, I've seen Dr Grossman. He says I'm just beautiful . . .'

'You are,' David agreed, holding her close again, 'you are a beautiful woman.' He seemed agitated, as if uncertain quite how he should act whilst still remaining a bit shell-shocked at the news.

Sylvia understood this. 'Well, and what do you feel about it?' she asked with a smile.

'I feel *great*, how do you feel?'

She looked into his beautiful face. 'It was a bit of a surprise initially . . .' She stopped, smiling to herself. 'Jesus, there's some good old British understatement for you!'

'A baby,' David said, 'I can hardly believe it.'

'Well, believe it, David, it will be evident soon enough.'

They held one another for a long time, unspeaking, Sylvia's head a muddle of thoughts, some joyous and some concerned with the practicalities of the next eight months or so.

'We'll get you home,' David began, 'we can both go back to England.'

'I've found myself a doctor I like, I think I'll have an American baby for a change!'

He thought about that for a while. 'What about your mother?'

'What about her?'

'Have you told her yet?'

'Of course not, allow me a little peace!'

'What do you think she'll say?'

'Something irritating, no doubt.'

David smiled. 'Do you think it's a case of history repeating itself?'

'You have to have a little faith, David. History doesn't repeat itself, it's just people making the same old mistakes.'

'My God,' he said, putting a hand up to his head, 'I can't believe it.'

'Well it's true, David, and within a few months your views about blessed parenthood may be altered considerably.'

He lifted himself on one elbow, looking down at her. 'Being pregnant definitely suits you,' he decided.

'Thanks.' She wasn't very convinced, though.

'You look beautiful.' He kissed her.

'When I was younger,' she began, 'when I was first married to Richard I went to a reunion of my old school mates.' She smiled. 'I went all alone and I can remember preparing for it very carefully. My mother supervised my dress, I can see it now . . . hideous!'

'Where was Richard?' he asked.

'God knows, some law thing, I don't know. Anyway, when I arrived at this hotel where the reunion was to take place, I walked in and suddenly realized that I was the only one to arrive without a partner. I turned on my heels and left, rushing home and dumping all my party clothes on the floor, feeling like a silly little schoolgirl.' She reached out for his hand. 'I tell you this to explain, to *try* and explain, why I decided to come back.'

David moved closer, lying on his side next to her. 'I thought we had already gone through this.'

Sylvia tugged at his hair, 'Well, I'm no longer very young and I'm far too old to be attending dances by myself and I wanted you very much . . .' She paused.

'What is it?' he asked.

'Oh, I don't know, I love you and I'm pregnant with your child and I just wanted to tell you that it feels wonderful . . .'

David put his arms around her. 'I think we need to get you back to work as soon as possible, you're becoming maudlin!'

'I feel I've surrendered.'

'Thanks a lot,' David replied with sarcasm.

'I love you, David,' she sighed. 'Thank God you don't care what I do, whether I work or not, whether I sell out my views, my ideological correctness, thank God you just want the things I can give you, that you're quire satisfied with them.'

'Who cares about anything as long as you're happy.'

'Isn't it odd to think that the one demand of yours I refused is now a fact . . .'

'There's still marriage,' he replied, smiling.

She lay back. 'I'm an absolute failure.'

'Because you're with me or because you're pregnant?' he asked.

'Because I can't survive on my own, I always need some human prop.' She rolled over on to him, resting her head so she could hear the beating of his heart. 'But I'm in love with you, so, perhaps that makes it all right.'

David laughed. 'You're quire insane. People aren't

supposed to go on alone, they need contact with others . . .'

'Yes, well, we've certainly had that.' She laughed making their bodies shake. 'Forty-one years old, pregnant, comfortable and feeling remarkably complacent . . .'

'You're absolutely bananas, Mrs McLeod, are you aware of that?' David asked, stroking her short hair.

'Being mad is as good excuse as any for this predicament . . . You know I'll get fat, I always balloon up, you've never seen me pregnant.'

'I love fat, it's good.'

Sylvia felt very sleepy, she lay still, listening to his heart and drifting like a child herself at peace now in his arms.

Sylvia called Peter who was surprised but seemed happy at the news.

'Congratulations,' he said. 'Are you pleased?'

'Are you shocked?' Sylvia replied.

'Sounds good to me . . . are we betting on a boy or a girl?'

'Either will do as long as it's healthy.'

'How's the farm?' he asked. 'Are you living there yet?'

Sylvia laughed. 'No, it will be months. We'll stay in New York until it's ready.'

'Dad and Miranda are off to the Caribbean. They asked me to go but I'd already accepted an offer to go to Norfolk.'

'Well, Mother's looking forward to seeing you, she's already packing up here!'

Peter laughed. 'Good old Gran.'

'You must come out soon.' Sylvia paused. 'You don't mind, do you, about the baby, I mean?'

'Mind? Of course I don't mind. What an odd question . . .'

'It's come as a complete shock you know, another example of Mother's bad timing!'

'I think it's absolutely great. What did Gran say?'

'I haven't told her yet. I'm seeing her tomorrow, though, and I'm dreading it, I can tell you.'

'She'll be thrilled,' Peter replied.

'Yes, I know, that's what I'm afraid of. We'll have our usual discussion about marriage, the baby gives her even more ammunition to fire at me.'

'Well, I'm sure you'll stand your ground, you're not contemplating marriage now, are you?'

'No,' Sylvia said firmly. 'Don't you go on at me, Peter.'

Peter laughed. 'Me? I never mind what you do.'

Sylvia wasn't very convinced about that but did not pursue the topic, it only enhanced her insecurity and feelings of recklessness. 'I have to decide what to do with the beach house,' she said, changing the subject abruptly. 'Do you want it?'

Peter was silent for a moment. 'What would I do with it?' he asked at last.

'You're seventeen, I could pass it on to you and you could make some use of it.'

'Can't you just keep it?'

'What use will I make of it living here?'

'Won't you use it when you visit, then?'

'I'm trying to divest myself of places. I no sooner get rid of one and I acquire another, it's positively ridiculous. You like the coast, you have a boat there and it's nice for week-ends.'

'Why can't you sell it?' he enquired.

'Your great grandfather built it for succeeding generations,' she informed him, 'after all, you may be married with children in a few years . . .'

'Come on, Mother,' he sounded scornful, 'you'll be married and have children before me!'

'Well, a child anyway. A half sibling for you.'

'I bet you'll end up marrying David,' he said.

'I don't particularly want to end up having to do anything, I certainly have no plans to marry again.'

'We'll see.'

'Well, darling, don't hold your breath waiting for it to happen!'

'I won't,' he said, 'I'll see you both in a few weeks then.'

'Take care, Peter,' Sylvia said at last, replacing the receiver and sitting back for a few moments, thinking about the future and the more immediate present concerning her visit to Natalia Fiodor.

Her mother had just returned from a series of concerts she had given in Washington DC. Sylvia arrived at the apartment bearing flowers just after lunch on a sunny cold afternoon.

'Thank you, Sylvia, how thoughtful you are.' She kissed her daughter before fetching a vase in which to arrange the blooms.

They sat in her mother's small book-lined study which caught the sun. Sylvia watched as she worked, crushing the base of each stem before placing the flowers into the tall vase. 'Something has happened,' Sylvia began, launching into her news as best she could.

'What is it?' Her mother looked at her, holding a flower mid-way between table and container.

'It's nothing terrible,' Sylvia smiled, 'at least, you won't think it is . . .'

'You've married David,' Natalia Fiodor said.

'I'm pregnant,' Sylvia replied, 'you're going to be a grandmother again, I bet you never expected that, did you?'

Natalia Fiodor stood and stared at her daughter, speechless.

'Say *something*, Mother,' Sylvia smiled.

'Sylvia,' she said delightedly, 'what wonderful news,' she smiled and then looked more serious, 'have you told David yet?'

Sylvia laughed. 'Mother, of course I've told him!'

Her mother put down the flower and crossed the room, sitting down next to Sylvia on the small thirties sofa, hugging her daughter and kissing her again. 'I expect you're depressed about this, aren't you.'

'No, Mother, I'm not depressed.'

'It's absolutely wonderful news, wait until your father hears, I'm calling him this evening. Are you quite sure, Sylvia?'

'Yes, Mother, I'm quite certain. It's wonderful for you because you don't have to go through the next nine months feeling like an old baggage.'

'Nonsense, you never looked anything other than superb when you were pregnant before.'

'I was twenty-one and twenty-three respectively,' Sylvia said, looking pained. 'I'm rather an ancient prospect for sublime motherhood now.'

Natalia Fiodor held Sylvia's hand firmly. 'You're a very strong woman, and you have those Russian hips . . . good child-bearing hips.'

Sylvia laughed loudly. 'What's that got to do with Russia? Mother, for God's sake, I'm just lucky . . .'

'Do you have a doctor here?'

'Of course, I have a very good doctor.'

'You're pleased, aren't you?' her mother encouraged her to talk. 'I know you . . . I can tell.'

'I'll tell you in a few months when it's giving me permanent indigestion and kicking me into shreds.'

The older woman clasped her hands together, beaming at Sylvia with pleasure. 'I'm so excited, what do you think it will be? What do you want?'

Sylvia regarded her mother with the kind of disdain she normally reserved for silly girls. 'I expect it will be a boy.'

Natalia Fiodor patter her daughter's cheek lovingly. 'It's wonderful, Sylvia, you'll see, everything will be fine.'

Sylvia didn't feel very convinced but smiled all the same.

'Wouldn't it be nice if it turned out to be a girl?' Natalia Fiodor returned to the flower arranging.

'You mean someone to take decent care of me when I reach my dotage?'

'Not at all. Perhaps a girl would reduce your venom, you could pass on your experience of womanhood to her.'

'Poor thing,' Sylvia answered, 'my experiences aren't necessarily to be relied upon to bring joy and happiness.'

'Don't be so negative all the time, Sylvia.'

'It will be a boy,' she repeated, what was the use of arguing about it? They chatted on about baby things, her mother anxious to get out and begin buying the supplies now. Instead they took a stroll in the park. It was a very cold afternoon and she took her mother's arm as they walked. 'I spoke to Peter, I told him the news, he seemed to take it very well.'

'Of course, he'll be thrilled.'

They were walking slowly down West Drive, the lake to their right. 'I've noticed something of Richard about him recently,' Sylvia said.

'Oh, but, darling, Peter is awfully like his father,

physically of course, but I've *always* thought they were alike in other ways.'

'Have you?' Sylvia felt surprised. 'Oh no, he's much more like Daddy.'

'He has Richard's streak of ruthlessness.'

'God, that's a bit harsh, Mother.'

'Not at all, what's wrong with a bit of ruthlessness mixed up with all the rest?'

'Because it contradicts the rest, that's why.'

'Richard has steam-rollered his way through life, you have to be strong in a profession like his.' Her mother saw it all as a casual fact of life.

'I thought you liked Richard.'

'He was a charming youth, he might not have become quite so unbearable if you hadn't been quite so difficult.'

Sylvia stopped walking, turning to the older woman, mouth open with shock. '*Me* difficult?' She looked away, thinking hard. 'Why are you telling me this now?'

'You left Richard because you were unhappy, you wanted to find yourself, develop a career, you were intent upon liberating yourself.' Natalia Fiodor checked off these points as though they were items on a shopping list. 'Well, you did all of that, you meet David, you fall in love, you're having his child now, but . . .' and her eyes widened in a sort of triumph, 'what ever happened to happiness, Sylvia?'

'Mother,' Sylvia began very patiently, 'you keep asking me this same question. Why won't you understand that I'm happy?'

'Because you never seem to express it in any way I can perceive. If you left Richard to achieve something – and you succeeded – why can't you just relax and let go? Why can't you enjoy life a little?'

'Oh, no, here we go,' Sylvia said, realizing just what

this was leading up to. 'Why not marriage? Now, that's the real question here, isn't it?'

Natalia Fiodor raised her eyes and began to walk on. 'You seem to take life *so* seriously, darling, why is that?'

'Because women always have to pay the price for everything they do with their guilt and because I lost a child and because I now have this . . . this thing inside me which I now have to be responsible for until I'm an old woman. It's all very well you telling me how simply wonderful everything is . . .' Sylvia stopped.

'A while ago you said you were pleased . . .'

'I am but it's not really what I would have wanted.'

'Fate,' her mother replied sagely.

'Balls!' Sylvia said crudely.

Natalia Fiodor didn't answer, instead she withdrew a crumpled paper bag of stale bread from her deep coat pocket and began to feed the pigeons. Sylvia sat down, her arms folded tightly against her chest watching the ugly, bloated birds pecking up the scraps of food, coming close and showing no fear.

'Do you want to have a go?' her mother asked.

'I'm not six years old,' Sylvia replied sullenly.

Natalia Fiodor laughed. 'Come on, don't be a bore.'

Her mother's infectious laughter made Sylvia grin. 'I don't want to feed those ratty-looking birds, thank you.'

Her mother tossed a few pieces of bread crust in Sylvia's general direction so that the pigeons were soon pecking at the ground near her feet. 'See, darling, they like you.'

Sylvia laughed. 'You're absolutely insane, Mother.' She stood up, the birds flapping away as she moved. 'You'll get a reputation for being the eccentric pigeon-fancier of New York!' Sylvia took her mother's arm, reaching into the paper bag to throw the food down and watching as the grey bird army scuttled on.

'The eccentric pigeon-fancier *and* her mad daughter strike again.' Natalia Fiodor began to laugh. 'Come on, darling, just thank your lucky stars that you're not a pigeon, you'd be sitting on eggs all the time!'

Sylvia had a vision of herself sitting high up on a perch above Central Park. 'At least I could fly away, then.'

'You've been doing that all your life, I think you're only now just beginning to settle.' Her mother crumpled up the bag and dropped it into the nearby waste basket. 'Come on then, I'll feed you now, we'll have some tea.'

The following day Sylvia accompanied her mother to the airport. She was worried for her, holding her as they parted, feeling the old woman frail underneath the embrace. Sylvia cried, it was the first time she could recall being emotional at a parting with her.

'Good God, child, whatever is it,' Natalia Fiodor asked. 'I'll be back in the new year with Peter . . .'

Sylvia laughed at herself, feeling rather foolish, brushing away her tears. They would be together again in a month or so, just a matter of weeks really.

David was just getting up when she returned from Kennedy International. She looked at his nude body.

'Okay?' he asked.

'Mother was going on a bit, nothing I can't cope with. Her apartment always looks so dreary and cold when it's closed up.'

'What was she going on about? As if I couldn't guess.' He walked into the bathroom and turned on the shower.

She went into the living-room where she opened up the fire doors of the modern wood-burning stove and pushed in a couple more log pieces. She sat watching the flames beginning to take hold, outside the snow was falling heavily.

'Your mother has always wanted us to marry,' David said, walking into the room in his tatty bath-robe, rubbing his wet hair with a towel.

'Yes,' Sylvia replied, without taking her eyes away from the fire.

'Well, all I'm saying . . .'

'I know what you're saying, David.' She looked up at him. 'My mother thinks it's the logical thing to do, therefore, I should attempt to appease her and marry you for the sake of the baby.'

'It's an idea, yes,' he replied.

'What about for the sake of Sylvia?' she asked, 'why all this pressure upon her?'

'I'm not pressurizing you,' he said, holding up his hands.

'Yes, you are,' she said softly, 'you are because I know you want marriage and I could easily justify it now for the sake of our child's bastardization!'

David winced and looked pained. 'Why is it, Sylvia, that whenever you and your mother get together *we* always end up arguing. I've not even *mentioned* the word marriage for an age.'

'You've thought about it, though.'

'Of course I've thought about it, it's what I'd like.'

'What you want.'

'If your mother upsets you so much why bother to see her?'

'My mother is a brilliant woman, she has an international reputation, people consider her a genius, one of the world's best pianists, if I can't live up to her expectations of me of course I get upset.'

'She's just a little old woman now, can you still be bothered by what she has to say? You're two completely different people.'

'I'm still her daughter, I function as that, as a daughter . . .'

'You have independent lives, you weren't even together much when you were a child.'

'Well, perhaps she's trying to regain something of that now . . .' Sylvia felt a host of conflicting emotions for Natalia Fiodor, love, respect, awe, contempt, even hate. Through it all, however, she knew she still wanted her mother to have reason to love her – to admire her. 'Damn her,' Sylvia said suddenly, bursting into tears, confused and afraid of all that was happening to her.

By the time David had dressed, Sylvia had composed herself and felt calmer.

'Hi,' he said, a little sheepishly.

'Hello,' Sylvia smiled.

'What's that?' he asked, looking down at some papers Sylvia was reading in front of the fire.

'Come here,' she said, reaching out for his hand as he came to sit beside her. 'I want you to watch. This is my contract for another season of "The Arts Programme", now you see it . . .' she began, ripping it in half, 'now you don't . . .' She placed it carefully amongst the flames and then sat back to watch the pristine paper browning and curling in the heat, finally bursting into flame.

'We're all right, aren't we, Sylvia?' David asked her suddenly, sounding concerned.

'Of course, what a thing to ask, we're absolutely fine.' She turned to him and smiled, kissing him on the mouth.

He seemed relieved and sat back to watch the flames.

Sylvia moved across to the large window, the heavy snow almost obliterating the view of the street and the buildings opposite.

'What are you thinking?' he asked.

'Nothing much,' she replied, coming back to him.

'Nothing?'

Sylvia laughed. 'I feel like a woman who, resigned to her fate, has come, accepting, to rest at last.'

David took her into his arms. 'You mean you'll settle down and make an honest man of me?' he joked.

She did not answer him. Nothing seemed impossible to her now.